Wolf
FLOW

To Peter—

Wolf ▬▬

K. W. JETER

FLOW

St. Martin's Press New York ▬▬▬▬

Best,
K. W. Jeter

DESIGN BY DAWN NILES

Library of Congress Cataloging-in-Publication Data

Jeter, K. W.
     Wolf flow / K.W. Jeter.
       p. cm.
     ISBN 0-312-07125-6
     I. Title.
   PS3560.E85W64   1992
   813'.54—dc20   91-38999
                                             CIP

First Edition: April 1992

10 9 8 7 6 5 4 3 2 1

To the Chocholaks—Michael and Misha, and Aaron, Adrienne, Justin and Thane.

When I first heard Howlin' Wolf, I said, "This is for me. This is where the soul of man never dies."

—SAM PHILLIPS OF SUN RECORDS

One

The car must have been doing fifty when they threw him out. One of the ropes snapped, the one binding his wrists, and his arms flew out in a pinwheeled crucifix as he hit the ground.

A long straight road, with nothing at either end. A hawk drifted lower in the sky, then caught the cross-beam of a telephone pole. The road's asphalt wavered in the shadowless heat. The hawk furled its wings and watched for small things to eat in the dry scrub underneath the wire.

For a few seconds the hawk's gaze checked out the thing that had rolled and flopped into stillness among the loose rocks and gravel. Whatever it was, it was still alive; the hawk's eyes scanned blood trickling through the dust on the thing's face, and the lift and fall of the breath moving inside. But it was too big. Maybe later, when it would be fresh dead, the blood still warm inside, then the hawk could tear at it with the sharp machine of its appetite.

Charlie looked in the rearview mirror and saw the

hawk sitting up there on the pole, watching. The world was yellow out here, and grey and brown—dry colors—the hawk the only scrap of life visible, and it just sat there, watching and waiting. Shit like that had a lot of patience, he figured. It'd have to.

"Slow it down a bit." Beside him, Aitch twisted around in the passenger seat and looked back behind the car. There wasn't much to see of what they had dumped out, except a cloud of dust rolling up from the ground—Charlie could see in the mirror just the top curve tumbling about like a slow explosion. "Come on"—Aitch sounded impatient, like a child—"slow down, will ya?"

He let off the gas and eased on the brake, allowing the car's own dust to catch up with it. They came to a stop. In the silence filling the car, broken only by the engine's idling murmur, he heard the voice coming off the tape deck.

It sounded terrible, more of the old junk that Aitch was so nuts about. Some old black guy shouting and moaning, the music sounding as though it'd been recorded with tin cans and string. That was all they'd listened to, all the way out from the city. With Mike sitting between them, his battered head lolling back and forth, and Aitch's arm around his shoulders to keep him upright. "This is good stuff," Aitch would say, reaching out to turn up the volume. "You should like this stuff, man." Grinning into Mike's face, with the eyes rolled up to show just whites and the blood smeared and drying into a black crust all over his nose and mouth and throat. Aitch'd been having so much fun, he hadn't even cared that the blood seeping through Mike's torn clothes, and the dirt and grease, had got on his pricey Italian jacket. He'd just kept on grinning, eyes sparking, and saying funny shit.

The dust settled behind the car. And farther back, it drifted down on something at the side of the road that looked like a bundle of rags.

"Go back," said Aitch. He had turned all the way

2

around in the passenger seat, rising up and leaning over the top to look through the car's rear window.

"What?"

Aitch gave him one of those looks. "Just go back—all right? Just put it in reverse and go back there."

Charlie said "Shit" under his breath. Wondering what weird crap Aitch was up to now, as he put the car in gear. He laid one arm along the top of the seat and steered one-handed, the wheels kicking up gravel where he let the car swerve off the road.

He didn't know why he put up with some of this shit. He had fifty pounds of muscle on Aitch and was a good head taller, with a reach to match. But he also knew full well why he put up with Aitch's shit. The money that rolled off of Aitch was good, that was why. It was good as long as you didn't get stupid and greedy about it.

Mike had forgotten about that last part. Charlie stopped the car, letting it rock and nod on its suspension. Mike was over there on the ground now, with the flies already promenading on his face.

There was too much action around this spot, too much coming and going, for the hawk's taste. It flapped off, the tips of its wings fingering the still air. Charlie turned his head and watched the hawk's shadow slide across the stubby weeds and bare, dry dirt.

Aitch rummaged around in the glove compartment. These big honking American cars that Aitch preferred had miles of space tucked away inside them. Charlie didn't care for them—like driving a boat or something. You just wallowed all over the road. He'd rather squeeze his bulk behind the wheel of some little Porsche or the like. He still had a wistful remembrance of a red Alfa Romeo that Aitch had made him take back to where he'd found it. The air-conditioning in these American jobbies was nice, though. He had to admit it. They'd have been roasting, coming out here without it.

A handful of Aitch's cassette tapes clattered onto the

3

floorboard's carpet. Aitch was practically elbow deep into the glove compartment before he came up with what he wanted.

Aitch held up a Polaroid camera, an SX-70 that looked like a square clam. He popped it open, and the round lens in front stared at Charlie. "Come on." Aitch pushed open the door on his side. "Let's go take a look."

Aww, man . . . Charlie shook his head, his hands resting on the top of the steering wheel. "No thanks. You go ahead." *Have yourself a ball.* He didn't need to see what a body dumped out of a moving car looked like. They might not have been going quite fifty—he'd eased off the accelerator instinctively, out of some leftover sympathy for the poor bastard, when Aitch had wrestled the limp form up against the door, then reached past Mike for the handle, with his other hand right in the small of Mike's back. But they'd still been going a good clip when Aitch had done it.

The worst of it was that they didn't even necessarily die when they hit the ground. Probably because they were already unconscious, or close to. If they knew what was happening, they'd naturally tense up, and the impact would probably bust them all to pieces. This way, they could just roll with it. But they were still pretty messed up by it. Like that Tony guy that they'd dropped off somewhere around here, just a couple of months ago. He'd gotten out of the car with Aitch that time to go take a look, and he still wished he hadn't.

The camera thing was something new, though. From the car's cooled sanctuary, he watched as Aitch walked over to the bundle of rags. The dust had all settled by now, except for what was being kicked up by Aitch's shiny black shoes. A gritty brown layer had draped over Mike, pulling him down into the landscape, making him part of it, like the outcropping of rocks a few yards distant.

Aitch put his foot on one of Mike's shoulders, pushing it back so that Mike's face rolled into view. Aitch bent

4

down with the camera, to get a good shot. When he took his foot away, the body flopped back the way it had been.

Finally heading back to the city—they had a long way to go. It gave him a little bit of the creeps, just a cold finger tracing up his spine, to see Aitch sitting over there, looking at the Polaroid snap in his hand, watching the image in it swim up into view. He could already see the outlines of Mike's fucked-up face, and the green blotch of the hospital-type shirt he'd been wearing, with his last name stenciled on the breast pocket.

Aitch glanced over at him. "I decided to start keeping a scrap book—okay?" He smiled to show that he was just joking around about being on the defensive. "That all right by you?"

Charlie shrugged, his hands loose on the wheel. He didn't give a fuck what Aitch got up to. He sighed—quietly—as Aitch slid another one of his cassettes into the dash, and more rotten old music filled the car.

The hawk wheeled back to the telephone pole and took up its station again. The big, noisy things had gone; the quiet of the high desert country had returned. That was the way the hawk preferred it.

There was still a big thing on the ground, though. It wasn't moving. It hadn't moved for a long time. The hawk dropped down to the ground in front of it.

It smelled like meat and blood. The noon sun hammering down had crusted the face's broken skin with black. The dark hair around one ear and across the top of the skull was stiffened into pointed fingers. One cheek was pressed against the gravel and dust, and the mouth was open, as though trying to suckle from the dry earth. A spot of red-tinged spittle had formed there; in its center was a fragment of smooth bone, sharp and red at the end where it had been broken from the jaw, then coughed out here like a flawed pearl.

The hawk tilted its own head, looking into the big

thing's eye. The lid had twitched and pulled open a fraction of an inch, showing a dull, unfocused stare. The hawk stared back into it, the same as he would to the bright bead eye of a field mouse he had trapped on the ground. A moan shuddered the big thing's ribs, and the dull eye closed. The sound hadn't been enough to alarm the hawk; after a few moments more, it flew back up to the pole.

The thing on the ground beneath it had looked promising. Maybe a coyote would come down out of the hills and rip it into smaller pieces. The hawk had no taste for scavenging, but the blood-soaked ground would attract others, the smaller things that the hawk could swoop down upon.

It was worth waiting around to see.

In the cab of the diesel rig were three copies of *Hustler* magazine, one as old as 1979. They were part of the general mulch that had collected around and under the seats, along with flattened Dunkin' Donuts cartons and cracked styrofoam coffee containers, the big economy size, with brown sludge coagulated at the bottom; orange hamburger wrappings, shiny and translucent where the grease had soaked through; a Harold Robbins novel with the front cover torn off; a couple other strips that had cost a nickel apiece at a flea market in La Grande; and other shit. In the sleeper behind the seats was more of the same, including a black brassiere with a safety pin holding together one strap, that was a souvenir of either an ex-wife or a thirty-five-year-old road bunny working the parking lots at the Burns Brothers truckstop near Reno.

Everything smelled like sweat and Prince Albert hand-rolleds. The driver smelled that way, too, as though he'd been steeping inside the Peterbilt's hermetically sealed box so long that the diesel stink had started to come out of the pores of his skin. The trucker had had his name painted once on the door of the cab, by a famous and expensive pinstriper named Von Dutch, but the sun had chewed away the swirling letters. Nowadays, he mainly seemed to live in the truck. There was a house somewhere, too—the remnant, along with his son, of his busted marriage. The house was good mainly for catching a shower and a three-day stretch of sleep between long-distance loads, checking out his mail, and fudging the interstate cheat sheets.

Right now, he had to take a piss. The pneumatics on the driver's seat were about shot, and his kidneys were overstimulated from the vibration traveling up from the asphalt and concrete. The roads out here were all shit, anyway; he'd have been just as well off, he figured, barreling straight across the sand and rocks.

The air brakes sighed as the Peterbilt came to a stop. He left the engine ticking over, its murmur and clatter the only sound in the still desert air, as he climbed down from the cab. The heels on his Dan Posts were worn round in back from working out on the accelerator and clutch pedals; it took him a moment to catch his balance when he stopped from the last chrome rung to the ground. From the open cab door above, the yellowed Robbins paperback and miscellaneous trash spilled and fluttered down.

The trucker walked stiffly toward the rocks a few yards from the edge of the road. His spine felt as though it had been welded together into one straight rod. He was getting too old for this shit. Maybe—he'd been thinking about it a lot lately—maybe he could line up a dispatcher's job with some outfit. Sit in some air-conditioned office somewhere, letting his ass grow wide and horsing around with whatever divorcee did the bookkeeping.... That'd be nice. A lizard peeped at him over the top of a rock, then scurried away, leaving an S-shaped trail in the dust.

Over by the big rocks, he unbuttoned his fly. A little river formed at their base, flowing past the toe of his right boot. The piss rounded like a thin black snake, crawling a couple of feet before sinking into the dust. His bladder eased, signaling its gratitude. He looked around, scratching the side of his face with his free hand. He had time; this was a long one.

He drew his squint down tighter when he spotted something lying by the side of the road, some twenty, thirty yards up from where he'd pulled the truck over. He couldn't make out what it was—just a shape sprawled out in the dirt—but he had a good idea. He'd come across shit like this before, out here. He finished his business, then did up his fly. He ambled toward the thing, whatever it was, in no hurry. It wasn't going anywhere.

As he figured—some poor sucker had been laid out here. Or thrown out: there were skid marks in the gravel, leading up to the body. The guy's arms were spread out, his face cocked into the dirt, ankles bound together with rough jute rope, a loop of the same stuff dangling from one wrist. A fly lifted from one of the red and black patches on the face and buzzed angrily away as the trucker squatted down and rolled the body over on its back.

The guy didn't look too good, but he was still alive. Barely. The trucker could see the shallow rise of the chest, and a bubble of red at the corner of the mouth. A young guy, though you could barely tell, he'd been worked over so good. He had on jeans—the bottom few inches of one leg seam ripped open, the denim fabric darkened where the blood had soaked through—and some kind of green-ish shirt without a collar. The shirt's thinner fabric had torn, showing the bruises and abraded skin across the guy's ribs. It wasn't all from getting thrown out of a car. The guy had been in bad shape before he got here.

The trucker stood back up. His shadow fell across the guy's face. The eyes in the battered face fluttered open. They looked up and pulled into focus for a moment, then drifted back into unconsciousness.

"Hey." The trucker prodded the guy in the ribs with the toe of his boot. Likely a couple of cracked ribs there, at the least. Maybe the new pain would bring the guy around again. "Hey, you with us, buddy?" Another poke. "Knock-knock, anybody home?"

He didn't get an answer. The eyes stayed closed, and the guy's shallow breathing slid over the red wetness filling his mouth.

"Well, hell . . ." The trucker dug out his pocket knife, bent down and cut the rope around the man's ankles. The guy's feet—one bare except for a dirty white sock, the other with a scuffed Adidas running shoe on—flopped disjointedly, as though they were held to the rest of the body by nothing but the jeans legs.

"Come on, buddy. Let's go for a walk." He pulled the guy upright by the arms, managing to get the body's limp weight onto his own shoulders. He held the wrists in front of his chest, with the arms draped across his neck. The guy's face, open-mouthed, with a string of red spittle dangling out, lolled against his head. He carried the weight toward the truck, leaving behind him his own bootprints and two parallel lines from the guy's dragging feet.

In the Peterbilt's cab, the body slumped against the angle of the seat and the righthand door. The trucker got in on the other side and slid behind the wheel. He could see some of the guy's injuries better now. Somebody had whaled on his head with what looked to have been a steel bar; the straight imprint was plain along the side of the guy's skull. That was what had broken open the scalp and left the hair matted and spiked with blood. If they'd wanted to, whoever had done it could just have easily taken off the whole top of the guy's head. They must have wanted to leave him alive, or just dying slowly, and then dump him out here: the high desert got cold enough at night, even at this time of year, to have finished him off. Not a fun way to go.

The guy was moaning, his face contorting after a series of quick, gulping breaths. The trucker watched him, then rooted through the stuff behind the seat and came up with a thermos bottle. The coffee in it was over a day old and stone cold, but it was something wet at least. He poured the plastic cup half full and leaned with it toward the guy.

"Here you go, ace." He held the cup to the guy's mouth, pulling him forward with a hand at the back of the head. "Try and get a little of this down."

Some of the coffee dribbled out of the corners of the guy's mouth, but the muscles of his throat clenched, working the rest along. Then he coughed, shoulders jerking, and the last mouthful welled over his chin and onto the torn green shirt. The head slumped back, but the panting breath had slowed and deepened.

The trucker screwed the cup back onto the thermos and set it down between the seats. He dropped the Peterbilt into gear and eased it back onto the road.

They had hardly picked up any speed at all when the guy opened his eyes—slowly, as though they were working free of stitches. He winced as he turned his face toward the trucker.

"Where . . ." The guy could barely speak. The voice sounded like an old man's. "Where we going . . ."

The trucker grunted. "Where the hell do you think?" He glanced over at him. "I'm taking you to a hospital."

The guy's body stiffened, the spine coming up from the seat and shoving his shoulder blades back. Underneath the dried blood, his face whitened with the sudden effort. He shook his head, teeth gritting against the pain. "No—no hospital—"

He couldn't believe he'd heard that. "What're you talking about? You're in a world of hurt, fella. You need some taking care of."

The guy leaned forward, with agonized slowness. He twisted around so that he could reach down between the seats. The trucker saw that the guy's right arm and hand weren't working too well; they flopped loosely as the guy reached for the thermos bottle. He managed to one-hand the cup off, then the plug at the bottle's opening. He got

10

the bottle to his mouth and gulped at what was left inside, a mix of blood and coffee running in rivulets down his throat. The empty bottle fell to the floor as he collapsed back against the seat.

The trucker looked over at him. The road was a perfect straight line, nothing between here and the low horizon, so he could keep his eye on the guy for several seconds. "I ain't shittin' ya, man. You need a doctor."

A smile, or the lopsided fragment of one, came up on the guy's face. Even a little laugh. "I *am* a doctor."

He looked at the guy for a moment longer, then turned back to the road beyond the windshield.

TWO

The hawk had watched the hurt thing being taken away. That had been hours ago—nothing to the hawk's slow patience—when the sun had still been slanting across the world. Now the hills had started to turn red, sinking toward black, and the seeing of things was getting harder.

Nothing was left on the ground below the wire except the scuffed-up earth, the traces of the thing's impact on the ground and then its being dragged away to the road. There was still the smell of blood and meat, though, soaked into the dust where it had lain.

Something, a loping four-legged shape, came out of the rocks at the edge of the low hills. It snuffled head-down at the discolored soil, the long teeth in its muzzle bared as it caught the scent of what had been there. Others like it were back in the rocks' hidden places, ears pricked for any sound other than the wind rising.

The animal looked up at the hawk. For a few seconds, the two carnivores' eyes met, blank gold coins above, red dots of fire below, the reflections of the sun burning behind the hills.

Then the hawk flapped away from the pole, turning above the shadowed ground. Its hunting was over for the day. The others could begin now.

He woke for little bits of time. Not really waking, not sleeping, but just drifting in and out of a blackness where the pain didn't go away but became something endurable, a red tidal motion timed to the slow beat of his pulse.

He knew he was in a truck, a big rattling diesel kind. He remembered somebody lifting, carrying him up into it, a long way from the ground. The same person was behind the wheel now, and the noise of the engine and the wind against the glass told him they were moving. Going somewhere—he didn't know. When he'd opened his eyes, he'd been able to focus for only a couple of seconds, just long enough to make out a face darkened to creased leather below one of those hick-looking billed caps. Then the double vision had come, the face blurring and splitting and dancing around with everything else inside the small space of the truck. He'd had to close his eyes and go back into the soft dark.

Back in there . . . the pain came over in a slow wave, pulling him under. He let go, watching himself disappear. Then that part was gone as well.

Harley and his buddy would be working away at the pit mine—the trucker knew it. Both of them liked to work, liked to have sweat pouring down their shirtless backs, rivulets trickling through the dust thick on their necks and forearms. The only other thing they liked to do—that he knew about—was go someplace where they could get shit-faced on cold beer, to make up for all the body fluids they'd lost out in the sun. And to make up for the time they'd lost, when they'd been in the can.

The pit mine was a hole in the ground. With a tin shack and piles of rusting equipment up on the top level and down in the hole. Tons of stuff—that was why Harley and his buddy were out here, and why he came dragging out here with his rig two times a week. As he steered the Peterbilt along the curving dirt track that led off the main road, he saw a hoisting tower at the edge of the pit sag, lean, then come toppling down, raising a cloud of dirt.

Harley's beater, an old Jimmy pickup with bald tires, was parked by the shack. His buddy was in the little rag of shade it threw, with a welding mask over his face, working with a cutting torch on a pile of scrap. The torch hissed and sent sparks popping over the dirt.

The trucker pulled the Peterbilt around by the shack. As he pushed the door on his side open, he saw Harley—big, hairy; both he and his buddy looked like badly shaved apes—come ambling over from the wreckage of the hoisting tower. Harley had a sledgehammer dangling from his meaty fist.

He jumped from the cab's last step to the ground. "Check it out," he said, pointing over his shoulder with his thumb.

Bristle-jawed Harley stood and looked at him for a moment, then walked past; he dropped the hammer and mounted a couple of steps up the side of the cab so he could look in its open door.

"Shit!" Harley jumped back down. His face had been red and sweaty before; now it blackened with anger as he confronted the trucker. "Who the fuck's that?"

He shrugged. "Found 'im. Out on the road."

Harley's buddy, with the welder's mask pushed up on top of his head, came around from the other side of the shack and looked in the truck. He was smiling, gaps showing in his yellow teeth, when he came over to them.

"Looks like somebody doesn't like him too much." Harley's buddy scratched his bare chest, grinning away.

"Shit. Jesus fucking Christ." Harley shook his head. "What the hell did you bring him here for?"

"What was I supposed to do?" The trucker gestured

14

toward the Peterbilt and the slumped figure visible inside. "Leave him out there?"

Harley put his hands on his hips and nodded. "Yeah, actually. That's *exactly* what you should've done. This stupid fucker, whoever he is, he gets his ass in a jam, it's no skin off our noses."

These assholes . . . The trucker kept his face impassive as he listened to Harley. *How the hell did I get hooked up with them?*

"Why do you think somebody like that gets dumped off in the middle of nowhere? Huh? Tell me."

The trucker shrugged.

Harley looked over his shoulder, then back to the trucker. "He probably burned somebody in some fuckin' dope deal. So he gets what he deserves, the stupid shit."

The other ape laughed, just thinking about that.

"Yeah, but . . . come on . . ."

"Don't give me that shit." Harley's face looked as if it were going to explode. "I don't want to hear it. What the hell do you think we're doing out here, man? We got thirty, forty tons of scrap to break up and get hauled out of here before somebody finds out what we're doing. This is *illegal,* man. You know what that means?"

"I know what it means." The shit he had to take from this guy; it wasn't worth it.

"No, you don't. It doesn't just mean that if we get popped, you don't get your share of the profits. It means that if we get popped, me and my buddy here, we go back in. And I've been in before, and I don't want to go in again—you got me? We get popped, the D.A. hits me with the fucking bitch—you know? Fuck, man, I'll get fucking seven just for breaking my fucking parole. And you want to haul some beat-up, dying dope dealer in here? You're out of your fucking mind."

"So what the hell am I supposed to do with him, then? Look, the guy's gonna die anyway—"

Harley cut him off. "Hey, I don't give a fuck. So let

15

him die somewhere else, okay? Just get rid of him. Haul him back out to where you found him. . . ."

The voices woke him. Shouting, somewhere in the distance.

He managed to drag his eyes open, a slit that let in stinging light. His face was against glass, the side window of the truck's cab. He turned his head—slowly; there was a rod of dull fire under his spine—until he could see where the voices came from.

Through the open door of the cab, he saw them. The man who had been driving the truck, who'd picked him up. And another one, with a red, sweating face. That one's voice was louder, angrier. He could just make out the words.

. . . get rid of him . . . haul him back out . . . found him . . .

The voice twisted in his ear, echoing. At the same time, the faces blurred and doubled, the truckdriver's and the red, angry one. He couldn't see them anymore. He closed his eyes, and part of him, the small part that heard and remembered, drifted in night over a blind world. The darkness welled beneath him, in synch with the heavy tide of his pulse, carrying him farther from the earth.

Farther away. The last thing, before there was nothing.

. . . get rid of him . . . The echo *. . . rid . . .*

He looked at Harley in disgust.

"Oh yeah, that's a great idea." The trucker's own anger was starting to rise. He shook his head, one corner of his mouth twisting up. "With my goddamn tire tracks rolling right by there—"

"Well, just dump him anywhere, then." Harley gestured off to the distance, to the dirt road behind the truck. "Some place out of sight. Find some flat rock to stick him under." He rubbed the dust from his hands onto his trousers, already filthy. "And then get your ass back here. We got plenty ready to load up." He turned away and walked toward the metal shack.

The trucker stared after him. Harley's buddy was already plopped down in the little bit of shade, working on a beer he'd taken from the cooler inside. He handed it up to Harley, who guzzled it nearly empty, his red-creased throat beating with each swallow.

Fuck these guys. For the hundredth time, the trucker wondered why he'd let himself get hooked up with them. Fuckin' yardbirds. He turned on his heel and headed for the Peterbilt.

Now it was dark outside as well; he could tell even without opening his eyes. The sun must have set. Under the edge of his eyelids he could just make out the green, spectral glow of the truck's dashboard lights, making the driver's hands into skeletonlike forms clutching the wheel. He squeezed his eyes closed tight, the corner of his forehead against the cold, vibrating glass of the side window. Black inside . . .

He came to again when he felt the truck come to a stop. Or it had been still for a while; he had no way of knowing. Except that the driver was gone from behind the wheel, leaving him alone in the dim, green-lit space.

The pain had gotten worse. Every breath brought a stab of fire around his chest. The one arm, his right, was useless; he couldn't move it from where the weight of his body pinned it against the door. That had been the first place he'd gotten hit, when he'd raised up his forearm to ward off the blow swinging down on him. A metal pipe, just under three feet long, with one end wrapped in electrician's tape for a better grip; he'd seen it before, propped up in a corner by the front door of Aitch's apartment, and had suspected what it was for. Now he knew.

The double vision had let up for a moment. He could see outside the truck, through the window his cheek rested against. Some big shape blotted out the bottom part of the night sky, closer than the low hills and made up of straight lines. The truck's headlights weren't aimed toward it, but enough of their glow leaked to the side that he could make out the size of the building, a big one, with a double row of windows. A couple of the windows on the top story were broken out, leaving jagged teeth glinting with the moon's cold blue light.

He saw the truck driver, or somebody, moving around the front of the building, a human shape stepping off what looked like a covered porch running across the front of the building. The man walked back toward the truck.

He closed his eyes and waited. He was too tired to care where the hell this was.

"There you go, buddy." The trucker had stripped the blankets off the narrow bed in the Peterbilt's sleeper and wrapped the guy up in them. He'd laid him down by a section of wall where the windows were all still securely boarded over and the chilling night wind couldn't get through, or at least not much of it. An angle of moonlight reached down the big flight of stairs at the far end. The guy's face, white underneath the bruises and crusted blood, gazed up at the old lobby's ceiling, breath dragging in and out of his open mouth.

The trucker peeled off his denim jacket, wadded it up and slid it under the back of the guy's head. The unfocused eyes screwed down in pain, then relaxed but still stayed closed as he lowered the fragile skull onto the makeshift pillow.

"There's water in here now." He set the thermos bottle down, with the plastic cup, already filled, next to it. He'd dipped the water up from a stagnant puddle he'd stepped in outside. But it was better than leaving the guy with nothing at all. "Right here, where you can get to it. Okay?"

The guy managed to move his head. "Yeah . . . thanks . . ." His voice sounded a million miles away.

If this sorry bastard didn't want to go to a hospital, the trucker figured, it was no skin off his ass. It would've been less trouble if he'd just left the guy at the side of the road, out where he'd found him. Taking him in to an emergency room, he might have had to come up with a cover story about why he was working his rig out in that butt-end of nowhere. Especially since this guy hadn't gotten so banged up by falling out of bed. And he didn't feel like explaining to the police his little business with the two cons at the pit mine. So if this fellow wanted to take his chances without benefit of medical attention . . . that might save everybody a lot of trouble.

"Hope you make it." He rubbed his chin as he looked down at the guy. "Look, uh . . . I got a good idea why you didn't want to go to a hospital. You're not the first dumb sonuvabitch somebody's found out there like that. You're just the first one—least that I ever came across—who was still alive."

The guy tried to raise his head; he grimaced, teeth clenched, and let the back of his skull hit the wadded-up jacket. He sucked his breath in through his teeth.

"Yeah . . . well . . ." The words barely crawled out. "Whatever . . ."

The trucker shook his head.

"I gotta take off now." With the toe of his boot he pushed the thermos closer to the guy's hand. "I'll send somebody around when it's light, to check up on you."

He turned and walked away, his footsteps echoing from the bare wood floor. He wondered what would be left of the guy by the time he came this way again.

The truck rumbled away; Mike heard the grinding of its gears as it headed down whatever road had brought him here.

He was in a room, someplace inside; he could tell that

19

much. Stiffly, he pulled his arm, the left one that he could still move, out from under the blankets swaddled around him. A curtain dangled to the floor beside him. He clutched at it, and the white rotten stuff came away in his hand. The dust from it drifted in the faint blue light.

He managed to rise up on his elbow. The room tilted around him, blurring and doubling. The pain binding his chest sang, rolling up his spine and battering at the pivot of his skull.

The window behind the curtain was boarded over. There was only a small gap through which he could see outside: night, and the darker hills blotting out the stars; blackness layered on top of itself.

Something moved out there, or inside his head; it was hard to tell which. He thought he saw two red points, set close as though they were eyes. And then others like them, moving at a slow pace in the unseen footing of the hills and turning their gaze toward him, sensing him in his frail shelter, the scent of his blood carried to them in the dark air.

The red points blurred, becoming gaseous and cloud-like, overlapping each other. The pain and dizziness sucked the strength from his arm, and he collapsed back to the floor and the nest of blankets.

He tried to listen as the soft darkness welled over him, but he could hear only the laboring step of his own pulse. Then nothing, as he fell and kept falling.

Three

They hadn't gone back to the apartment—Aitch's place, though Charlie lived there, too—when they returned from dumping Mike off. Which bugged Charlie; he was hungry and tired, tired from all the driving in this goddamn Detroit gunboat that Aitch had latched onto. Next week, or tomorrow, it'd be something different, but just as big. Right now, though, he felt as if he were drowning in the soft world of the Cadillac, or whatever it was, that Aitch had made his own with all that fucking boo music on the stereo.

Aitch lounged back in the passenger seat, one arm thrown along the top, his fingers almost touching Charlie's shoulder. Slumped down behind the steering wheel, Charlie watched—what the hell else was there to do?—the apartment building across the street and a little way down the block.

They were parked somewhere over in the northwest section of the city. He knew vaguely his way around here. There was a health food co-op a couple blocks away, he remembered, which had been full of hippie types with hair straggling down to their asses years ago, and which was now considerably more upscale. He'd had a girlfriend, off and on, back when he'd been taking classes at the campus downtown, who'd make him drive out here so she could buy huge sacks of whole grains that'd looked to him like the stuff you'd feed to horses. She was probably still out here, schlumpfing around in her Indian print skirts, getting maybe some grey streaks in her hair, living in some Lesbian poetry-writing commune in one of the funkier old houses—he didn't want to know. A huge crock of lentils soaking, and a dozen cats. This whole area, he knew (Aitch had told him; info some of Aitch's customers had passed on), all these ratty houses with sagging porches and peeling fish-scale shingles—it was all slated for being bulldozed and replaced with skinny packs of row houses. What's-her-name would have to migrate, with her cats and lentils, down the I-5, to Eugene maybe.

Those were the kinds of thoughts that came drifting by—thoughts about old girlfriends—hanging around late at night in a pilfered Caddy. At least Aitch had burned out finally on those goddamn cassettes; now they had the graveyard shift on the classical station oozing out of the speakers. That was okay—he just had to be careful not to nod out to all that Mozart shit. All this driving back and forth—you figured it up, it was like ten, twelve hours of driving—along with all that pounding away on Mike beforehand . . . no wonder he was tired. Plus—he rotated his hands on the steering wheel to look at them—he had a really nasty cut across the back of his left hand, deep enough to have drawn blood and scabbed over by now. He'd gotten it from one of Mike's teeth, he supposed, from giving him a crack in the mouth when he'd still been trying to fight and yell.

What he really wanted to do—besides go back to Aitch's apartment and get something to eat and go to sleep—was to wash out that cut with some kind of disinfectant, even just that raw isopropyl that Aitch always had lying around. Something like that could get really infected. Christ, a *dog's* mouth was supposed to be cleaner than a human's. And a dog would eat its own shit if you let it. So you had to figure this was a lot worse . . .

But instead, they were hanging out here, waiting for Mike's girlfriend to show up. Some other horseshit idea of Aitch's. He took his hand off the wheel and pumped his fist, brooding over the cut on its back.

"Hey, there she is." Aitch raised his head, peering out through the windshield. "Here she comes."

Charlie followed Aitch's gaze and spotted the Corvette heading up the street toward them. A red number, a convertible; some flashy piece of shit, as far as he was concerned. A teenager's idea of a neat car. Good for blowing off old ladies in Plymouths at the stop lights, and that was about it. It figured Mike's girlfriend—Charlie had met her before—would have something like that.

He tried to rouse himself, bracing his arms against the wheel and flexing his shoulder blades to work the stiffness out. "She's got a big surprise coming," he said, getting with Aitch's sense of humor, "when she finds out her boyfriend's gone bye-bye on her."

Aitch made a little laughing, snorting sound and nodded. They both watched the Corvette pull up to the curb in front of the apartment building. It was easy to spot the girl's blonde hair and the big sunglasses from here.

The girl matched the 'Vette; Charlie looked at her, those high-heeled fuck-me shoes clicking up the cement path to the building's front door. Maybe it had been Mike's idea to get her the car, so he'd have some kind of matched, Barbie-Gone-Bad ensemble on his hands; it had certainly been his money. It was nice enough, if that's what you liked: bubble butt just covered by an elastic-looking black skirt. She got a can like that from spending three days a week pumping a Nautilus machine. Same with her hard little tits shot forward by her winged-back shoulders—that's what the butterfly machine did for girls, gave them that arched back like the invisible man was trying to snap their spines with the point of his knee.

Tough little face, though he couldn't see it from this angle; she was already fiddling with her key at the front door's lock. He'd just remembered what she'd looked like when he'd met her at Mike's place. One of those doll faces with a mean red mouth. Figure a flat 100 IQ points, fifty of them given to shopping, the rest to the kind of sex that left marks.

If that was what Mike had wanted to spend his money on—everything was past tense with Mike from now on—then fine. Except anyone could've seen it, like a cancer on an X-ray, as though it were fated—that he'd wind up getting greedy and stupid. Just to keep up with her. You sleep with greedy and stupid little twats, it rubs off.

These little rock-and-roll numbers, with the big hair—the ones that Charlie always figured were supposed to look like they'd just gotten out of bed, where they'd been fucking their brains out—they weren't anything he himself went for. What he liked was to sit in the coffee house at Powell's, maybe while he was waiting to connect with Aitch for some kind of business, sit right up close by the big windows that faced on the sidewalk on Burnside, sit there with a decaf *latte* and gaze at the windows of the ballet studio, up on the third floor of the building across the street. Like on a real rainy night. And catch quick heartbreaker glimpses of those little dance student types, with their sweet faces and their hair pulled back into those little crocheted bun things—chignons, they were; he'd asked somebody once about it. The dancers knocked him out, and they didn't even know it. And he wasn't likely to meet one in his line of work. Though he'd read about some famous ones, like back in New York, who'd been all strung out on shit. He would've had mixed feelings about supplying somebody like that, getting to know them on that basis. That would really suck, he decided. In the meantime, if he caught any lowlifes from the transient hotel hanging around in the doorway of the ballet studio's building, littering the place up with their cigarette butts and dog bottles, he'd lean on them and tell them to take a hike.

"Jesus," said Aitch. "Look at this airhead."

Mike's girlfriend hadn't noticed them watching her. She was having a hard time getting into the apartment building. Probably already blitzed, Charlie figured, coming home from some party with her equally mindless little friends. Carrying the refreshments with her in her little spangly purse. Something else that she'd gotten from Mike. She finally managed to get the building's front door open—she was *really* fucked up; Charlie glanced back to the Corvette at the curb and saw a sideswipe scrape along the right front fender, looking like a fresh wound—and dropped the key into the metallic bag. Dumb shit—Charlie shook his head—she'd have to go through the whole routine of digging it out again when she got upstairs.

The apartment was in the front of the building. The two of them sat in the Cadillac, watching and waiting, until they saw the light go on in the window.

Charlie looked from the corner of his eye, without turning his head. Aitch sat there, gazing up at the square of light, one of his little smiles on his face.

She stood in the doorway, with her hand still on the light switch. Just standing and looking, her bright red mouth coming open, the strap of her purse sliding off the shoulder of the white acrylic fur jacket. She blinked, her forehead creasing into lines. Trying to figure it out, what she was seeing. Or even to see it all. It was as if the messages coming up her optic nerves had to slog through a chemical bog to get into her brain.

The place was trashed. Totally fucking *ruined*—that one word ping-ponged around inside her head. The furniture was overturned, except for the big Italian leather sofa she and Mike had had to go all the way up to Seattle to find, and that had been slashed open with a knife; the butter-soft cushions had mouths now, grinning and vomiting up white cotton stuffing.

One of the torchères had been bent double, as though somebody had snapped it across his knee, then thrown it out into the middle of the floor, its cord trailing behind it. On the far wall, by the dining room doorway, the Warhol Mao, and the Liz, that Mike had had before she had hooked up with him, had the glass smashed from the chrome frames and the prints cut into dangling ribbons.

She took a step into the apartment, looking at the rubble strewn across the floor, the sparkling shards of glass, the books broken-backed and flopped onto their faces.

"Mike . . . ?" she called.

There was no answer from the bedroom or from anywhere else in the empty apartment.

"Shit . . ." A whisper, her eyes grown wide. The edge of panic had cut through the fog. Her heart sped inside her.

Then she turned and saw on the wall behind her, near the door, the caved-in place in the plaster, just the size of a man's face. A wash of dried blood smeared down the wall, broken by a red handprint.

It was kind of funny to picture her up there, stumbling into the middle of their handiwork.

"Hey—what do you think?" Charlie smiled and nodded toward the windshield, and beyond to the lit window in the apartment building. He nudged Aitch with the point of his elbow. "Think I should pick up on that action? Little Miss Bimbo up there? She's going to be awfully lonely now."

Aitch gave him a disgusted look. He shook his head,

26

as if he couldn't believe he'd heard what Charlie had said. "Come on. Let's get out of here."

Now he wanted to go. Just when things were getting good. Who knew, maybe Mike's girlfriend—what was her name? Something with an *L*—maybe she was about to come running out of the building, all freaked out. That'd be funny, too.

He turned the key in the ignition. Still, it'd be worth remembering this address. He wasn't so hung up on those ballet types that he couldn't try a hit of something else.

Four

Something had happened, and he could move. He could walk.

This is dreaming—the thought slid through Mike's head, the whisper of his own voice inside himself. The space around him had become suffused with blue light, as though the roof and the floors above had melted away, letting the moon wash up against the walls. He lifted his head and looked, but didn't see the night sky. Instead, he saw a ceiling of carved beams intersecting with one another, forming squares and triangles and the shape of a six-pointed star right in the center. The white plaster between, stencilled with vines, shone luminous. From the center star hung a chandelier, unlit; the dark pieces of glass chimed like small bells as a current of air touched them.

He looked down at his hands, turning them over to see the palms. They seemed almost translucent, as though he could discern the veins and tendons, the perfect, undamaged workings inside. There was a smear of blood across his right palm; he rubbed it with the thumb of his other hand, then closed both hands tight, the fingers curling into the fists.

The right hand and arm had healed; and the walking, the dream light . . . He didn't care. *Maybe I'm not dreaming. Maybe I'm dead.* He knew he'd been hurt badly enough, by Aitch and Charlie. His fingers touched the side of his head, feeling for the place where the steel bar had struck, bearing him with its eclipsing weight down to the angle of his apartment's wall. Nothing; he took his hand away.

He looked down to the nest of blankets on the floor. He half expected to see himself curled up there, his real body, the hurt one, the blood and life having slowly leaked away. But he wasn't there. He squeezed his fists again, feeling the blood coursing around the bones inside.

This place was different, too. Its silence held him deep, the blue light an ocean pressing against him. He looked up from his hands and saw the curtains, not torn rotting stuff, but white gleaming rivers, billowing with the night wind sliding through the uncovered windows.

He stepped over the blankets and looked out, the window glass cold against his fingertips. The black hills were etched with the blue light, the stars slowly turning behind them. The red specks of fire, the watching eyes, drifted with the other, blacker shapes ranged against the hills. He let go of the curtain, and its silky weightlessness flowed past his gaze.

He turned back to the room. The walls receded, opening the space they enclosed to empty miles. He knew he could walk, hand reaching out, and in the motion of dreams never reach the far door that opened onto the columned entranceway. He was inside; he wasn't meant to leave. He knew that. Not until he'd been shown everything: the circular reception desk, with its mahogany panels buffed to dead mirrors, its marble top etched in silver and black—he rested his hands flat upon it, the stone the same chill temperature as his flesh—the rack of room keys behind it, the grid of mail slots for the guests; a switchboard, an antique, with its headpiece dangling from a hook, a curved black flower to speak into; the black cords snaked from one hole to another.

That wasn't it. There was something else. The blue light lapped against his chest, drawing him as though it were an ebbing tide.

A dining room. Tables with cloths draped to the floor, candles in silver holders. High-backed chairs. A grand piano beside a little stage at the far end. He stood in the wide doorway, his gaze searching across the empty space.

He went back to the lobby and stood at the foot of the wide staircase that curved up to the next floor. The light spilled down the steps and pooled at his feet.

His hand gripped the banister, just past the carved wooden post at the end, an eagle's claw holding a polished globe. He pulled himself onto the first step, looking upward at all the ones to follow.

Dreaming . . . He told himself that again, as he took another step, his hand sliding along the smooth surface of the rail.

A landing halfway up, with a window; he pressed his face close against the glass. Another section of hills circling in the distance outside the building. The red points were there as well, watching him, as if they had tracked his progress from the space below.

The last step; he let go and stood in the middle of a hallway, with numbered doorways down either direction. A window, curtainless, at the far end; through it, he heard the distant sound of voices and laughter. He walked toward the sound.

They were down there, the others. The window overlooked the gardens in front of the building, a white-gravelled drive circling through manicured lawns. The moonlight tinted everything white and blue, leaching away all other colors. The people down there moved in the pale light, touching one another, their voices sounding like crystal glasses breaking.

The women laughed, a chime of small bells. Dressed in long gowns, with lace collars that clung to their throats like the petals of flowers. High-waisted dresses, with more lace across their breasts and sleeves that puffed big at the shoulders, then tapered to rows of pearl buttons at the wrists. Their hair upswept, a few feathers left loose to drift along their swan necks.

A costume party, in the dead of night. He spread his hands against the frame of the window, bracing himself as he leaned toward the darkness and the chill night air. But that was what it looked like. Gibson Girls, the turn of the century. A long time ago.

The scent of flowers that bloomed in summer nights, jasmine and something sweeter, thickened the air. And mingled with that, the smell of money. This was what rich women had looked like, back then.

There were two of them, younger ones, with drawn-in waists a man could circle with his hands. They had little skinny racquets in their hands, and a net between them, set up right on the groomed lawn. Badminton; he saw the shuttlecock, held by the feathers in the delicate hand of one of them, as she laughed and said something to her friend on the other side.

Men also, in old-type fussy suits, with high, stiff collars, one in something with bright checks, knickers showing plaid stockings. Mustaches and muttonchops. They talked in low voices, their laughter, rarer than the women's, barking out suddenly.

Some of the people were in wheelchairs. The old kind, with high wicker backs and wooden arms. Pushed by nurses with starched white caps, bigger than those nurses wore now. They looked like pictures of Florence Nightingale, with those short blue capes just covering their shoulders.

It all looked like a picture, some period-piece engraving, an old photograph, silver etched on glass; a photograph come to life, or the shadow of it. In the moonlight, the figures in their old-fashioned clothes moved languidly, as though under a becalmed sea. Their voices and laughter drifted up to his ear as he watched their slow grace. One of the younger women moved her racquet in an underhand arc, and for a moment—and longer, forever—the shuttlecock hung motionless over the net.

Then it lay on the grass. He hadn't seen it fall. Time had moved again, but differently now. The voices and the chiming laughter had stopped. The figures on the broad manicured lawns held still, only their heads turning.

All toward him. Their faces lifted. The young women and the older ones; the men with their stiff collars and heavy mustaches; the ones in the wheelchairs, and the nurses standing behind them . . . They looked up to the window. At him. The pale light silvered their eyes, like coins or sparks of ice. They saw him—not smiling, not moving, their faces darkening as though a cloud had rolled across the moon. They watched him, their eyes locked on to his.

One of the young women, the prettiest one, raised her badminton racquet up to her face as though it were a fan, her small hand touching its curved rim. She bent her head, her gaze shadowed by her lashes. Perhaps she smiled at him; he couldn't tell . . .

He drew back from the open window. Before he could take a step away from it, he felt a hand touch his shoulder. His breath sucked in, a gasp, as his eyes darted around to the side.

"Come along now."

A nurse had laid hold of his shoulder, easily pulling him around, as though he had only a child's strength. She had on the old-style uniform, the same as the ones pushing the wheelchairs on the lawn, with the starched, winged hat, but without the short blue cape—that was for outdoors. A no-nonsense face, mouth set firm; she was older than the pretty ones outside.

She took his arm, gently but firmly, and walked him down the corridor.

"You're late." The words clipped out of her thin-lipped mouth. "The doctor's already waiting for you."

He couldn't say anything—they were already at the end of the corridor, in front of one of the doors. This one wasn't numbered; in precise, gold-edged black letters, it read Examining Room.

The nurse pushed open the door. "In you go." Her hand pressed at the small of his back, and he was inside the room.

He heard the door close behind, but he couldn't tell if the nurse was still there with him. A light glared, blinding him; he raised his hand, shielding his eyes. The light burned between his fingers; tears welled under his squeezed-tight eyelids.

The light swung away. Its afterimage swirled molten in the center of his gaze. He could just make out a figure in a white coat, head silhouetted black by the light behind him.

"Lie down on the table, please."

A doctor. He could make out the looped tubes of a stethoscope protruding from one of the pockets of the white coat. He saw the white-sleeved arm come up; a hand pressed against his chest. Pushing him backward—his own hands caught the edge of the table behind him.

Then he was lying on his back, on the table. The glare dazzled his eyes again as the examining lamp was swung over him. He still couldn't see the doctor's face beyond the light. He turned his head on the table's thin pillow. The room tilted about him. He could see the cabinets mounted on the far wall, glass-fronted, bottles of dark blue with handwritten labels inside. The cabinets and other fixtures in the room looked like antiques, but new somehow, as if they'd just been built and put in here.

There was something else, closer to the table; he could almost reach out and touch it with his hand. A machine, of black lacquered metal, with gold lettering and flourishes painted on. It took him a moment to realize what it was. An X-ray machine, an old one, a museum piece. But it was new as well, shiny and functional. A faint smell of ozone came from the machine.

The doctor had turned his back to him. He heard the clink of metal as the doctor sorted through some small objects on a chrome tray.

He couldn't move. He tried to raise his head from the table, but his strength had ebbed away. Only his eyes, straining to the side to see what the doctor was doing . . .

The figure in the white coat turned around, stepping closer to the table. Light sparked from the scalpel he held up in his rubber-gloved hand. Behind the edge of the blade, the face moved for the first time from shadow into the glow seeping from the side of the lamp.

An old face, carved down to the skull beneath the parchment skin, translucent enough that the teeth could be numbered behind the unsmiling lips. Black hole eyes that swallowed the light and gave none of it back.

"Just relax." The doctor turned the black gaze to the scalpel in his hand, then to the patient on the table. "This won't take long . . . not long at all . . ."

He watched the scalpel being lowered down toward his own face.

Nothing more than the random firings of neurons— he told himself that. Disorganized cortical functioning. All of it: the figures outside on the lawn, the blue undersea light lying heavy on the grass, the badminton shuttlecock hung suspended in the warm night air of summer, the nurse, and the doctor. *Dreaming . . .*

"A very simple procedure . . ."

The point of the scalpel touched his cheek, a few centimeters under his eye. He felt it pushing; then the skin parted, and the thin metal sunk in. His breath caught, his heart laboring under a fear that he'd forgotten, that he'd thought had gone away forever—that made him a child again, frozen at the sight of broken glass sparkling around his hand and red welling up to hide again the things that had been revealed to him, white things like wet string and snot, inside him; and it scared him, more than the pain, it scared him to see those things . . .

"Very simple . . . you'll hardly feel it at all . . ."

The scalpel moved, cutting downward. Deeper; his tongue tasted the metal.

Something was wet upon his face that wasn't the blood welling over the scalpel and the thin rubber fingers that held it. He squeezed his eyelids even tighter, and the tears broke through and ran, trailing down to the angle of his jaw. A sob, a child's, fought past his clenched breath.

"Don't worry . . . everything's coming along fine . . ."

The words inside his head were louder than the doctor's whisper.

Dreaming . . . He shouted it, teeth grinding together, trying to swallow the fear that had clotted on his tongue.

Or else he was dying. He knew that could be true as well. And that would be all right, too. As long as it ended.

"Just fine . . ."

Far away now. The light gone; deep inside. The familiar dark had come out of the hole at the center of the doctor's eyes, and wrapped him up in its comfort, forgiving him. He had been stupid to have been so scared. Like a child.

He let go and fell.

Five

He woke up, the hinges of his jaw aching. He wondered—dimly, at the edge of his consciousness—whether he had been shouting, or screaming, his mouth stretched open wide.

With no one to hear him. He opened his eyes and saw early morning sunlight, thin and pale, seeping through the ragged curtains in narrow cuts between the boards nailed over the windows. The pieces of sun made straight-edged marks across the bare floor.

The dream's panic eased away with his slowing pulse. But he remembered that other world, with its own light . . . its heavy motion, as though he'd been mired in some soft, perfectly transparent crystal. Until at last he'd been unable to move at all—that was the worst, to remember that. He closed his eyes again, working on one trembling breath after another, feeling each ache against his ribs. Something about . . . an examining room. He'd been up on the table, with the light pressing down on him. Everything in the room around him had been old-looking, period pieces: the cabinets, the black X-ray machine with its swirls of gold lettering, even the light itself, the fixture on its double-hinged arm. But all new at the same time, as though the cabinets had just been built a little while ago, the X-ray shipped out from the factory . . . that had been the weird part.

More of the dream came back to him, as he drew one breath after another, letting the sleep weight drain from him. The people who'd been out on the lawn, in their funny old clothes . . . but not old. Old-fashioned; that was it. Costume party stuff. Or like they'd been shooting a movie, and he hadn't spotted the cameras. Something like *The Great Gatsby*. No; he shook his head, wincing at a stab of pain up his neck. That'd be too late. Flappers and shit. Maybe something by Henry James. Cybill Shepherd in *Daisy Miller*. That was it. Parasols and those high-waisted long dresses that made girls' breasts look so nice, choker lace up to their chins . . .

He burst out laughing, eyes squeezed shut, his throat barking dry, realizing that he'd started to work himself into a hard-on. *Must not be dead . . . yet.* Fat lot of good it would do him—*you dumb shit*—and it was already dwindling away, chased by the pain that the laughing had pulled out of his ribs. Like some goddamn old Lenny Bruce routine: you're dying, you've been beaten to death and kicked out in the boonies, and what do you think about? *Shit.* He gulped little shallow breaths, letting the pain fold back in on itself, become something small enough so that he could stand opening his eyes to the strip of sunlight he felt on his face.

Still, the girl with the badminton racquet, the youngest one, had been good-looking enough. Skinny little thing. Even if she had stared up at him with the same dead face and coin-blank eyes that all the rest of them had had, the other women and the men with their muttonchops and walrus mustaches. All of them, the whole costume party on the lawn. The dream.

Lindy would have looked good in one of those old

period-piece dresses. He felt a little sad thinking about that; a different tear welled at the corner of his eyelid. With her hair pulled back and lifted off her neck, instead of all tangled-out to the width of her shoulders. That fucking bimbo style. If he pulled through this, if he ever made it back—big ifs—he'd do that, he'd get her one of those dresses, he'd have it made for her. She might go for it if she thought it was kinky enough, some particular fantasy of his that he was dressing her up for and inserting in place. A change from all those little numbers that just barely covered her ass, and all that Melrose Avenue crap. It'd be nice . . . something to think about . . .

He felt himself falling again, into the soft dark, and pulled himself back up. If he went under, he knew he might not make it back to the light. He was that close; he could feel it, like working on a cardiac arrest in the ER and sensing it slipping away, beyond the reach of his hands and all their cleverness.

He forced his eyes open. The wedge of sun fell right on them, dazzling him for a moment. He turned his head away. With his cheek against the bare plank floor, he could see across the space to the round, marble-topped counter and the grand staircase curving beyond. The same as he'd seen in his dreaming, only now covered with dust and dust-clotted cobwebs. One of the mahogany panels at the front of the counter had been kicked in, leaving jagged splinters. A big section of the reception desk's marble top had been pulled away and thrown to the floor; the pale, veined shards were scattered across the floor like bits of sugar candy.

Something else was different. Different from when the truck driver had dragged him in here and laid him down on the floor. He lifted his hand—the left one; his whole right arm was still a floppy, useless appendage—and touched his side. He didn't feel the bare skin and crusted blood over his ribs; instead, the texture of soft cloth, bound tight. Lifting his head from the blanket underneath, chin pressing against his collarbone, he saw the white bandages wrapped around his chest. They were smudged with dust from the floor, and red had started to leak through, from a torn place in the skin beneath his arm. His breath strained against the bandages, the broken ribs twinging sharply.

The effort of moving had drained him. He fell back, his head thumping on the blanket. The ceiling above him blurred, his eyes losing focus. Raising his hand, he touched the side of his head and felt the bandages there. He could even catch the faint scent of some kind of disinfectant.

He let his hand flop out to the side, and it hit something soft. He clutched his fingers into it, and drew it to him. He could just make out its color, but that was enough—it was his green scrub shirt, with his name stenciled on the breast pocket, from the hospital laundry. He held it close to his bandaged chest, panting from the exertion of the last few moments. The ceiling's cracked plaster kept on blurring and swimming about; he had to close his eyes.

Thinking about it kept him from slipping back under. Somebody had bandaged him up while he'd still been unconscious—maybe that was what the dream, at least the doctor part of it, had been all about. Though it wouldn't have had to have been a doctor; a boy scout with a merit badge in first aid could have done as much as this. Still . . . the image of the bony face, the skull with skin over it that he'd seen, came back unbidden. With the scalpel, and all that other creepy shit. His eyes flew open, to the comforting sunlight.

Getting up from the floor almost killed him: the pain burst and sparked along his spinal column, his breath hammering against his broken ribs as he rolled onto his side, then pushed with his good hand. On his knees, with his paralyzed arm curled under him, he looked across the room to the counter and staircase, miles away. He knew he'd never be able to crawl that far, not with the one hand useless; he was already hunched over, his weight borne on his other forearm. If he could get to his feet, stay upright . . .

The rotted fabric of the curtains came apart, into dust and threads, as he grabbed it, dumping him onto the point of his shoulder. But the fall had brought him closer to a chair, an oval-backed wooden one, against the wall; his fingers closed around the curved leg, and he drew it toward himself.

The chair's seat was broken out, spilling cotton stuffing and canvas tatters toward the floor. He dragged himself upright with it, finally resting his stomach on the back's rounded top edge. Jackknifed, his good hand gripping the wood, he let his breath fill up his lungs again.

He was afraid to let go of the chair. If he fell from this height and struck his head, the chances of staying conscious were slim—if it didn't kill him outright. The fragile tissues inside his skull were already swollen with an influx of blood, like a balloon filled with strawberry jam; one good jolt, and the overstretched rubber would split. There weren't any boy scout bandages that would fix that one up.

The chair slid forward a couple of inches as he shifted his weight on it. He saw how he could do it now. He pushed with his feet and the chair scraped across the planks, leaving its thin marks in the dust.

He reached the reception desk. Raising his head, he looked over the counter's marble top. He already knew what he'd see. Just as in the dream—the funky old switchboard, with its snake's nest of cables, the woven black covering frayed next to the brass-tipped plugs; the pigeon holes for the guests' mail, with the room numbers on tiny enameled badges under each one. A bell sitting on the counter, like another prop from a movie. *Boy! Take the doctor's luggage to Room 309, right away!* He balanced his weight on the chair, reached out and struck the bell's little

40

plunger with the palm of his hand. It made no sound except for a muffled thunk. He had to grab the side of the chair to keep from falling. *And have the maid draw the bath; the doctor's been traveling a long way.* He closed his eyes, letting the fantasy unreel inside his wobbling head. *There's a shiny new quarter for you if you're quick about it . . .*

His sight was starting to blur when he opened his eyes again. He could just make out a sheet of paper, yellowed, with curling brown edges, stuck with a pushpin by the switchboard. The ink scrawled on it had faded to a few grey curlicues, but a sepia-toned vignette of a building remained visible in the upper left corner: three stories, rows of windows, some kind of covered verandah or walkway around the front, big letters on a metal framework at the top that spelled out THERMALENE. Printed under the engraving in tiny italics were the words *Your Health Is Your Only Treasure.* Then the piece of paper doubled and swam about in his vision, and he couldn't see the words anymore.

Some kind of hotel, or health resort, then. He looked back across the lobby to the boarded-over doors in the distance. He wondered how long ago the place had folded. Long enough for the dust to have seeped in, the curtains and the chairs to have rotted, the air to have thickened with the silent years.

He heard a voice niggling at the back of his head. *Get rid of him . . . haul him back out . . .* The truck driver had managed that well enough. It didn't look as if anyone had been inside the place in half a century, at least.

A coughing spasm, the dust lodged in his throat, bent him double over the chair back. He spit a red wad out onto the floor and pushed himself upright again. The lobby tilted, his blurred view of it speckled with swarming black dots. The dots took several minutes to fade away.

He pushed the chair along the length of the reception counter. At the counter's end, where the marble had been

41

broken off and shattered on the floor, he leaned his shoulder against the mahogany. The foot of the grand staircase, which swept on up to the next floor, was a few yards farther on.

A real bad idea—he knew that, as he looked at the stairs mounting like a frozen waterfall. What he should do was to creep back to the nest of blankets in the middle of the floor, collapse in them, and use as much of his strength as he had left for the simple acts of breathing and moving his blood through his damaged frame. Just try to keep living, for as long as he could. He had a dim memory of the truck driver saying he'd send somebody around to check up on him. If he could hold out that long . . . then maybe he could make it. All the way through to the other side. Where he wouldn't be dead, and he could take care of the things he had to do.

Go back and lie down . . . just breathe, one after another . . . The water that the truck driver had left for him was back there by the blankets, and he suddenly realized how dehydrated he was, his throat dry and cracking like old leather.

If he lay back down, though, he knew he wouldn't be able to get up again. He'd just have to lie there and wait for somebody to come, for anything, just hoping that the guy with the truck hadn't been lying to him, hadn't already forgotten about him.

He leaned against the counter for a few more minutes, gathering his strength.

The stairs were only a couple of yards away. He could push the chair that far, and then lunge for the curved wooden banister. A ball in an eagle's claw—he recognized that from the dream. If he could manage to keep hold of the rail, he'd be able to stay upright.

He pushed himself away from the counter, sliding the chair across the floor, a few inches with each dragging step, like an old woman with a chrome walker—he could see a picture of himself inside his head, creeping along.

The chair's legs bumped against the bottom stair. He leaned farther over, reaching for the banister. His weight went too far to the side, and the chair suddenly skittered out from under him, toppling onto its side. His good hand gripped the rail, squeezing the dust-covered wood tight. His knees sagged, but he managed to keep his legs under him.

The strain of reaching had torn something loose under the bandages. He looked down and saw a line of red seeping from under the cloth and trickling down his skin to the waistband of his jeans.

Tilting his head back, he could see above him a window at the landing where the stairs turned. The glass wasn't boarded up like the ones all around the ground floor lobby. Bright sunlight poured through and washed down the stairs.

He pulled himself toward the light. Every two or three steps he had to stop and let his heart ease down from hammering against his breastbone.

The rail ended at the landing. He leaned against the wall and looked out the window. The glass was clouded with dust, but he could still see low hills, the sun pressing down on the dry brown scrub. The empty landscape rolled on toward the horizon and a distant blue-gray range of mountains without interruption.

He worked himself around, hands pressed against the window's frame, to where the stairs continued.

The black spots were dancing in front of his eyes again by the time he reached the end of the stairs. Panting for breath, the back of his head against the wall, he saw another piece of his dreaming: the corridor, the numbered doors, one after another. The narrow space was dark, lit only by the one window at the end.

That was where he'd looked out, in the dream; he remembered it. The glass was broken out, one triangular shard hanging from the top. He didn't have to go to it—in the dream, he'd been able to walk instead of crawling and creeping—to know he'd see nothing from it. The party on the lawn, the women in their high-breasted dresses, the young one with the badminton racquet—they were all gone. Long ago. Now there were just the dead hills, baked to stone.

He moved in the other direction, sliding his shoulder against the wall, the way the nurse in the dream had led him.

The gold letters had chipped off the pebbled glass. He could only make out "xamin" and "oom" on the door at the other end of the corridor. The rusted knob turned in his hand, the hinges scraping as he pushed the door inward.

More pieces of the dream. Battered by time, like everything in the building. The cabinet doors sagged open, the blue glass bottles with their hand-written labels now broken or tipped on their sides, gummy black tar leaking through their corks and making dark trails down the white-painted wood. The antique X-ray machine looked like the carapace of some giant insect, huddled in a corner and dried to a hollow shell.

He leaned against the examining table; it creaked under his weight, as though the rust-specked metal legs might split apart. His forehead bumped against the lamp, and it swayed away on its spidery articulated arm. Something snapped in the wheeled base, and the lamp toppled over, crashing to the floor. Bright splinters of the bulb inside scattered through the rising dust.

A counter underneath the cabinets was close enough to reach. He picked up a scalpel from a tray and brought it up to his face. For a moment, the end of the dream, all that he could remember of it, moved inside his head. The blade had been perfect and shining then, a mirror that he'd been able to see his face in, until it had been too close, pressing its fine edge into the skin under his eye. His breath stopped, trapped behind a stone in his chest.

The scalpel in his hand was dulled with rust, scabbed

44

over with orange and brown. He dropped it, and it clattered against the other ancient tools on the metal tray.

He leaned across the examining table, his forearm flat against its frayed padding, his head below his hunched shoulders. The dream had been another world, separate from this decay. It wasn't here now.

This was where they had left him. Aitch and Charlie. In this dead place.

With a sudden cry of anger, he lurched over the table, his good hand smashing across the rows of bottles on the cabinet shelves. They scattered and burst against the floor, the pungent odors filling the air with rot and age.

The swing of his arm sent him sprawling to the floor, the impact setting off a burst of fire behind his eyes. His hand clawed through the broken glass, digging into the wood beneath, slippery with the blood from his palm.

His legs weren't strong enough to get him upright again. He made it as far as the head of the stairs, dragging his useless arm, the back of his hand smearing through the dust.

The stairs blurred and spun, a hole deepening before him. The black spots swarmed up his face, became one, bigger than the light and the walls and the floor. The last of his strength bled out of him, and he crumpled forward, falling.

He didn't feel it when he hit. There was nothing left to feel.

Six

The red eyes watched the building. The sun's heat, even this early in the morning, battered the hills; the watching animals stayed in their shaded burrows, the cool spaces beneath the rocks, and waited.

The scent of a hurt thing was in the air, the smell of blood, dried to a black crust, and fresh, still wet. The fine trace, a thread in the air, drifted out of the building; different from the aged, layered smells of dust and splintering wood.

Different now, but the same as what had been there before. The ones in the hills, waiting through the long brilliant hours for night, knew what it was. They remembered. The building had been full of that smell once, of hurt things, and then things that stopped hurting. And became something else.

That had been a glorious time. If they'd had words to speak, they would have said it of that time, handing the memory around to each other like a golden coin worn smooth by each one's touch, over and over.

They had no words.

They could only watch and wait, in their cool shaded places. A hurt thing was in that place, where hurt things had been before, and hadn't been for a long time—too long a time. The other hunger, the one that wasn't in their bellies, stirred and moved, awakened.

One raised its muzzle and drew in the hot, laden air. The scent was still there, red and clear. The hurt thing hadn't died, not yet.

Later, in the dark, they would come down from the hills and drink in the scent, the sharp points of their muzzles pressed close to the boarded-over windows and doors. They would circle around the building, ears pricked, every sense trembling. In their own silence . . .

Now they waited, for the sun's time to pass.

The sound of the motorbike's two-stroke engine spattered against the hills and bounced off. It sounded, even at a distance, like a string of firecrackers going off inside an empty metal trash can. A continuous mechanical fart— that was what one of Doot's English teachers, the little snippy one that everybody figured was a homo, had called it, after hearing it rasping around in front of the high school.

He didn't give a shit what that guy, or anybody else, said about the bike; it got him where he wanted to go. A car would've been better—he was already saving up money for that—but in the meantime, the buzzing little mongrel beat walking. A person could fry his fucking *brains* out, trying to walk from one place to another out here. Big spaces, and nothing in between. That was the high desert for you.

Still, when there wasn't anybody around giving you shit, it was kinda nice. Doot's father, when he'd told him what was going on and what he wanted him to do, had said that he should get an early start, knowing that the bike had a top speed that only beat a slow trot because it could keep it up longer. So when he'd heard his dad's truck pulling out, before the first light, he'd already been awake and drawing on his jeans and T-shirt. And he had been on the road, with the stuff his dad had told him to pack, when the hills were all red with the sun coming up, the air still smelling like night, cool in the lungs, and unbroken by any human sound. He'd fired up the bike with regret; if he could've gotten to where he had to go by walking, with the food and the water and the other things in a backpack, he would've done it that way. The bike's engine had sawed apart the quiet, and it wouldn't come back together again until nightfall.

The road cut straight across the landscape, low brush on either side. He hadn't bothered putting on his helmet, leaving it strapped to the bike's frame. Out here, the world was so flat that he could see miles off anything that might give him trouble. Like one of the shit-for-brains types from the high school, horsing around with his daddy's pickup truck. He'd already taken a bad spill in the center of town, the one spot where there was an actual traffic light—not that the rednecks around here paid any attention to it. That Garza fellow, who should've graduated a couple of years ago and was still hanging around looking for trouble and finding it, and one of his buddies from the county correctional farm had pretty much taken dead aim at him, laughing and pounding their beer cans against the dashboard as they'd come barreling around the corner. He'd had to dump the bike to get out of their way—the pickup had gone right over the bike without touching it, thank you, God—and he'd gotten up without anything worse than a bleeding road rash underneath the left sleeve of his denim jacket. Those fuckers had just headed on out of town, braying away and tossing the empties out the side windows.

That was a big reason it was so pleasant out here. The absence of assholes. As long as he kept an eye open for potholes gouged out by the winter's snow and ice, it was clear sailing.

The building, the old clinic, showed up ahead, still a couple of miles away. It looked like the stump of a broken tooth, dirty white except for the blackened part to the side where the fire had been. A faint sulfurous smell moved in the wind, like duck eggs that had been laid in a barn and then forgotten until a pitchfork had broken them open in the old straw. Behind the clinic building, the first set of low hills interrupted the flat terrain.

A lane curved off the county road, leading to the clinic. The tires of the motorbike bumped over the rusting metal of the rail line that had run out here, ages ago. Brown weeds bristled up from between the ties. A stagnant-looking pond, the surface coated with swirls that reflected oily rainbows, stretched to the right, with one of the clinic's outbuildings, a little stucco hut, at its edge.

Doot halted the motorbike halfway down the lane. From here, he could see the boarded-over windows all along the ground floor, the shingles of the covered verandah sagging or broken through to the planks beneath. Up at the top of the building, braced by a framework of iron grown fragile, big letters spelled out THERMALEN. There had been another E at the end, but it had fallen off in a windstorm and now lay facedown near the steps going up to the building's front doors, stenciling itself into the dry weeds.

The bike's racket snapped back from the looming front of the building, the echo fluttering at his ears. He walked the bike through the deepest rut in the lane, then lifted his feet to the pegs and rolled on a touch of the accelerator.

When he got off the bike, pushing down the kickstand, he combed his hair back into place—or close to—with his fingers. Tooling around without the helmet always left him looking like he had yellow straw sticking straight up from his forehead; with the helmet on, and sweating into it, made him look as though the straw had been glued all over his skull.

The hills' silence wrapped around him, now that the bike's engine was shut off. He glanced over his shoulder as he untied the bundle from the carrier rack. The blank windows in the stories above stared down at him.

"Shit." The hook at the end of the bungee cord had snagged his fingertip; he hadn't been watching what he was doing. A drop of blood oozed up. He stuck the finger in his mouth for a moment, then shook it dry. Another drop seeped out, smaller than the first. That would have to do for now. He lifted the pack's strap onto his shoulder and mounted the buckling steps up to the clinic's door.

"Hey—anybody here?" He squeezed his chest past the boards and looked around what had been the clinic's lobby. It was a dumb thing to say—as if the guy could have gone off somewhere, the way his dad had said he was all busted up—but he didn't know what else would've been appropriate. He didn't want to just burst in on the guy. *Maybe I should have knocked.* That was a dumb enough idea to be a joke.

He pushed the boards farther back, so he could work his way in with the bundle. His dad had been the one who'd pulled loose most of the rusted nails around the door's frame, leaving just a couple at the top and bottom that could be wiggled back into their orange-rimmed holes. So that anybody who came along wouldn't think people had been going in and out of that place. That had been a long time ago, too—he'd been only ten or so when his dad, right after the divorce, had gone through a phase with a metal detector. A buddy had laid it on him as partial payment for helping him out with a load of cauliflower that had broken down on the pass through the Blue Mountains. His dad had been working a reefer truck back then, making good enough money that he had been more interested in dumb toys than cash.

Seeing the lobby again, with its raggedy curtains and

the mahogany and marble counter at the far end, busted-off pieces and all, set a little movie ticking away inside his head. Him and his dad, the round flat snout of the metal detector sniffing at the floor, his dad watching the dial on the box up at the top. He'd tagged behind him, keeping a carefully calculated distance to show that he wasn't really worried about any horrible shit happening, like ghosts or hoboes—either or both—raving down the big staircase with knives and hard-ons. The older kids in school had told him back then that that was what 'boes did to you, if they caught you snooping around where they had their fires and did all the rest of their hobo business. The knife up to your throat while they pulled down your pants with their other dirty, black-nailed hand. Ghosts he hadn't been so sure about back then, as a kid. Could ghosts get hard-ons? Something poking up under the white sheet, like a pup tent?

That showed how long ago he'd been a kid. Nowadays, kids that young didn't know from ghosts in white sheets. Now they wore hockey goalie masks and had chain saws and knives on the ends of their fingers and shit. And even the little kids laughed their asses off, or said *"Wow, gnarly"* at stuff like that when they watched them on their folks' VCRs. That was the way things went. It made him feel old to think about it already, and he was just goddamn seventeen.

The smell of the musty air inside the building, cooped up and baked by long days of sun—he remembered that, too. And dust motes drifting in and out of the thin slices of light coming through the window boards. And the quiet.

He and his dad hadn't found any treasure with the metal detector. Now that he'd thought about it, he'd realized his old man hadn't really been expecting to but had just been in some goofy screwing-around mode. The only thing had been a silver dollar, an old Standing Liberty cartwheel that had fallen down in a crack between the floorboards, and that his dad had pried out with his jack-knife blade and given to him. It was under his clean socks now, in a drawer of his bedroom dresser, back home. They had never come back out to the place, after that one time.

"Hey," he called again; nobody had answered him from before. Maybe the guy was asleep, or passed out still. Or dead—his old man had told him the guy looked pretty close to it. Being in this place with some fuckin' corpse wasn't an idea he wanted to think about. "You here? Come on, man."

Silence. His eyes had adjusted enough to the dim light that he could see a couple of blankets, a deflated ghost, crumpled in the middle of the lobby's floor. He recognized them as the ones his dad usually kept in the Peterbilt's sleeper. That was probably his dad's thermos beside them; he'd said something about leaving the guy some water.

Well, shit . . . Doot walked farther into the lobby, looking around him. The guy wasn't here. Maybe he'd crawled outside. And pounded the nails back in that held the boards over the door? Not likely.

He stood by the counter that had been the old clinic's reception desk. There were marks, like somebody had dragged his arm through the dust on the marble top, and one clear handprint.

"Just tell me where you're at, okay?" He raised his eyes, listening to his voice bounce off the carved, interlocking beams of the ceiling. He held his breath; when the echo faded, he heard the other sound. Someone else breathing.

Around the end of the counter, Doot saw him. The guy was sprawled out on the landing up the big staircase, shoulder and head against the wall, one hand flopped down the steps. Blood leaked through the bandages wrapped around the guy's chest.

The guy moaned when he raised him up. Doot squatted on the stairs below him, trying to get the weight onto his own shoulders. It flashed on him then that maybe he was fucking it up, maybe the guy had one of those injuries where if you tried to move him, you'd just killed him right there on the spot. But it was already too late; he'd got the guy up into a fireman's carry, or as much of one as he could manage—the guy seemed to weigh a ton, all loose and uncooperative like that—and had already stumbled with him down to the lobby. Besides, he didn't see how he could have left him all bent up like a rag doll on the landing.

He dragged the guy over to the blankets and lay him down. The eyes fluttered open as he stood back up; they drifted, then fastened on his face.

The man's lips were dry and cracked; the point of his tongue moved across them, then drew back in. His voice rasped out, "Who . . ." He closed his eyes for a moment, then opened them again, having pulled up some fragment of strength inside. "Who are you . . ."

He wiped his hands on his jeans. He'd gotten the guy's blood on them. "Uh . . . my dad sent me. He told me you were out here. Said you might need some stuff."

He'd dropped his pack down by the blankets when he'd walked over to the reception counter. Now he squatted down, opened the pack and started pulling out things.

"I got something to drink here—Pepsi; is that okay?" The words tumbled out of him. He'd never seen anybody in as bad shape as this fellow. "And I made you some sandwiches, and I brought along some canned chili—we could make a fire or something, you know, to heat it up . . ."

He managed to get the brakes on at last. He stayed squatting on his heels, holding the can of Nalley's Extra Beefy in his hands. The focus of the man's gaze had moved from Doot's face up to the ceiling.

"Is there . . ." The rasp had dwindled to a whisper. "There's water there, isn't there . . . He said . . ."

Doot filled up the cup from the thermos bottle and held it to the man's lips, cradling the back of the bandaged head with his other hand. Some of the water trickled out of the mouth's corners, turning pink as it sluiced through the red-black crust and down to the throat.

The man drew his head back from the cup, and Doot laid him back down as gently as he could. One hand lifted from the blankets and smeared its palm across the man's mouth, drawing the blood and water into ragged stripes across his cheek.

"Thanks . . ." The voice was a little stronger. The gaze came slowly back around to Doot. The pupil of one eye was bigger than the other; it looked like a hole somebody could drop a nickel down. "So—that was your father? The guy with the truck?"

Doot nodded. "Yeah—he told me you looked like you'd got in a bit of trouble."

The man grunted, even managing a faint smile. "Bit of trouble" was the understatement of the year. He rolled onto his side, pushing with one hand—Doot could see that the other one, the right, was no good, paralyzed or something. The man grabbed one of the sandwiches, pinning it against the floor to tear off the clear plastic wrapping. His teeth tore at the white bread and pink lunch meat.

Doot let his own voice go softer. "He said it was like . . . law trouble, or something . . . That was why you couldn't go to the hospital."

The eyes with their mismatched pupils looked over the sandwich at him. The man chewed and swallowed. "Is that a problem for you?"

He shook his head. "Hell, no—I don't care." He'd learned a long time ago to keep his mouth shut about certain things. Like what his dad was up to these days. "I was just . . . you know . . . curious. That's all."

Another chew and swallow. The man took smaller bites now. "There's just some people in this world," he said slowly, nodding his head, eyes looking at some point past Doot, "that you just have to watch your step around them."

The man fell silent, working away at what was left of

54

the sandwich. His face darkened, brooding, as Doot watched him. After a moment, Doot figured that was all the explanation he was going to get for now.

He filled the plastic cup again for the man, who drank it down greedily.

"So where's your father, then?" The man breathed hard after gulping the water. "Is he going to come back around here?"

Doot shook his head. "He's off on some job. Hauling something—I don't know." He shrugged. "He's gone a lot. Said he'd be back in a week or so. I'm on my own most of the time. My mom walked out on him a long time ago." Immediately, he regretted saying that last bit, and wondered why he had. This guy didn't need to know shit like that.

The man didn't even seem to have paid any attention. He rolled on his damaged arm, bringing his face closer. Under the bruises and the dark hair matted with blood, he had sharp-angled features, eyes deep set; maybe in his late twenties. It was hard to tell, with him being so fucked up.

"What's your name?"

He felt a flush of embarrassment creep up his throat. "Everybody around here calls me Doot." There was no point in trying to hide it. The guy would find out sooner or later. He pointed with his thumb toward the lobby's door. " 'Cause of that little bike I got. You know—doot, doot, doot?" Now he really felt like a jerk.

An impatient nod from the man, his eyes wincing in sudden pain. "Listen, Doot." He locked his unbalanced gaze onto him, speaking slowly. "I need you to do me a big favor. I've got to get to a telephone. Right away. And without anybody seeing me. Think you can handle that?"

This was too weird. He'd never even *seen* this guy until, what, a quarter of an hour ago? If that. And Christ knew what kind of deep shit he was in. To get worked over like that, and tossed out on the road in the middle of nowhere, the way Doot's father had described it to him—

that meant the guy had been keeping some unpleasant company. Heavy-type people. So this guy was probably something along those lines, too. Plus all that business about not wanting to go to a hospital—you didn't have to be a genius to figure that one out. The guy was looking to avoid the police.

The way he figured it, he'd already done his good deed by coming out here and checking up on the guy, bringing up all this food and stuff. His dad had felt sorry for him, because he'd found him out there where he'd been dumped. Well, fine; they didn't owe him anything more. Not to the point of wading hip deep into whatever shit it was that had gotten the guy into this predicament.

What was the smart thing to do, he knew, was to leave the guy here, with the rest of the sandwiches, and the chili and the Pepsi, and the flashlight and can opener he'd brought along. And go home and think about what to do next. Do not, he told himself, get involved in this dude's spooky business.

The man's voice poked at him. "Well? Can you?"

He hesitated a minute, then tried to keep his eyes from going too wide and making him look like a fool. He nodded yes.

Seven

Aitch had gone down to L.A. with an empty briefcase and came back with it full. Charlie waited for him at the airport gate, actually across the walkway at another gate where nobody was sitting. He could see from there when people started getting off the plane. Somebody in the crowd filling the rows of seats over there was smoking a cigar that smelled as though he'd taken a shit, then set it on fire for some personal reason; that was why Charlie had moved.

What a bunch of horseshit, to have smoking and no smoking sections right together, separated by some diddly sign hanging from the ceiling. Like that fart smell was going to percolate along in the air, right up to there, and then stop. All the way on the other side of the building, he slouched down in his seat—they were leathery plastic slings, suspended together from a long chrome frame— and looked at the neck of the business suit with the cigar. Put 'em all in their own little room, that was the way, and close the door. Jesus—now the smell was coming over here.

He picked up a folded newspaper that somebody had left on the seat next to him. The headlines were all yesterday's; he dropped it back onto the empty seat and wished that Aitch would hurry up. The first passengers had already come up the narrow slanting tunnel that went out to the plane. That fuckin' cigar smoke was going to make him puke.

Aitch finally appeared, swinging along with the briefcase dangling from his hand. It was full, Charlie knew, not from the apparent weight of it or anything like that—what Aitch had gone down to L.A. for didn't weigh that much—but just because Aitch wouldn't have been smiling like that if he'd come back empty-handed.

Charlie got up and walked over, just in time to see Aitch curl his lip, nose wrinkling, and hear him say to the schmuck with the cigar, "Hey, mac—there's kids around. You know?"

He grabbed Aitch by the arm, right above the elbow, and pushed him out toward the walkway. "Come on, let's get out of here."

They walked past the metal detectors. "How'd it go?" asked Charlie.

"Oh, fine. Fine. No problem. We're dealing with reasonable people." Aitch looked back over his shoulder as he walked. "Christ, did you *smell* that thing? What the—"

It was dark outside the terminal. Aitch had been gone all day. Charlie unlocked the car's trunk and Aitch tossed the briefcase in.

"That's the last time I fly in and out of LAX, though." Aitch lounged back as Charlie paid the girl in the parking garage booth. The barrier went up, and he headed for the freeway. "Fuckin' nightmare," said Aitch. "And I don't mean because it's crowded. I can deal with that. It's those goddamn wimpy takeoffs you gotta endure. You know LAX is a black star airport?"

"What's that?" He swung the car up the on-ramp.

"I read it somewhere." Aitch was hopped up and

talkative from too much caffeine; Charlie recognized the symptoms. "The airline pilots get together and give a black star to airports they think are dangerous. L.A. rates because of the noise restrictions. They gotta creep out of it on low throttle until they're out over the water, then they can give it the gas. Meanwhile you're hanging up there, wondering if this bastard's going to make it. No, man, next time I have to go down there, I'm going to use Ontario. You ever fly out of Ontario? Not Ontario, Canada; I mean the one down in Southern California."

He moved the car into the center lane and picked up speed. "No. Never have."

"It's a trip." Aitch stretched his legs out, arching his spine away from the seat, head rolled back. "Full power takeoff. People who live around there don't like it, they can move. Boom, you're up in the air like a slingshot. Real E ticket ride."

Charlie grunted, noncommittal. Everything was a trip for Aitch.

Now he was leaning forward, prowling through the glove compartment for a tape he wanted to hear. He gave up, falling back in the seat and leaving the radio tuned to the murmur of the classical station. "Hey, you know Hollis, don't you? You've met him."

Hollis was the source in L.A. that Aitch had flown down there to talk to. "Yeah, I know him." Hollis was Mister Smooth—he *looked* like a doctor—which made it easy for him to turn the ones that got in over their heads. It was like dealing with a fellow professional. Or maybe a priest: they got to confess their sins and do their penance. Which was where the margin of profit for Hollis, and for Aitch and him, came from. Things like the stuff the briefcase in the trunk was filled with. Stuff like that, on the loose instead of being locked up in a hospital cupboard, meant that somebody was fucking up.

"Hollis told me something interesting." Aitch watched the cars over in the next lane. "About skeletons.

59

You know how hard it is, getting hold of a good skeleton these days? He hears about these things 'cause of his line of work, you know, hanging around with all these doctors. Some of 'em teach and do university stuff, and they're telling him about the problems they got. And it seems—" Aitch spread his hands out. "Seems there's a real drought in the market right now, for really good Grade A human skeletons. Everybody's gotta make do with these plastic ones, or fiberglass. They used to get 'em, the real ones, out of India and places like that, he told me—a real Third World export product, you know—but a lot of those places have clamped down. Politics and stuff. Plus now— catch this—a lot of the ones that do come up for sale, they get snagged by these interior decorating places. Some yuppie, he's into like a *bone* motif, he's already got a water buffalo skull or something up on his wall, then he wants like real human bits and pieces. Plus, you figure, he's only ever going to buy *one,* so he can pay whatever they want. Drives the prices right up."

He knew Aitch was watching him out of the corner of his eye, checking his reaction to this kind of talk. Seeing if he was squeamish about it. He kept his face composed, just watching the traffic. The talk was more cold-hearted than actually grisly.

Aitch stroked his lower lip, musing. "You know, what else Hollis told me was that you got your different quality skeletons. Especially in the skulls. Like A, B, and C grades. Depending on how much of their teeth they got left in their heads. They got all their teeth, maybe a few fillings, that's a Grade A. I wonder . . ." He pinched the lip between his thumb and forefinger, then let go of it. "Hey, you remember our buddy Mike?"

He was talking about it as though they'd dumped Mike off months ago, instead of just the other day. As though he had to really work to dredge him up out of memory.

Charlie nodded. "What about him?"

"He had pretty good teeth, didn't he? I mean, with him being a young guy, and a doctor and all . . . he took pretty good care of himself. Maybe a couple teeth got busted, when you hit him with that bar."

Aitch had been the one that had hit Mike with the bar, a roundhouse swing that had laid Mike out on the floor. Charlie looked over at Aitch. "What do you want to do? You want to go back out there and get him, scrape the meat off his bones or something?"

"No, come on . . . shit." Aitch shook his head. "I mean, he's out there in the middle of nowhere, he's gonna *be* bones after a while. You don't have to pick meat off him. The sun just, you know . . . dries him out. Bleaches him."

"Um, I don't think so. There's coyotes out there. They'd pull him to pieces. Crack the bones to get at the whatta-ya-call-it, the marrow inside. You'd go back out there and you wouldn't find any pieces bigger than your thumbnail." He didn't know if that was true or not, but it sounded right.

"That's a pisser." Aitch stared out the windshield. "Coyotes, huh?" He mulled it over. "That's really too bad. Because you can get a pretty good price for a nice human skeleton, with all its teeth in good shape. I don't mean tons of money, but still . . ."

Charlie knew that Aitch wasn't interested in the money at all. Some bent yuppie has a human skeleton in his bone collection, then Aitch had to have one. That fucker Hollis had put the idea in his head. Plus to have it be somebody you had known . . . a former business associate, instead of just some dumb Indian peasant . . . that would appeal to Aitch. He could hang it in the corner of his bedroom, maybe with some artistic lighting on it, and make little sly comments about it to the girls. *Oh, that?— just somebody who had a, uh, little accident.* Mysterioso gangster vibes. They went for that sort of thing.

Aitch lifted the sleeve of his jacket to his nose and

sniffed it. His face curdled. "Christ! All I did was walk past that guy, and I can still smell his fucking cigar!"

"Yeah, it really gets in there." Charlie let the traffic pull the car along, on toward the city. "Hey, did you know I used to smoke?"

"You did, huh." Aitch still looked disgusted.

"Gave it up—'cause of the smell, and all the other stuff. The first time I woke up in the morning, went to the bathroom, and coughed up a big yellow wad in the sink— looked like some kinda prop from a horror movie—I said that's it. No more for me. The way I quit, this old guy I used to know told me how to do it. It was the same way he'd gotten himself off pills."

"Yeah? What's that?"

Charlie lifted a forefinger off the wheel. "What you gotta do is, you take all the stuff you don't want to do any more, like the pills or the cigarettes, and you throw 'em in the toilet, and you watch it all go down. Then you go out and get some more of it—you go out and *buy* more—and you take it home and flush *that*. And you keep doing that until you don't want the stuff any more." He took his hand from the wheel and used the finger to tap the side of his head. "See, what it does, it makes a connection in your brain between that stuff and shit. Shit goes in the toilet. That's what it's for. And who wants shit? You know?"

Aitch turned his head and looked at him for a long moment. Then he nodded. "That's very good. That's smart. Lucky for us, the people we deal with aren't that smart." He slumped back in the seat, gazing back out the side window.

It'd been the longest spiel he'd ever had, talking with Aitch. Usually he didn't say that much, at least not all in one go. But he'd wanted to change the subject, get Aitch off all that b.s. about skeletons—Mike's bleached bones— and stuff. *That* was sick.

He glanced over at Aitch. The man was thinking,

whatever it was he thought about when he shut up and his eyelids came halfway down.

"Maybe . . ." Aitch's voice came from far away. "Maybe we could go out there and put like chicken wire over him. So the coyotes wouldn't get to him."

Shit, thought Charlie. The guy never let up.

Eight

Mike lay on the building's verandah, his back against the boards over the door. It had been so hot and airless inside, the sun making the place into an oven, that he'd had the kid drag him out there. Along with the water that was left in the thermos, and the big bottle of Pepsi. He'd nearly finished them both. He'd lost a lot of fluid, both from the beating and then from the hours he'd been lying unconscious at the roadside.

The sloping roof over the verandah—it ran all the way across the long front of the building and turned the corner to the side—had shaded him. What breeze there had been brought a faint sulfur smell from, he supposed, the pond he could just see out at the side of the lane. It probably had some kind of mineral content, fed from underground. That was why it hadn't evaporated away in this heat.

On other hot days, long ago—he'd drowsed, thinking about it—the people in the wheelchairs, with their nurses behind them, must have stationed themselves up here in the shade, watching the young women playing badminton.

Or would they have played, in that kind of heat? Maybe just strolled about, with parasols trimmed with lace to match their dresses. And those little straw hats with blue ribbons, that sat up on top of their hair. A pretty picture. With his eyes closed, he'd almost been able to see it.

After sunset, the temperature had started to fall. The kid—Doot, whatever—had pulled Mike's green scrub shirt back on him, working it over his useless arm. The kid had also hauled out one of the blankets, though Mike hadn't seen the point of it at the time. Now he was glad the kid had done it. He managed to wrap it around his shoulder, crouching forward into the well of his own body warmth. The kid lived out here, he was part of this world; he knew what it was like.

The kid had had other things to take care of, all of his little scooting-around errands. Skinny kid; he looked like a scarecrow in faded denim, with yellow hair sticking out in all directions. Bright enough to do what he was told, but not any brighter than that—which suited Mike fine. He'd instructed the kid to come back when it was dark. They'd make the push to get him to a phone then, when nobody would be likely to see them.

If he made it till then. He'd used up what strength he'd had, just pulling it together long enough to talk to the kid and make plans. Plus, pitching down the building's stairs—he'd known going up there had been a bad idea, but the dream's shifting memory had pulled him on—had left him more fucked up than before. His vision was going; when there had been light enough to see, the doubling and the blurring had gotten worse, much worse. All the well-established indicators of the blood seeping inside his skull. He'd had only a brief glimpse of Doot's face before it had diffused into something like a pink cloud with a voice attached to it.

The pain had become something he could handle—or he couldn't handle; he had no choice about it. It made him think of something a cop had told him once, about how phony movies were where somebody gets the crap beat out of him, then the next day is up and doing shit, like he's Dirty Harry or something. *Man, you get hit in the gut hard enough, next day you don't even want to live.* He didn't have a choice about that, either. If he wanted to look up Aitch and Charlie again . . .

His arm worried him, though, the one he couldn't move. With his good hand, he gathered the blanket tighter around himself; underneath it, he tried again to clench his right fist. He couldn't even feel it. Plus the leg on that side was starting to numb out as well; it had flopped and dragged behind him when the kid had carried him out to the verandah. Nerve damage, probably from one of the blows to his spine, or another symptom resulting from the swelling of the brain tissue. Either way, it was getting worse.

The last thing Mike had the kid do, before he'd gotten on his little motorbike and taken off, was to help him stand up at the edge of the verandah, over to the side and away from the stairs. With his good hand, he'd been able to get the fly of his trousers open. His piss had been red with blood, leaving his bladder and kidneys aching. It made a dark puddle soaking into the ground.

So where was the kid now? Doot and his motorbike. *Doot doot doot.* Mike raised his head, trying to hear anything that might be coming down the road, out past the lane that ran through the weeds in front of the building. Nothing. Complete night had wrapped around the hills; overhead, the stars blurred and danced as he looked up at them.

"Come on . . ." He murmured the words deep in his throat. You stupid little shit. Get your ass back here. He hunched down, feeling the night's cold penetrating the blanket.

Another light moved, closer to him, in the darkness around the building—red, instead of the cold blue-white of the stars up above. He squinted, trying to make out what it was. He managed to focus well enough that the red light condensed into two points. Like eyes—the eyes of an animal regarding him, silent and watchful. And there were others, pairs of the red sparks, creeping down out of the hills. They stopped at a certain distance, as though an invisible line were drawn there, several yards away.

"Shit." This was all he needed. Fucking coyotes, or something even worse. He hoped they were just coyotes. Was he far enough out in the sticks for there to be wolves around? How far east, he wondered, had Aitch and Charlie driven before they'd dumped him off? Start getting close to the Idaho border, and there were forests and mountain lakes that got socked in good and tight during the winter, real "Mutual of Omaha's Wild Kingdom" stuff. All kinds of shit out there, including wolves.

These were coyotes. He was sure of it, he wanted to be sure. Not much more than skinny dogs, clever and cowardly. The smell of the blood, probably from the piss he'd taken off the edge of the verandah, had brought them slinking around, soon as it had turned dark. Now they were hanging back, waiting to see if he were dead or alive. Essentially chickenshit; the ones down south, in California, had to be completely desperate from hunger to come out and snatch a toy poodle from beside a Beverly Hills swimming pool.

"Beat it!" His shout croaked out of his throat. "Come on, get out of here!" The red eyes—there seemed to be about six or seven pairs in the dark now—didn't move from the positions they had taken. And the fuckers looked too big to be coyotes. He leaned forward, sweeping his hand across the verandah, trying to find something to throw.

He came up with a piece of wood, a pointed fragment a couple of feet long that had been knocked loose from the boards over the door. Straightening back up, he whipped the piece around by the end and let it fly. The effort sent him sprawling forward; he caught his balance with his good hand, the palm sliding in the layers of dust.

Moonlight caught the wood as it flew; he looked up in time to see one of the pairs of eyes shift aside, in an unhurried fluid motion, as the piece hit the ground.

The watching eyes stayed where they were. *Maybe I should've kept it.* The sharp point would have at least given him a weapon to defend himself with, if the animals grew bold enough to sidle up onto the verandah. If they determined, however their minds worked, that he was weak enough to make easy prey . . .

They gazed back at him, unmoving and patient. Where was that stupid kid? Mike glanced from the corner of his eye toward the distant road, then quickly back to the animals out in the dark. A couple of them had shifted, padding silently to new positions, to crouch down and watch. Even that small movement of his eyes brought on the blurring, the red sparks hazing out of focus.

"You fuckers . . ." Blinded, he sensed that the coyotes had edged closer. "Sonsabitches . . ." That brought a laugh rasping in his throat. *Of course; what else would they be?* A salt taste welled up on his tongue, and he spat it out.

A sputtering mechanical note sounded in the distance. He turned his head and saw another blurred point, yellowish white instead of red. The motorbike's beam swept around toward him as the rider slowed for the turn off the road, onto the lane.

The patient creatures melted back into the hills' darkness. He had a glimpse, for only a fraction of a second, of one of them, the loping, sharp-muzzled figure disappearing into its own shadow running before it. Then they were gone.

The motorbike came to a halt in front of the building, its engine wheezing to silence. Mike could just see the kid Doot climbing off it.

* * *

Up ahead, Doot saw the pickup trucks and a few spavined old Chevys and Fords parked around the front of the hamburger place. Most of the guys were lounging against the fenders, shooting the breeze with each other. Their girlfriends—only a couple of those—looked bored. A few guffawing bursts of laughter floated across on the still night air.

He'd pulled the bike over to the side of the road, about fifty yards away from the noise and the lights. Nobody over there had turned around from talking and caught sight of him.

"How you doing?" Doot looked over his shoulder. "You okay?"

The guy looked like hell. His face was just a few inches away, the guy's chest pressed close to Doot's spine. That had been the only way to get him out here, this far away from the old clinic building; the guy hadn't strength enough to stay upright on the seat behind Doot. He'd had to take the bungee cord off the bike's carrier rack and loop it around the man's frame, then fasten the hooks together in front of his own chest. To conceal the cord, he'd draped his denim jacket over the guy's shoulders, fastening the top button to keep it in place. That way, anybody who might have seen them on the road would've just thought Doot had a passenger holding on tight behind him. He'd brought along a knit watch cap of his dad's and had pulled it on over the bandages around the guy's head to make him look even more normal and less like some escapee from a hospital ward.

Breathing through his mouth, eyes closed, the guy didn't answer him. Underneath the bruises, the face was drained white as the edge of the bandages peeking out from the cap.

Maybe the vibration from the bike's engine had busted loose whatever was hurt inside the guy. Plus the road from the old clinic building wasn't in any great shape. Doot had tried to avoid the biggest holes and ruts, but even so, there had still been plenty of good hard jolts coming up the bike's frame. The last couple of miles, the guy's head had lain against his shoulder, jiggling with each bounce in the road. The idea had come into Doot's own head that the guy was dead, that the trip had killed him off and he was actually scooting down the road with a corpse tied to himself. Arms and legs flopping loose, and blood running out of its nose and mouth. That notion had spooked him so much that he'd goosed the bike to its fastest speed, trying to get here as quickly as possible.

"Hey, mister." He reached across himself and pushed the guy's shoulder. "Hey, we're here. Come on."

The man's head tilted back, and the eyes came open. Their focus wobbled to some point drifting yards beyond Doot.

"Phone . . ." The word whispered out of the man's cracked lips. "Where's the . . . where's the phone . . ."

"It's up ahead a little ways." Doot took his hand from the bars and pointed.

The hamburger place down the road had started existence as an A & W Root Beer franchise. A long time ago, maybe back in the fifties, it had gone bust and been reincarnated as Arnie's Place, then gone bust again, and now it was Big Lou's Burgers. It was probably going to go under again; nobody came around except the high school kids, and they didn't spend enough to keep the place going. Lou and his little fat Mexican wife didn't even bother to try chasing them away anymore; if the kids weren't around, the place looked so abandoned that anybody coming down the county highway might not have been able to tell that it was open for business.

Lou and his wife kept opening up the place every day, because there was nothing else to do except go on marching toward bankruptcy. The kids from the high school hung around because there wasn't shit else to do in what passed for a town out here. Like flies hanging around a last melon left in a field, the rind split open by the sun. It didn't have to be sweet, it just had to be there.

The phone booth was around the side, at the edge of the parking lot. The pickup trucks and the old beaters were out front, where the lights were. Night bugs orbited the fixtures.

Doot had debated with himself about bringing the guy here or taking him home. But the house was clear on the other side of town, another couple of miles away; the guy looked like he was barely hanging on, as it was. He didn't want to push it.

The guy squinted, trying to follow Doot's pointing finger. He took a deep breath, forcing himself upright. "Okay." He nodded stiffly, as though his spine had welded into a solid piece. "Take me . . . on over there."

None of the teenagers at the front of the hamburger place noticed them pulling up beside the booth. Inside, Lou was scraping crud off the grill with a metal spatula. Doot unhooked the bungee cord, holding onto the ends to keep the guy from toppling off the seat. He hopped off, and helped the guy stand up.

In the phone booth, the guy slumped back against the glass. Doot held his arm above the elbow, keeping him upright.

The guy dug his good hand into his jeans pocket, then pulled it out empty. "Shit . . ." Even that little effort had his breath coming in shallow gasps. The slitted eyes turned toward Doot. "You got any money? Coins, I mean . . ."

"Yeah, I think so." Doot searched his own front pockets and came up with a quarter and two nickels. He told the man what he had.

The other shook his head. "That's . . . not enough. It's long distance . . . where I'm calling. Need more than that. You got . . . any folding money . . ."

"Couple dollars." The man started to slip, back scraping the glass, and Doot strained to pull his weight back up. "That's about it."

The man nodded. "Go get change . . ."

He propped the man, head lolling back, into the booth's corner. Then he turned and sprinted toward the front of the hamburger place.

"Hey, Doot! What's happenin'?" Stevie Garza called out to Doot as he came up to the counter window; he'd slowed down to a quick walk, trying not to attract attention. Garza, perched on the fender of his father's Ford Ranger, had spotted him coming around the building's side. "Where ya been keepin' yourself?"

Doot leaned his palms against the chipped edges of the Formica counter. Inside, Big Lou was still scowling at the heat-blackened grill. Doot rapped on the glass with his knuckles.

"Yeah, yeah," Lou called over, without looking around. "Keep your pants on."

An alcohol-laden breath hit Doot. Garza had draped his arm around Doot's shoulders. A Bacardi pint bottle dangled from Garza's hand, and his loopy smile pressed close to Doot's face. "Look what *I* got."

Doot knew it wasn't Bacardi. Garza had been carrying around that one bottle so long that the label had started to fray white around the edges. He made something from raisins and sugar and yeast, in a gallon jug that he hid up in the rafters of his parents' garage, and then poured it into the bottle with a plastic funnel. It smelled like vomit.

"Yeah, that's great. Lucky you." Doot slipped out from the other's embrace. Support gone, Garza stumbled a few steps away, barely regaining his balance. He looked up, mouth dropped open, eyes filled with sudden puzzlement.

"What d'ya want?" On the other side of the glass, Lou took a pencil from behind his ear.

"I need change." Doot pushed the dollar bills across the counter and over the metal track of the little window. "Quarters and dimes."

"You get change at a bank. This ain't a bank."

One of Garza's buddies, a little less drunk, was pulling him back over to the Ranger; Doot saw them out of the corner of his eye. "Uh, just a Coke, then. Small one."

Lou looked disgusted and waddled over to the dispenser. A few seconds later, he turned and slammed the cup down on the counter.

Doot snatched back the two dollars and held them up. "Break 'em both?"

"Jesus Christ." Lou's face went even sourer. He grabbed the bills and stepped over to the cash register. He slapped the change down, ignoring Doot's outstretched palm.

"Doot! Hey, Doot!" Garza, propped up against the Ranger again, called out to him as he turned away from the counter. The raisinjack's hilarity had come bubbling up in the other kid again. "We'll see you around, man! We'll see you *around . . ."*

He ignored the slurring, drunken voice, and all the rest of the guys hanging out. Soon as he was around the corner and in the dark, he ran across the empty sector of asphalt.

The phone booth looked empty. When he was a couple of yards away, he saw the man crumpled at the booth's floor, knees folded tight. He yanked the door open, and the face rolled toward him.

"Come on." He got a grip under the man's arms and lifted him up. The man was still alive; he could hear the shallow, ragged breathing. "Look—I got the change."

The eyes opened partway. He raised his good hand and rubbed his face, bright with sweat. His shoulders flopped back against the glass.

"Fuck." The man tilted his head forward, panting. "I can't even see the sonuvabitch." His hand gestured vaguely toward the pay phone. "You gotta do it for me . . . I'll tell you the number . . . you dial . . ."

Doot squeezed in closer so he could turn toward the

phone. He took the phone from its chrome hook and held it to his ear; with his other hand, he thumbed a quarter into the coin slot.

"Okay . . ." The man spoke with his eyes closed. "You gotta dial one first . . ."

She usually didn't get this loaded when she was by herself. She lay on the bed with the sheets all tousled and wadded up underneath her. On the floor was a Scotch bottle, some single malt that tasted the way fertilizer smelled, which had been the only liquor Mike had kept in the apartment. The bottle had fallen over on its side and made a big spot on the carpet. On the pillow beside her head was a plastic baggie, empty except for a couple of tabs and one blue and yellow cap. Her blonde hair trailed over the baggie's open mouth.

Getting seriously fucked up was for when you were with other people, as far as she was concerned. Not just because of having more fun—a real party, a *damage yourself* good time—but also because if you went too far, loaded up your bloodstream with more fizzy chemicals than your body could take, there'd be a good chance that somebody would be around to pull you through it. At the least, roll you over on your face so that you wouldn't aspirate your own puke and strangle yourself, drowning on your lunch. Calling the police about a dead body was the absolute most comedown way to end a party.

Not that she had to worry about puking anything up. She hadn't eaten since she'd come back to the apartment and found the place trashed and Mike gone. Not gone like out to the store, or gone to the hospital to pull down his shift, but *gone.* Gone like not coming back. Gone like dead.

That's what the blood on the wall over by the apartment's front door had meant. The place hadn't been trashed as though somebody had been looking for something—she'd checked Mike's stashes and had found them all in place, untouched—but instead, from people fighting and rolling around. Mike had given them a tough time. For a little while, at least. It had probably been those two guys, the mean, smart-mouthed one and his bigger companion, who'd done it. And then they'd ripped up the sofa cushions and done some other shit—she'd found one wall in the kitchen, with a puddle on the floor beneath it, that looked like it'd been pissed on—just for fun. Just to give her a good scare.

It'd worked, all right. She'd dived right into the stash Mike had kept in a plastic baggie taped to the bottom of the stereo preamp: Mexican boots, stuff he didn't get from his hospital sources because the pharmaceutical companies didn't make them anymore. They'd fuzzed her right out, the way they always did. But when the fear was gone, hammered into oblivion, the new loneliness stayed solid as a rock. Methaqualone, even at shitty boot potency, always made her feel tragic. By now, her face was puffy and damp, like a red sponge, from weeping over Mike. She'd really loved him.

The radio on the little table beside the bed murmured. It had gone off the station it'd been tuned to—probably one of those fuckers had kicked it or something—and now it emitted more static than voices and music. She hadn't bothered to switch it off. It didn't matter.

Another sound cut through the static and the distant, eroded voices. The telephone was ringing. Its note was muffled by the bed's other pillow, which had flopped over on the table, hiding the things on it.

The phone went on ringing. She heard it—the ringing was inside her head now, bouncing back and forth—but she didn't stir. If she ignored it, eventually it would go away. Everything went away—eventually.

It didn't. It went on.

"Motherfucker." She spoke the word into the pillow under her face, feeling her numbed lips move against the cloth. She raised her head. The whole side of her face felt numb, as though the blood had been drained from it.

Pushing the dry tangle of her hair away from her eyes, she fumbled her other hand toward the noise. The pillow fell off the bedside table, and the phone's ring shrieked louder.

She managed to get it to her ear.

"Yeah?" Her tongue felt like some alien creature that had taken up residence in her mouth, a space too small for it. Mumbling: "What d'ya want?"

"Lindy, it's me . . . it's Mike . . ."

The words, the voice, jolted her into full consciousness. As if the chemicals in her blood and brain had evaporated, replaced by adrenaline. She sat upright on the bed, drawing her legs underneath her, clutching the phone, the most valuable thing in the world, with both hands.

"Mike—" Her brain raced ahead; it took a second for her own words to catch up. "Where are you? How did you—"

His voice, an unsteady whisper but his voice, cut her short. "Never mind . . . we can talk about that later . . . when you get here. First . . . you've got to help me." For a few seconds, she heard nothing but his breathing, dragging and rough. Then he spoke again: "I'm going to need some stuff . . ."

Doot had had to stay in the phone booth, his butt sticking out past the folded-up door, to keep the guy standing so he could go on talking. Some of the things the guy said, to whomever was on the other end of the line, made sense—it sounded like doctor stuff, things the guy needed to try to take care of himself—and other things he couldn't figure out at all. That part didn't sound too good.

"All right . . ." The man's voice had dwindled down to a whisper, a breath. "Just hurry . . ." The phone fell from his hand and dangled at the end of its cord.

He draped the man's arm over his shoulder and carried him out of the booth to the motorbike. The guy looked even worse than before. Maybe he really was dying.

The bruised face lifted toward his. "Let's go back . . ." The lips barely moved. "Just gotta wait . . ."

They'd have to do the whole bungee cord routine again. Doot pulled the cord out of the back pocket of his jeans and looped it underneath the denim jacket, the man's weight sagging against the elastic. He got him straddling the bike's passenger seat, then climbed on and hooked the cord around his own chest.

The bike sputtered to life. Its headlight swept across the empty reach of the parking lot as Doot swung the machine back out onto the road.

She flew through the apartment, grabbing things and running back to the bedroom to stuff them into the suitcase.

Some of the things were easy to find, even in the apartment's trashed-out state. Things that were legal, that had never had to be hidden. Mike's doctor stuff, antibiotics and simple shit like that. She threw them in on top of the clothes, both his and hers, that she'd snatched out of the dresser drawers.

Other stuff . . . She stood for a moment beside the bed, eyes closed, gathering her breath. Then she swiftly knelt down and tugged at the carpet underneath the bed frame. The deep pile's backing had been slit; the point of a triangle peeled back in her hand. From the hiding place cut in the floorboards, she took out a small cardboard box, its flaps held down by a rubber band around it. She straightened up and threw the box into the suitcase. The rubber band snapped, and an assortment of hypodermics and glass vials and orange-capped plastic containers, their contents rattling, spilled out.

She stood up and slammed the case's lid shut, snapping the locks into place.

With the suitcase in one hand and her coat draped over the other, she couldn't manage to pull the apartment's front door shut behind her.

"Fuck it."

She left the door open and headed for the stairs. Through the building's glass door at the bottom, she could see the Corvette waiting at the curb.

Nine

Doot left the guy lying on the floor of the old clinic's lobby, wrapped up in the blankets he'd had to fetch back in from the building's porch.

"I gotta go now." Doot slid the water bottle and the Pepsi and what was left of the food closer to the man, then stood up. "I'll be back in the morning, see how you're doing. Okay?"

The other nodded weakly, his head barely moving. He hadn't opened his eyes in all the time Doot had been half carrying, half walking him back into the building.

He watched the man for a moment longer, the slight, quick motion of the chest rising and falling. Then he reached down and switched off the flashlight sitting on the floor. The lobby's walls vanished into darkness. He turned and headed for the moonlit outline of the door.

What the fuck have I gotten myself into? Doot beat himself over the head with the question as the motorbike sped as best it could down the road. He'd left his denim jacket buttoned around the injured man, and now the night's chill tore through the thin cotton of his shirt. It was more than the night that shivered goosebumps up his arms. Now that he had time to think—riding the bike at night always drew out his thoughts—there was also time to get spooked.

He didn't even know who the fuck this guy was. He'd thought he'd heard a woman's voice coming over the pay phone's line, calling him Mike—that was all. Whatever the guy's name was, he was in deep shit. If Doot's father hadn't found him, the guy would already have sunk in the shit, and the brown waves would be rolling over his head. That was what worried Doot: if somebody had wanted this Mike character dead, then they probably wouldn't be too happy to find out he was still alive. And they wouldn't be too friendly with anybody who was helping him stay alive.

You idiot. He squinted into the cold wind. What a fuckin' mess—he'd already gotten himself into it far enough that he didn't see how he could pull his foot out. If he just left the guy out there, and didn't go back again . . . Maybe, maybe not. The guy couldn't have dragged his ass all the way out to that old clinic building by himself, not the way he was beat up. Somebody would've had to have helped him. And if the people who'd beat the crap out of this Mike were still around, or came back, they might want to know who the local good Samaritans were. Which would mean more shit, heavy shit, for Doot and his dad.

He didn't even know why he'd stepped in it. Going out there and dropping off some food and water for the guy, like his dad had told him to—that was one thing. But strapping him onto the bike and hauling him all over the place, right on the road where any pair of headlights could have caught them . . . *Jesus H. Christ.* He must've been out of his flipping mind.

That was the big problem with living out here in the middle of nowhere. It was something Anne, his buddy from school, was always talking about, why she'd been scheming since she was ten years old on how to get out of here. People got so stupid and bored in a dump like this—he could see Anne flailing about with her hands when she said it, making *bored* a two-syllable cry up to the ceiling of her bedroom—that they'd jump off a cliff, with a six-pack, every can opened, pressed up to their guzzling faces, just to break the monotony.

He knew she was right. This was a great place to live, if all you ever wanted to do was get blasted out of your mind and pile your daddy's pickup into a telephone pole, with a Metallica tape cranking away in the dash.

Look at the way he'd fallen right into doing whatever that guy had asked him to do. He'd already been able to see the deep shit coming in like a tide—you didn't have to be a fuckin' genius to figure these things out—and *still* he'd gone and done it. He bit his lip, shaking his head over the bike's handlebars. How stupid could you get?

He didn't know. *I suppose I got a good chance of finding out.* What he needed now was to get some sleep, maybe think about all this stuff in the morning. He could call up Anne and talk to her, tell her what was going on—she could keep a secret. He'd told her all kinds of things that nobody else knew. Maybe she'd be able to figure out what he should do now.

Underneath the cold pinpricks of light, he rolled on the bike's accelerator, heading for home.

Mike listened to the rasp of the kid's motorbike fading away—a million miles, then more, down the straight road that ran through the night. If there had been any other sound, it would have blotted out the tiny engine's sputter.

He worked at his breathing, each pull into his lungs forced by his will. He'd tried opening his eyes—that had taken an effort as well—but he wasn't going to try again. The sensation of darkness spinning—of not even being able to *see* anything, yet sensing that the dark was twisting and blurring around him, as though he were falling down an endless, unlit mine shaft—had frightened him. A small calm voice in his head had announced, as though speaking of some stranger anesthetized on the table: *So this is what it feels like to die.* The fingers of his good hand had dug into the kid's arm as he'd been carried into the building.

If he just kept quiet, just stayed submerged under the wash of the pain and the dizziness . . . if he could just make it to the morning, and then the bright hours after that . . . however long it took for Lindy to get here . . .

If he could take another breath, and then one after that . . .

Easy, he told himself. *It's the easiest thing in the world.* He didn't have a single other thing to do now. The whole world had shrunk down to this, a dark, empty, dust-smelling room in some shabby old building falling down around him.

I should've asked—his thoughts wandered, his breathing going on by itself; that was a good sign, he knew. *I should've asked him where the fuck am I.* What this place was; some kind of hospital, he figured, if the things he'd seen upstairs were really there, and not just part of the dreaming. And that would be funny—he could feel the skin of his face tightening in a rictuslike smile. What he needed was to be in a hospital, and here he was in one, only it looked as though he were about a hundred years too late.

You missed your appointment, doctor . . . A snippy little receptionist's voice. *Perhaps we can reschedule you . . . perhaps you can come back tomorrow . . .*

A laugh scraped out of his throat. It died, and he had to roll onto his shoulder to spit out a sour wad of blood and phlegm. In the silence that flowed back over him, as he let his shoulders fall back onto the blankets, he heard something moving outside, nearly silent itself—a motion that touched the air, parted it like a weightless curtain, and left it in place, unchanged. The easing of weight onto powdery dust, the step of a tracking animal, leaving nothing but the marks of its passage.

Mike's eyes opened, involuntarily. Adrenaline seeped around his spine, pointing his senses. He could hear the creature outside, the slow investigation of its muzzle around the building's walls. And the others, the rest of them—all that had come down out of the hills, toward the scent of blood.

He could see the walls and ceiling in the faint blue light seeping inside; the adrenal rush had brought things into focus. He turned on his side and pulled himself toward the window. Levering himself up with his elbow on the sill, he peered through the largest crack between the boards.

Outside, the red eyes prowled back and forth, pacing the limits of their night territory.

He brought his gaze up, toward the crest of the hills. Another creature was there, gazing down at the building. Upright, a silhouette against the black of the sky, a hole where the stars were blotted out in the shape of a man.

The figure in the distance stood unmoving, watching, the same as the others.

Mike drew back from the window. He lay on the floor, wrapping the nest of blankets around himself. Already, the world out in the night was slipping away, another darkness welling up inside him. He closed his eyes and let go, feeling the floor yield beneath his weight, the earth beneath gaping open to receive him.

Doot saw the lights spilling out from the house. Even before he switched off the motorbike's engine, he could hear the raucous laughter and the voices shouting. Somebody's boom-box added thudding bass notes to the mix.

"Shit." He said it out loud, gazing in dismay at the house; his house, or really his dad's. Invaded by a party that was news to him. Sitting on the bike, out in the gravel driveway, he could hear a girl's shrieking, high-pitched laugh and an answering male guffaw. Then glass breaking; it sounded like an empty beer bottle hitting the concrete steps out in back.

The front door was unlocked and open a couple of inches. He pushed it the rest of the way, and the noise and light washed over him. His heart sank.

"Doot! Doot, my *man!*" Stevie Garza grabbed him around the shoulders, slopping beer onto his chest. The can dangled loose from Garza's other hand. The face looming into Doot's was all red and sweaty. "I told ya—didn't I tell ya—we'd see ya around." He poked his finger into Doot's breastbone; more beer fizzed onto his shirt. "We brought the party to *your* place!"

He pushed Garza away, the drunk kid staggering back against his buddies. Doot shoved his way through the crowd—there were at least a couple dozen other teen-agers packed into the tiny living room—and toward the kitchen. Some of the laughing faces he recognized from the high school, others he didn't. The cigarette smoke and smell of spilled beer, and the pounding metal from the box sitting on top of the TV, made the place seem even smaller.

"Jesus *Christ!*" The narrow door to the kitchen's broom closet hung open; they'd found the cases of beer his dad kept stacked up in there. His dad got them cheap from a buddy of his that worked in the distributor's warehouse. Now the six cardboard cartons were spread out over the floor and on the sink counter and were empty except for crumpled-up cans.

Doot grabbed the arm of one of the guys leaning up against the wall. The floor around his feet was littered with ground-out cigarette stubs. "How the fuck did you get in here?"

He didn't have to wait for the guy's answer. He saw now the window broken by the back door, the sparkle of the glass shards across the linoleum. "Aww, shit . . ."

He heard a couple of the assholes snickering at him.

Somebody pushed a half-full beer can into his hand. "Hey, lighten up, man—"

Another voice joined in. "Don't sweat it. Your old man's out of town."

A couple was going at it over by the refrigerator, her back against it, the guy's hand roaming under her tank-top. A line of white elastic showed under the opened top button of her jeans.

Doot took a hit off the beer and wandered with it to the other side of the house. Through the bathroom door-way, he saw somebody hugging the bowl and making outboard motor noises. The guy's spine arched as though he were trying to bring his kidneys up. The sour odor of beer puke floated out.

Slumped against the hallway wall, Doot worked at what was left in the can. The music's pulse came through the plaster and into the back of his head.

There were too fucking many of them to get rid of. And there was no way he was going to call the cops; they'd haul his ass off along with everybody else's, and his dad would hit the fucking roof if he had to come down to the station. Which would be days from now, anyway, before his dad came back from his run. All of these jerks would be prancing around on the streets, and he'd still be cooling his heels in the juvie slammer.

He'd have to ride it out. In the morning, he could check out the damage. In the meantime . . . He crumpled the empty in his fist, dropped it, and went back to the kitchen to see if he could scout out another.

The sun poured down on the green lawns and the people there, standing and talking or moving about in a langorous summer haze.

Mike felt his arm being taken by the young woman, her hand pressing softly above his elbow. "Let's go inside. It's so hot out here." She smiled at him. The feathered wisps of her hair traced across her neck as she reached to place the badminton racquet on one of the canvas and wood folding chairs.

She had eyes like Lindy's, or the way Lindy's were without the chemical glaze. But the smile was sweeter, more demure and secretive. She tilted her head to one side, still smiling at him, her other hand joining the first in its light grasp. He could feel each small finger, and the stiff lace at her wrists poking against his skin. The touch pulled at a wire that ran directly to his groin.

One of the blue-caped nurses pushed a wheelchair past them, with a gray-haired woman fluttering a paper fan. The girl tugged and led him up the curving path toward the clinic building, its windows glinting pieces of the sun.

He halted at the first step and looked across the lawns to the rolling, brilliant sky. Behind the sunlight, as though it were a backdrop painted on thin silk, he could see the night, the stars' points of ice glittering in darkness.

"Come on," said the girl in the antique dress, with the lace up to her throat. She had already mounted the first couple of steps to the building's verandah; she smiled and pulled playfully on his arm. "No shilly-shallying now."

"It's all right," he murmured. He looked up at her. "There's plenty of time. This is all just dreaming." Behind him, he felt the strolling forms on the lawn waver and shift, as though a breeze had fluttered the backdrop.

He brought his gaze around from her, and out to the hills. There were none of the animals with the red, watching eyes; they were back in that other world, where it was still night. But the figure he had seen in silhouette, up on the crest of the nearest hill . . . The man was there, standing in the exact same place, revealed in daylight. In a doctor's white coat, his arms folded across his chest. Mike could just make out the man's face, at this distance. The same face he'd dreamed before, the flesh pared down over the skull; the doctor who'd raised the scalpel up to the examining room's light.

The bright sun glittered off the face's wire-rimmed spectacles. Mike felt the doctor's gaze upon him, the eyes penetrating to the back of his own skull, inventorying everything inside him.

He hadn't seen it before, but now he did: a black, doglike creature, with a grinning muzzle and sharp-pointed teeth. Bigger than a dog, leaner and harder. It sat on its haunches beside the doctor, its red gaze tracking on the same line.

"No, you're wrong." The girl pulled him up beside her on the steps. "There's never any time to waste. You should've learned that by now."

The angle of the verandah's roof blocked any view of the white-coated figure on the hill. He turned toward the girl. "But I'm dreaming. I know I am."

She shook her head, the smile holding a secret. She stood on tiptoe and kissed him on the brow. "No," she whispered, bringing her cheek down beside his. "You've finally woken up."

He let her lead him across the lobby. He'd almost expected to see himself curled up in the blankets on the floor, but there were only the wooden planks, waxed and buffed to a glassy sheen, and the massive shapes of rugs with Indian designs, jagged lightning bolts and slit-eyed *kachina* faces. The clerk behind the marble-topped counter looked over his shoulder at Mike and the girl, then turned discreetly back to sorting the guests' mail.

"In here," she said. Her smile parted to show her white, perfect teeth. "They won't find us here."

She had taken him upstairs, to the corridor of numbered doors. To the door without a number that said Examining Room instead. She laid her fingers on the pebbled glass, and the door swung open as though weightless.

The room's smell, of disinfectant and sterile gauze, mingled with the girl's flower scent. Light sparked off the chrome and glass surfaces, the tray of sharp instruments, and the bottles in the cupboards, arrayed in the constellations of the night sky beneath. In that other world.

She pulled him down on top of her, on the examining table. "It's all right . . ." Her fingers twined in the damp hair at the back of his neck, drawing him closer.

"Here . . ." She let go of him for a moment, her fingers moving at her throat. The lace parted, and her breasts, white as the lace, rose as she arched her back and drew in her breath through the points of her teeth.

He cupped her in his hand, the familiar weight, the birdlike trembling, warming the skin of his palm.

"They won't find us . . ." She murmured the words, eyes closed.

"Who?" He had his mouth close to her ear, breathing her in. "Who won't?" It seemed urgent that he knew.

"My mother . . . and my father . . ." She turned her head, and he felt the motion of her lips against the curve of his jaw. The tip of her tongue against the flesh. "They brought me here . . . oh, I was so ill, I was so weak . . . they told me he'd cure me . . ."

He opened his mouth, tasting her. "He cured you . . ." He knew who she meant. The doctor that he'd seen standing up on the crest of the hill. His other hand had found its way under the folds of the long skirt; his fingertips grazed satin over an angle of bone and skin.

"Yes . . . yes . . . he cured me . . ." She put her hands on his shoulders and pushed him a few inches away. With a child's solemnity, she gazed through her lashes at him. She took her hands away, and touched herself, in the white space between her breasts.

A faint blue vein lay under the translucent skin. He balanced himself on his palms and elbows and watched her fingertips, the pearl ridges of her nails, pressing an indentation there. She gasped, a quick swallowing of breath, as the flesh yielded moisture.

A red line appeared. Squeezing her eyes shut tighter,

she let her fingertips sink a fraction of an inch under the skin.

He watched. His own breath hammered inside his throat, dizzying him.

Her fingers went farther into herself, then curled. The red opening spread apart.

"Look . . ." Her whisper. "You see . . ."

The opening grew, the points of the red line running up to her throat, down toward her navel.

"He cured me . . ."

Her ribcage spread open like wings. The white dress had fallen away into a bed of lace spilling from the edges of the examining table. Her nakedness as white as that, tinged with the blood running underneath the skin. And the secret place, the red center, trembling, revealed to him—

She lay open beneath him. The tracery of vein and sinew, the darker shapes clustered near the segmented wand of her spine, like fruit moistened by a summer rain that left them warm and soft. Her breath, pulled in through the teeth biting her lower lip, swelled the forms that had been hidden beneath her breasts.

And at the center . . . the motion of her heart, the contraction and pulse . . .

He had seen all this before; that was how he'd learned. But never in beauty like this.

Dreaming . . . He could barely hear the voice inside his head, his own voice. It had fallen away, back to that other world.

"Touch me . . . here . . ." Her hand took his wrist and guided him.

Inside her, the warmth seized him, the moistness of blood trembling inside flesh, soft yet urgent, yielding. A small, secret world.

"Yes . . ." A word not spoken, but hissed through the teeth breaking a drop of blood upon her lip.

His hand closed upon it, and the trembling was in his

hand. He was at her center, the pulse of her heart beating into his fist and up his arm into his own heart. The same pulse now, his and the woman's; the red blinding tide surging up into his head; the skull too weak to contain it any longer, breaking—

"... *yes* ..."

A cry, not of pain. Her face transfigured.

A drop of blood, his, fell upon the white silk of her cheek at the arch of the bone beneath. And in the drop's curved mirror, he saw his own face. His eyes glistened as though weeping.

The naked form beneath him; he fell, embracing ...

He woke up in the dark, the lobby's empty space around him, the wood of the floor beneath the thin blankets.

Dreaming. But not like dreams—he could remember everything, the girl's face, her body opening its red secrets to receive him; the heart beating in his fist.

And before—the figure in doctor's white up on the hill's crest, the animal with its grin of sharp teeth beside him.

He let himself drift in memory—the girl, her smile, the bite of her teeth upon her own lip, the blood there and upon her cheek ...

His own body remembered as well. He reached down, under the blankets, and touched the swell of his erection. His blood was only now starting to seep back from his groin, a tide easing into the sea of his flesh.

Outside, the watching forms paced and turned their red gaze toward him. He heard them there, as a sleep without dreams pulled him under.

Ten

The old man had a treasure trove about twenty miles past where the county highway split off from the Interstate—a constantly renewing source of wealth. The Arco station at the junction was the only gas for a long stretch in either direction. Most of the people who stopped there also hit the Coke machines at the side of the garage. In the summer's heat, it didn't take them long to drain the cans and toss them out their cars' windows. So there was money all up and down the highway, right in that stretch; money glinting in the dry weeds.

There was a trick to scooping up the cans without bending over so far that he'd screw up his back again. He could even stay on his bike—a girl's Schwinn, powder blue underneath the crusting badges of rust; it suited him because he didn't have to lift his stiff leg over the frame to get on. He had his clever stick, a sawed-off broom handle with a big ball of masking tape wadded at the end, held on with a couple of thumbtacks hammered into the wood. The tape was just sticky enough to snag a pop can off the ground. The trick was to make a good clean shot—he had to squint one eye to do it—right through the roadside weeds and hit the can dead on, without getting dirt and twigs and shit on the masking tape; if it got too dirty, he'd have to wind up a new ball and put it on the stick-end. The other trick was to rap the snagged can sharply in the open mouth of one of the black plastic garbage sacks hooked behind him on the bicycle so the can fell off and joined the others clanking around in there. The old man alternated— left sack, right sack—so the bicycle didn't get lopsided. He'd patched the fraying sacks so often with electrician's tape that they'd become more like nets, the bright valuable cans peeking through the holes.

He liked to get an early start, get a good bit of business done before the sun made him dizzy. It was not much past dawn—the air still had a touch of the night's cold in it—and he'd already snared four or five Coke Classics, a couple of Dr. Peppers (didn't see those too often, they weren't in the vending machines at the gas station; must've been tourists passing through), a Sunkist Orange and a Seven-Up. People were fools—they just *threw* their money away.

He worked the county road, heading up to the junction and the big blue Arco sign that people could see for miles. The pickings would be even better going down the other leg; lots more traffic on the Interstate. The black sacks would be bulging all the way out to the sides of the bike, like the pollen sacs of some kind of mechanical bee, by the time he was done. He already had the feeling in his gut that it'd be a good haul today.

He heard the car before he saw it. Somebody downshifted, slowing to make the swing off the Interstate. But not enough; the old man looked up and saw a cloud of dust as the car, something low-slung and red, fishtailed off the road and onto the loose gravel of the shoulder.

The car was only a hundred yards away from him before the driver managed to get it back up on the road. It pulled a storm of dust and pinging rocks along with it, which enveloped the old man as it shot past him. A convertible; he caught, through the the eye-stinging swirl, a glimpse of a blonde woman with black sunglasses. She didn't even glance over at him, but flattened the accelerator and rocketed on down the highway. The dust rolled behind her, slowly settling to the earth.

"Well, fuck me." The old man had gotten twigs from the dry weeds kicked up by the car's passage, and other shit, in his beard. He combed them out with his leathery fingers. "Fuck me for a nanny *goat.*"

Some people were in a hurry, all right. The car was already just a red dot near the highway's vanishing point. He turned back to the way he'd been going, pedaling slowly and scanning the ground. Some people were in a hurry, but he wasn't. There was a lot of ground to cover out here; it'd take you your whole lifetime, no matter how fast or slow you went.

He didn't mind. He had all the time he needed. Day like today, he could just go on forever.

The party had dwindled to the final dregs. The dregs being Stevie Garza and three of his total load-o buddies. Doot didn't even know who one of them was—he couldn't recall ever seeing him at the high school. Maybe he was some kind of half-brother or cousin of Garza's; the guy had the same scraggly beard, which looked more like he needed to give his face a good hard scrub, and the same faded denim and tour souvenir T-shirt outfit that was the uniform for the school's heavy-metal-and-downers crowd. Plus the same slack jaw, mouth hanging slightly open, and pink stewed eyes. But then they *all* had that.

The four of them were beached like flabby whales all over the living room, two of them slumped on the couch as though their spines had been surgically removed, Garza sprawled in the brown Naugahyde recliner that was the favorite chair of Doot's dad. The fourth stoner was flat on the floor, either playing his air guitar or trying to scratch the white pooched-out stomach that his rucked-up T-shirt had exposed—Doot couldn't tell which.

The music was coming off the TV, some local station that filled in its gaps with repeats of a syndicated rock video program. Most of the kids in town had memorized the dozen different half hours, and could recite the intros along with the freeze-dried fossil in the sweater. They wouldn't get cable out in this butt-end of the universe until the year two-thousand-and-fucking-something—probably sometime after New Guinea got it—so a 24-hour jobbie like MTV was out of the question. Even if somebody's folks put in a satellite dish, all it seemed to do was pull in more goddamned football than any reasonable person could stand, and weird Latino variety shows that were like watching Lawrence Welk on bad acid.

Doot moved through the living room, stepping over the sprawled legs of the pair on the couch, gathering up empty cans and cigarette butts from the floor. This wasn't even the dregs of the party, but the aftermath, like walking around and picking up shell casings on a battlefield after the warring armies had crawled away. It even smelled like a battlefield, or what Doot imagined one would smell like: a burned odor—that was all the butts and the cigarette smoke that had settled into the curtains—and a smell of puke drifting in through the screen door, where one of the beer ODs had stumbled out and upchucked in the bushes. Doot figured he could get out the garden hose later on and try to wash away the accident scene, soak it into the ground—maybe it'd make good fertilizer. Right now, his head was aching, his mouth tasting as though all the cigarettes had been stubbed out on his tongue.

"These people suck," announced Garza, his half-lidded gaze on the TV. A belch rumbled out of him. "The big hairy one," he finished.

"This ain't real metal." One of the couch pair raised his head, his eyes looking like those of a snake that had been prodded with a stick. Doot remembered seeing him

94

slouching around the high school in a hand-lettered T-shirt that said Death to False Metal. "Van Halen's like *pussy* metal. Fuckin' wimps."

The one on the floor gazed up at the ceiling. "They used to be good . . ."

"Yeah, but they're pussies *now.*"

Doot hauled the trash sack toward the kitchen. He'd turned down the sound on the TV an hour ago, and none of the hangers-on had objected. They all looked a little fragile and shattered.

The dickhead in the sweater came on again—he had a weird way of moving his hands, like he was trying to hit a fly with the tip of his forefinger—then some bright-faced teenage girl smiling and bouncing around and doing little kick steps. Garza and the guys on the couch stirred, hopefully scanning for perky tit action.

At least there was plenty of time to get the place cleaned up before his dad finished his hauling run and came home. Doot shoved the trash sack into a corner of the kitchen and studied the debris layers on the counters. He could shovel away most of this crap and air the place out. Even replacing the broken-out window—thank God the party hadn't gotten rowdy enough to have sparked any other real damage—that could be taken care of easily enough. He could take the motorbike into town and score a glass pane, and putty it in. Replacing the cases of beer would be a problem, though.

Maybe—he felt his brain turning over sluggishly, a battery cranked down flat—*maybe I should leave the busted window the way it is. Tell him that burglars ripped off the beer.* He wondered if his dad would go for that.

The other problem, the one he had to deal with right now, was getting Garza and the other basket cases out the door. They were all semiconscious at this point; at least they opened their eyes partway and made noises out of their mouths that weren't just snoring. He'd have to work fast, though, if he was going to boot them out before they

95

lapsed into sleep. The last thing he needed was a crew of coma victims draped all over the furniture, mumbling and farting away. When they got that way, you couldn't even roll them out onto the lawn and leave them. The trick was to get them stumbling off toward some other source of amusement or food or more beer. Let them pass out in Big Lou's parking lot—Doot figured it wouldn't be his problem then.

He opened the back door and bumped the trash sack down the steps, then lifted its clanking weight into the thirty-gallon can. For a moment, he sat on the can's steel lid, his legs angled out, arms folded across his chest, breathing in the still-cool morning air that didn't smell like stale cigarette smoke and party sweat.

The fog was clearing out of his head, but he still felt stupid and disgusted. Disgusted at himself, mainly. *Should've kicked all their asses out last night.* When he'd come home and found the party already rolling—it wouldn't have been too hard, Garza and the other hard-core hounds already having been too fucked up to put up much of a fight.

That hadn't been what he'd been afraid of—of having to swap a few punches with some staggering load-o—when he'd told himself there were too many to take care of, that he'd have to let the party ride. It was the weight of all the rest of them, squashing down on him, like they were sitting on his head or something, telling him what had already been decided: It's party time. They'd made the decision, and didn't give a fuck about what he thought.

Shit, it was like dealing with that spooky guy he'd left out at the old clinic building. That guy telling him what to do, and then his just going ahead and doing it, like he was some kind of zombie asshole on remote control—*Yes, master!* Whizz-click robot noises. *Your wish is my command!* That was all just more of what he'd been doing all his life. Leaning his weight against the trash can, he felt himself getting sick at his stomach, but not from anything he'd drunk last night.

It was something his buddy Anne had always gotten on his case about. You didn't want people to think you were a nerdy guy, a drag, unfun, so you let them walk all over you. If it wasn't that, it was the fucking teachers at the school. Your daddy drives a truck, so you let them tell you that you're stupid. He'd seen that in Miss Dickbreath's eyes all the way back in first grade; she hadn't even had to tell him that's what he was. Then they just went on telling you; you didn't get a chance to believe it or not believe it.

He looked out past the side of the house, across the scrubby lawn and the cracker-box houses, pink stucco or blue aluminum siding, and the scrubby lawns on the other side of the street. Nobody had come over while the party had been blasting away and told the kids to hold it down or threatened to call the police. In this part of town—the stupid part—everybody made noise: if not parties cranking through the hours to dawn, then all-out fights where the neighbors thought it was pretty mild if some guy's old lady didn't unload one of the deer rifles he kept under the bed, pow pow pow, right through their stucco *and* yours. So if you didn't call the cops about their noise, they wouldn't call 'em about yours—an arrangement that suited the cops fine, too.

Way past the houses, out in the distance, the black jagged line of the mountains . . . Except they didn't look so far away now; they looked as if they were bumped right up against the town, almost in his face, as though he could stick out his hand and touch them. Real close, but still big, too big to get over and escape. They made a fence around the town, a little world. If the mountains came in any closer, any tighter, he wouldn't be able to breathe. He could barely pull the air in now.

Screw it. He shoved his hands behind his back and pushed himself up off the trash can. He was going to go in there and tell Garza and his beer-hog buddies to take a hike. At least he could do that much.

The perky teenage girl with the beret and the dorky knee pants was gone from the TV screen. Now there was some flash bimbo with big blond hair and some kind of chain mail over her tits. When she wasn't singing, her red mouth pooched open as though she couldn't wait to get fucked.

"Okay, guys"—Doot's voice rose over the grind of the music—"come on, party's over. Let's go. I got all kinds of shit to do today."

"Wuh?" Garza rolled his neck on the recliner's headrest so he could see Doot standing behind the couch. "Like what?"

He'd come back into the house so pissed off that he hadn't worked out any lines beyond his first ones. He stared back at Garza and at the two other slack faces from the couch.

"Hey—you know—like shit." Doot spread his hands, palms up. "Like I gotta get this place cleaned up, and . . . you know . . ." His voice trailed away.

Garza waved him off, arm flopping against the recliner's padding. "Aw, man . . ." He sounded annoyed. "Don't be such a fuckin' dweeb." He went back to gazing at the blonde on the screen.

"Yeah, *Doot*"—one of the guys on the couch said the name like a joke—"why don't you just cool out for a while, okay? Don't sweat the housecleaning—you can do your fuckin' dusting some other time."

His buddy beside him giggled. "Yeah, man, you can borrow my mom's vacuum, you're so hot to clean house." They both got a laugh out of that.

There were still too many to deal with. One would have been too many. Doot looked over at Garza and saw the heavy-lidded gaze, like some kind of reptile, slyly checking him out from the corner of one eye. Garza didn't even have to do anything to win; he just had to lie sprawled out there, like some kind of black hole that soaked up the whole universe and everything in it, and he won.

That was what the look in Garza's eye meant. *I'm a fuckin' dweeb,* thought Doot. What was it, that somebody just *thinking* something like that made it so?

"Oh, man; this chick's o-*kay.*" One of the couch guys nodded at the TV. Doot knew he had ceased to exist for them—again—but they were still revved up from yanking his chain. "She sits on your face, got a snatch on her you could pull down over your whole fuckin' *head,* walk around with her like a fuckin' hat."

Shit, thought Doot; he'd heard that one before. It was this yo-yo's standard line. Talking as if he weren't the biggest jerk-off artist in town. He gazed moodily at the blond singer. Her breasts glistened with sweat, or else the whole chain-mail and leather outfit—what there was of it—had been doused with a bucket while he hadn't been watching. Smoke rolled past the hard angles of her bared hipbones. She looked out and knew he was a dweeb, too.

Garza's eyes narrowed at the screen. "Ooh, yeah. You kiddin'? She can use my tongue for her tampax, any ol' time." He and the guys on the couch were still yukking it up when a voice came from the floor.

"Holy *Christ!*" Their buddy on the floor sounded awestruck. He pushed himself up on one elbow. He wasn't looking at the TV. His hand shaking, he pointed to the screen door and the bright morning world outside. "Check *this* out."

Doot had retreated a couple yards behind the couch, almost to the kitchen doorway. His head turned a couple of degrees, tracking with everybody else's away from the TV and toward the screen door. The throaty sound of a big-bore engine floated in through the mesh, undercutting the bass line pounding from the TV.

A red Corvette had pulled up at the curb in front of

the house. The machine looked glossy and expensive even under its coat of road dust—a convertible, with its top down. Doot could see the driver as she reached forward and switched off the engine. Her blond hair looked like a gold explosion in the sun, streaked back and tangled as though the wind were still in it.

"Jee-zuss . . ." The guys on the couch pushed against the seat cushions with their hands, trying to bury themselves spine first in the upholstery behind them.

The woman had gotten out of the 'Vette—the street seemed dead silent with the machine at rest—and was coming up the cracked concrete walkway to the front door. Garza's eyes had gone wide open; his stare flicked back to the TV for a moment, then to the vision out the screen door, as though he couldn't figure out which was reality. Or if either of them was.

She wasn't the same woman that was on the TV. But she looked like a different model from the same assembly line. Instead of the chain mail and raggedy leather getup, she had painted-on jeans, the kind with the little zippers to snug them up tight around the calves, and a fur jacket thing, incongruous in the too-warm sunshine, that just came past her shoulder blades. Under the jacket was a tank top cut so skimpy that it not only showed the top curves of her breasts, but around on the sides as well. The little shoes with no backs to them clicked on the walk, tiny bullets that shot right into the house.

Marching right up to the door, she didn't have the TV girl's fuck-me look; the red mouth was set and determined.

The woman rapped on the screen door's aluminum frame. The clatter bounced against the walls. She pushed her sunglasses up above her brow, into the thicket of her golden hair. Shading her eyes with one hand, she leaned close to the door's mesh.

"Hey—"

Garza and the others shrank back from the apparition.

She could see them in there. "I'm looking for some-body." She dug a piece of paper out of the small purse slung over her shoulder. She looked at the paper, then back into the house. "Somebody named—*Doot?*"

A moment passed, the name falling like a leaf through the house's still air. Then, slowly, four faces turned, necks swiveling, and stared at him. From the floor and the re-cliner and across the back of the couch. They stared at him in amazement, their mouths falling open. Like cartoons of dumbfoundedness.

Doot didn't know what it meant, who she was. He just knew that already it was the greatest fucking moment of his life.

Eleven

She followed the kid—this Doot, or whatever his name was—on his motorbike, sputtering and coughing away on the road in front of her. It felt as though she were crawling along in the 'Vette, after having floored it all the way out here from the city.

The sun had risen up above the mountains, flooding the barren miles with light. Brown weeds and rusty-looking railroad tracks ran beside the highway. This was really nowhere—Mike's buddies, his ex–business partners, had really done a number in disposing of him.

Ahead of her, the kid had taken one hand off the bike's bars and was signaling something to her. She squinted behind her sunglasses to see. The kid pointed off to the side of the road, to something in the distance. She turned her head and saw the building, some big ramshackle thing with a sign up on top of it—from this angle, she couldn't tell what it spelled out. It looked like a hotel, or something, that had gotten plucked up from where it was supposed to be, like what's-her-name with the little dog in that old movie, and dropped down on some other planet. The whole landscape around it looked like god-damn Mars to her. Who the hell would build a hotel out here?

The red taillight on the bike's rear fender came on; the kid slowed down to make the turn off the road. She downshifted the 'Vette, slowing with him. The bike bumped over the railroad tracks and then down a lane bordered with weeds.

The smell hit her as she followed the bike toward the building. A dead-looking pond lay past the weeds on the right. The smell came from there. Her lip curled involuntarily; it was strong enough to taste on her tongue. Like rotten eggs, or as if everybody in that pokey little town came all the way out here on a regular basis to take a piss. Maybe that was what the whole lake was; maybe they'd managed to fill the low spot in the ground that way.

In front of the building—the hotel, or whatever it was—the kid turned the bike around and brought it to a halt, his long skinny legs straddling out to the sides. She brought the 'Vette up behind him and killed the engine.

As the dust settled, she could see the building more closely. The dilapidated appearance it had given from out on the road past the tracks was even worse this much nearer: sagging boards, gaps in the roof and walls that showed the beams underneath; boarded-up windows on the ground floor, and broken glass up above. And worse: a whole wing that stretched away from the main section had been gutted by fire, reduced to blackened timbers collapsed onto each other like jackstraws. It looked as if the fire had happened a long time ago. Weeds had sprouted up through the charred wood.

"Come on." Doot hopped off the motorbike. He tilted his head toward the building. "He's in there."

The front door was boarded over, but the kid pulled back the planks far enough for her to squeeze through. He swung in behind her, then drew the barrier back into place.

Inside, it smelled like dust and ancient, sun-baked air. Thin ribbons of light slid through the boards on the windows, motes drifting into brightness and then invisible again.

"Over here." The kid brushed past her, walking quickly to something darker on the floor. Her eyes adjusted, and she saw the figure lying on its back, a rumpled blanket spread beneath.

She ran to him and knelt down. "Mike . . ." He turned his head toward her, his face catching one of the thin sheets of light. A gasp broke from her throat. "Oh, Mike"—she ran her hand over his brow, looking at his battered flesh in dismay—"what happened? What did they do to you?"

His lips were dry and cracked. The unfocused gaze drifted past her face. He shook his head, a slight roll to either side, teeth clenched.

"Did . . ."

She had to lean close to hear his whisper.

"Did you bring . . . everything . . . everything I told you to . . ." His eyes closed. He had started to pant for breath.

She turned to the kid standing behind her. "In the car," she snapped. "Behind the seats."

The kid sprinted to the door. She turned back to Mike, lifting his head and cradling it in her lap.

In less than a minute, the kid was back with the case. She took it from him and opened it up on the floor beside Mike. With a sudden lurch, he rolled onto his side and reached past her, pawing through the case's contents. He dug out a hypodermic and one of the glass vials, then fell back, clutching them with one hand to his chest.

His breath laboring, he fumbled with the needle. She saw that he couldn't use his other hand; the arm flopped loose at his side. She pulled the needle from his fingers and quickly loaded it, pushing the point through the vial's plastic seal. She found the vein in the crook of his arm—he

104

had never shot there, always somewhere else that could be hidden under his clothes—and pressed the needle into it. A drop of blood welled up around the point.

She felt the change under her fingers, the skin of his arm loosening, as though the fine tremor in the muscles beneath had drawn it up tight as a snare drum before. His face changed; color flowed into the dead white flesh under the bruises. Back from the grave. She pulled the needle out and laid her fingertip on the tiny hole, to keep any more life from leaking out of him. His breath slowed, becoming strong and deep. Even a little smile, turning at the corners of his mouth.

Mike raised his chin, stretching the tendons in his neck, rubbing the back of his head against the angle of her lap and stomach. "Lindy," he murmured. "I was . . . waiting for you . . ." His voice slurred, the words slow and heavy. "I knew you'd get here . . ."

"I'm here, baby." She leaned over him, a bit of her blond hair trailing across his cheek. "You know I am."

They were silent for a moment, his hand finding hers and tightening upon it.

"Mike—" With her other hand, she wiped her eyes. "You're in bad shape, Mike."

He smiled up at her. "Think I don't know that?" A quick laugh jerked in his chest. "I'm all fucked up. What we're looking at . . . I figure some kind of cerebral hematoma; epidural if I'm lucky." His hand let go of hers and touched the bandages at the side of his head. The cloth was soiled and darkened with blood. "I think the fracture's pretty much just linear . . . bleeding's mostly from where the scalp got torn. If it's subdural . . . the hematoma . . . that's not so good."

She didn't know what he was talking about. All that medical stuff. But to hear him reciting it, in his dry, weakened voice—reciting it about himself, and not some body on a table—that scared her even more than just seeing the bruises and the battered flesh.

He went on, the words dragging under narcotic weight. "I think . . . some kind of spinal injury . . . I don't remember, I was already down on the floor . . . Brown-Séquard's syndrome . . . maybe . . . can't move that arm . . . they were kicking me, I think . . ." His voice had started to fade, then he pulled himself back. "Plus the usual . . . contusions, cracked ribs . . . shit like that. They did a good job on me. Maybe some renal trauma . . . I keep pissing blood . . ." The smile came back, rueful this time. "Those guys really worked me over . . ."

"Aitch did this?"

Mike nodded, slowly. "Him and Charlie . . . I guess . . . they didn't appreciate being cut out of their business . . ."

She saw him falling again, away from her. "Mike— we gotta get you to a hospital."

"No!" His eyes jerked open. "I know how he works . . . Aitch's friends; he's told them all about me . . . I know he has. The cops . . . they'd be on me before I got out of the emergency room. He's got friends . . . I don't." He shook his head, the same slight roll from side to side. "Don't worry . . . I can pull through. As long as you're here."

He reached and took her hand, bringing it close to the side of his face. Squeezing it tight, with all the strength left in him.

The fire crackled, sparks drifting upward with the smoke. Doot squatted by the shallow hole he'd scooped out of the rocks and dirt, and pushed a few more twigs into the flames. He hadn't built a big fire; they didn't need it. The evening air was only starting to cool, the ground beneath them still warm from soaking up the day's heat.

He and Lindy—he knew her name now; the guy had said it—had carried Mike outside, his arms slung over both their shoulders. Now he knew that name, too; knew for sure that was it. He had hung back and listened, and

106

watched, like somebody who was invisible, somebody who wasn't there at all. Until they needed him.

They needed him to do all kinds of stuff. This Lindy hadn't even been able to figure how to work the little can opener he'd brought out before with the other stuff. So he'd opened up the cans of chili, and built the fire, and put together the stick and string contraption for holding the cans over the fire until the contents were hot enough to eat. The chili got a little burned black on the cans' bottoms, but that hadn't seemed to bother Mike; he'd wolfed the stuff down like he was starving. Well, he probably was. His girlfriend Lindy held the can, with a corner of one of the blankets wrapped around the hot metal, and spooned it up for him.

His girlfriend—that's who she was. Anybody could see that. Doot didn't care one way or the other. He'd just wanted to know, and now he did. The flames licked at his fingertips, and he dropped the last half inch of the twig.

They'd gone several yards away from the old clinic building, far enough to find a skeletal tree that Mike could prop his back up against. The other blanket was spread underneath him, as though he were out on a picnic. Lindy sat cross-legged next to him, tilting her head back to drink straight from the Pepsi bottle.

"Hey, Doot."

He looked up from the fire and over to Mike by the tree. The guy didn't look so bad now, but not by much. As if he'd been beat to hell, all right, but not like he was going to die, at least not this minute. Whatever had been in the needle—and Doot had a pretty good suspicion what kind of stuff it had been—had fixed him up to a degree. At least he was functioning.

Doot stood up, stretching a crick out of his knee. "What?"

"Is there somebody else around here?" Mike used his chin to point to the building and the shadowed landscape around it. "I mean . . . somebody that hangs out here?"

Some of the lethargy that had flowed over him had dissipated. His words came faster.

Doot shrugged. "There's some old guy, least I think he's still around. Named . . . Nelder; something like that. He's kinda like the caretaker or something. He's got like a shack up in the hills. But you don't have to worry about him." Doot glanced at the uneven line that marked off the stars, then back to Mike. "He's just some old fart. If he's not dead by now."

Mike turned his head, scanning across the building's silhouette. "Who owns this place, anyway?"

Another shrug. "I dunno. My dad always told me it was some folks back East."

Leaning back against the tree, Mike nodded. He lapsed into silence for a moment, then looked over at Lindy. "You know," he said slowly. "I could use another . . ."

She knew what he meant. Doot watched as she got up and went into the building, squeezing past the boards over the front door. When she came back, she had the needle and another one of the glass vials in her hand.

Doot looked away as she knelt down beside Mike, picking up his arm and turning its pale underside toward her.

The lobby was filled with light. Not just from the sun pouring through the crystalline windows, the curtains stirred by a caressing breeze. Everything glowed, lit from within. Mike stood in the center of the room, hands outstretched, bathed in opiate bliss.

Everything made new again, the past revoked, as though it were the dream and not this. The wood polished to mirrors, the marble top of the reception desk unbroken; pieces of brass, the rings of the curtains and the bits on the switchboard, all burning bright as fire.

He walked across the space, the Indian rugs yielding beneath his feet. At the edge of the grand staircase, he looked up into the sunlight flooding down from the landing window. He grasped the banister and ascended.

The doctor was waiting for him. He saw the white-coated figure, back turned to him, standing by the counter, sorting through his instruments.

The gaunt face turned and looked over his shoulder at Mike. And smiled. He gestured for Mike to step closer.

"I'm glad you made it," whispered the doctor. "We've got an awful lot to do . . ." His rubber-gloved hand extended something toward Mike.

He felt his own fingers close on cold metal. He looked at his hand and saw a scalpel, its edge glistening as though made of silver fire.

"Here we are." The doctor stood by the examining table. A white sheet covered the figure lying on it.

Mike looked down at the table as the doctor reached over and swung the examining lamp into place. Its light caught a spill of blond hair tumbling from beneath the sheet's edge.

The doctor drew the sheet away from the body, exposing the feet and legs first, then the naked groin.

A corpse, already dissected. The skin had been split and peeled back, exposing the shafts of bone and striated muscle tissue. The female organs lay nestled in the pelvic basin, like unborn things that had never taken human shape.

"You see?" The doctor's whisper again. He drew the sheet farther back, to reveal the coiled viscera, the knotted spine running underneath, a snake in a soft, moist garden. The woman's breasts lay against the slender biceps muscles, as though giving suckle to the red tissue, the clotted blood speckling the nipples. The cage of her ribs guarded the spongy lungs and the fist shape between them.

The sheet was bunched around the figure's neck, her face still covered. Mike leaned over her with the scalpel. He didn't know where to begin, what he was to do. The flesh, naked beyond what the skin had ever shown, glistened with wet jewels.

A rubber-gloved hand moved at the edge of his vision. The doctor pulled the sheet away, off the table and the figure's head. The golden hair trailed across the padded surface beneath.

Lindy's face, eyes closed, mouth parted as though stilled with its last breath—the throat beneath her chin had been opened, showing the windpipe and the tendons running next to it, but the face hadn't been touched. The skin there was still perfect and unmarked.

He brought his face close to hers, marveling at her beauty, his own lips parted for a kiss.

Her eyes snapped open. Her gaze, perfect black at its center, locked into his.

Her mouth widened, smiling.

The scalpel clattered on the floor as he fell backward. His hand hit the examining lamp, its beam arcing across his face.

Lindy sat up on the table, smiling as her breasts slid across her ribs and dangled on straps of skin against her viscera. Smiling at him.

Her red hand reached for him, the fingers curling, wanting to draw him into her kiss. Her embrace.

The lamp swung again on its arm. Its glare burst and blinded him as he fell.

He woke with a flashlight shining in his eyes. From across the room—the beam was small enough to blot out with his upraised hand.

For a moment, he thought it was the kid, come back again. Doot had gone puttering off on his motorbike, heading home. He'd told Doot that he and Lindy wanted a little privacy.

Lindy . . . Next to him, she pushed herself upright, holding one of the blankets across her breast. Her eyes scanned confusedly across his face.

"Mike—" The remains of her own sleep, and whatever she'd helped herself to from the case, still tangled about her. "Mike, what is it?"

The flashlight beam swept across her. She shrank back from it, the edge of the blanket pulled to her chin.

It wasn't the kid. With the flashlight turned away from him, Mike could see the taller, thinner figure behind it.

The beam pointed to the floor, making a bright oval there. Enough light scattered to the sides to show the outlines of the lobby, the ragged curtains over the windows.

The dim light also showed the gaunt face that Mike had seen in the dreaming. Skeletal, flesh carved down to the angles of the bone beneath. But without the gold-rimmed spectacles. The face had dark sunglasses on—the round black lenses looked like bored-out holes into the man's skull.

There was no white doctor's coat, either. Mike could see that the bony man had on old denim work pants, the legs bagging loosely on his frame. And a shabby-looking plaid flannel shirt, buttoned up to his Adam's apple. The cords of his neck were stretched taut beneath the frayed edges of the collar.

It's the caretaker—he realized that now. Just some old fart with a flashlight, prowling around. The one that the kid had told him about.

The man smiled, a crease lengthening in the narrow face.

"Don't worry, folks." Dry voice, paper and dust. "I just came around to see how my guests were."

Lindy had scooted over close to him. He felt the bare skin of her arm touching his. He kept his eyes on the old man.

The caretaker stepped closer, the puddle of light floating ahead of him. "How you folks doing?"

Mike watched the man as he stopped a couple of yards away. "We're okay," he said after a moment.

The black lenses regarded him. "You didn't look so okay the other night." The voice even drier, as if it couldn't even be bothered to laugh. "When I fixed you up."

Mike glanced down at the bandages wrapped around his ribs, then back to the man.

He nodded. "Thanks."

"You're in a bad way, son." The flashlight's beam moved across the floor, then slid partway up a wall, the man's hidden gaze following it, then turning back to Mike. "You should be in a hospital. There's only so much you can do with some bandages."

"I'll be all right."

"Suit yourself."

The caretaker turned away and walked toward the lobby's door. Mike watched him, until he was gone. He didn't have to push the boards far to get outside.

"It's okay." He looked over at Lindy. "I don't think we have to worry about him."

They lay back down, the side of her face resting against his shoulder. But he didn't sleep.

Twelve

"This was quite a place at one time." The caretaker stopped and looked back over his shoulder. "People used to call it 'The Mayo Clinic of the West.' " His thin lips formed their mirthless smile. "It was really something. Or so I've been told."

The old man was giving them the grand tour. Nelder—Mike had remembered the name the kid had told him. That was it. Old Nelder, with his grey William-Burroughs-plays-Mister-Death face, had come sliding back into the building's lobby, with a skillet of bacon and bread fried in the grease. He must have been outside as soon as dawn had come over the hills, building the little fire and squatting down beside it. At least in the morning, with the bright daylight scraping in, the dark glasses on the skinny face didn't look so strange.

"Used to be the biggest train stop between here and Lincoln, Nebraska." Nelder kept walking, turning his head toward his shoulder when he spoke. "Folks came from all over to take the cure."

Mike hobbled after him, one foot dragging. The old

113

man had dug up a crutch, a real antique with a cracked leather pad and a grip that looked as though it were carved from yellowed ivory. That, plus Lindy on his other side, the side he couldn't move, kept him upright. Most of the time, at least—he'd already taken one fall when the tip of the crutch had slipped out from beneath his weight and Lindy hadn't been able to catch him in time. He'd hit the floor hard enough to knock out what little breath he had left. Gasping, he'd looked up and seen the caretaker standing there, waiting and watching, face expressionless behind the black glasses.

They were in a ground floor corridor now, in the burned-down wing. Up ahead, they could see where the blackened timbers laced across the sky, the walls and ceiling collapsed together.

Mike stopped, resting his weight against the crutch and Lindy's grasp on his other arm. "What cure?" he called after Nelder.

The black glasses looked around at him.

"The waters." Nelder pointed a bony finger toward the floor. "Place is built on top of a natural mineral spring. What they call geothermal—water just comes steaming up out of the ground, boiling hot. Some doctor back around the 1800s came out here and discovered it. 'Course, the Indians knew all about it, already. But they'd been cleared off. So the doctor built the clinic here. Thermalene, he called it. You can still see the letters outside, up on top of the building—most of 'em, at any rate. Claimed the water had all sorts of medicinal properties—cure anything, from impetigo to swooning fits."

"Yeah?" Mike lifted his head. "Did it?"

The old man shrugged. "People maybe thought it did."

Mike watched as Nelder went a few steps farther along the corridor and pushed open a door. Nelder tilted his head toward it.

"Come on—" Mike jerked the crutch tip ahead of

himself. Lindy's grip tightened on his arm. "Let's go see whatever the fuck it is."

Her nose wrinkled in disgust when the smell hit them.

It looked like an old-fashioned steam room. The years of neglect that had decayed the rest of the building had settled here as well. The tiled walls were covered with mold; the concrete steps going down from the corridor were slick with damp. The far side of the room was filled with stone basins set close to each other, oblong cavities the size of bathtubs. A network of pipes mazed above them. The spigots mounted into the ends of the basins were chained shut, with large rusting padlocks dangling from the links.

"Jesus." Lindy looked as though she were going to puke. "Smells like something *died* in here."

Nelder gave his thin smile again. He had gone ahead of them, down the concrete steps; he stood near the circular drain in the middle of the room's floor.

"That's the water," said Nelder. "Folks used to pay a lot of money to come here and soak in it. Drink it, too."

Lindy made a gagging face, tongue sticking out.

Mike ignored her. He let go of the crutch and grasped the iron rail running beside the steps. The metal was wet and peeled rust flaked against his palm as he dragged his dead foot behind. He managed to get to the bottom without falling. Lindy hurried after him and helped pull him upright.

He leaned his hip against the rail—the metal creaked, the bolts straining in the stone wall—and looked around the room.

"So what happened?" The patches of mold, with their baroque edges, were the size of eagles nailed up. "It doesn't look like anybody's been around here in a while."

Nelder shrugged. "That was all a long time ago." The smile again. "Before my time, even. Scandals, maybe—the old quack who ran the place probably got into trouble. Telling people they'd get cured, then they came out here and died on him. Something like that, I figure. Then there was a fire; as you saw, most of the east wing is gone." The smile went away. The black glasses gazed across the mottled walls. "And then people just forgot about this place after a while."

"Hey, I'm not kidding." Lindy tugged on Mike's arm. "This place is really making me sick."

He let her pull him back up the steps. In the corridor, they waited, and finally heard Nelder clumping up after them. The old man pulled the door shut, but the smell still hung stifling around them.

He'd been in the examining room before: in the dreaming, and when he'd managed to drag himself up the big stairs that opened onto the lobby.

It wasn't the way it had been in the dreams, all bright and shiny and new. This was another outpost of the decayed world. Rust and broken glass, and the dirty cotton stuffing straggling out of the examining table's padding. The bottles, dark blue with hand-written labels, lay on their sides in the cabinets, mired in cobwebs.

"What the hell's this thing?" Lindy had found the contraption hulking in the corner. She leaned close to it, peering at the gold decorations on black enamel, all under layers of ancient dust.

Nelder stood in the doorway, his skinny arms folded over his chest. "That, young lady, is the first X-ray machine brought west of the Mississippi."

Mike, propped against the edge of the examining table, looked around at Nelder. "Really?"

The caretaker paused a beat before answering. "So I've been told." His flat voice scraped through the room.

The counter underneath the glass-fronted cabinets was close enough for Mike to reach. He prowled through the contents of a metal tray.

"You got some real antiques here." He picked up a suture needle, laid it down, then something like a hemostat. He didn't recognize it. "Last time I saw stuff like these was when I was in med school. We had one instructor who had a collection of antique surgical instruments. All kinds of strange stuff. Pretty grisly when you got into the Victorian obstetrical devices—decapitating hooks and shit like that—"

Nelder's round black gaze turned toward him. "You're a doctor?"

Mike dropped the instrument into the tray. They were all specked with rust, the blades dulled by time.

He nodded. "Yeah, I am." He looked up at the old man. "Well, practically. I was finishing up my residency when . . . some shit happened."

The skeletal face stayed expressionless. The silence goaded him on more than any questions could.

"I got started doing some shit I shouldn't have. You start doing things . . . and then they catch up with you. That fuckin' fentanyl . . ." He laughed, a dead imitation of laughter. There was still fentanyl working its way through his bloodstream, from the shot Lindy had given him a couple of hours ago. That was the only thing that enabled him to move around without feeling the pain of his damaged flesh. "That's some high-powered stuff."

"This is some kind of drug you're talking about?" Nelder spoke as if they were discussing something to do with a frog dissected on a lab table. "A narcotic, I take it?"

Mike nodded. "Synthetic opiate. Good for terminal cancer, major trauma, deep-tissue burn injuries. Just about a hundred times more powerful than morphine. Good for anybody who's screaming his head off; one shot, agony all gone, pink clouds come rolling in." He turned his own death's-head grin at Nelder. "Know what else it's good for? It's good for getting high as a fuckin' kite, that's what it's good for. And you know what else? For getting strung out like a telephone wire. And for getting stupid and doing stupid things. I was signing shit out of the pharmaceuticals cage like I was checking books out of the

117

public library." The words kept pouring out of him, dizzying. "Shorting patients, giving 'em saline, keeping the good stuff for myself. Hoarding it. And then . . . once you start screwing up . . . you can hide it, you can hide it for a *real* long time, but somebody will know. Like they can smell it on you or something. And I'm not talking about cops." He shook his head. "Other people . . . they just know. And they come around, it's their business to know, they come around and tell you about the money. They got other people doing it, why not you? And pretty soon you got the fentanyl, and everything else, *and* the money." He laughed again, feeling his ribs begin to ache beneath the bandages. "And then you're really screwing up."

"You weren't much of a doctor." The thin lips barely moved. "Were you?"

"On the contrary." Mike picked up an instrument from the tray and tested its edge against his thumb. "Actually I'm a very good doctor. I know my stuff. I'm just not a very good criminal." The tool made a pink line in his skin. "Good criminals don't get stupid and burn the wrong people."

"I wouldn't know about that," said Nelder.

Lindy had come over from the X-ray machine. She took Mike's arm and laid her head against his shoulder. He felt disgusted for a moment, as though a fingertip had been set down in his gut. He knew she was still rolling under her own dosage.

There was a swimming pool behind the building, at the end of a path bordered with red brick. It looked as old as the clinic itself, with the same tiles set around the sides as covered the wall in the room with the stone basins.

Empty now—the contents must have been drained out a long time before, back when the clinic had been shut down. The bottom had filled with debris over the years: tree branches—a dead-looking grove lay a few yards farther on—and brown leaves; charred timbers that had been hauled out and dumped from the burned wing. Other trash had been browned by the sun, old cardboard boxes and papers, all of it piled together in a thick, interlaced mulch, a stratum of decay.

Mike leaned on the crutch, looking across the tile-rimmed hole. "What, they went swimming in the stuff? The water, I mean."

Beside him, Nelder pointed to a group of control valves near the pool's edge. The iron wheels on a pair of U-shaped pipes rising from the ground were also chained and padlocked. "They used to fill it up every morning, then drain it at night. Least, that's what I was told." His finger moved a couple of inches, indicating a third wheel set in a metal housing, larger than the other two. "So it'd always be fresh." He turned, pointing in another direction, to a rock-lined culvert yards away, with a pipe spout horizontal at its end. "Came out there—so it could soak back in the ground."

Mike closed his eyes. A vision lit the interior of his head for a moment. Of the women in their old-style bathing costumes, down to their knees, and with those funny ruffled hats.

"So that's it?"

Nelder was walking away, through the dust and loose gravel surrounding it. The brown weeds scratched at his legs as he headed toward the low hills.

Mike hobbled after the caretaker, then stopped, exhausted. He leaned over the crutch, gasping. The shot of fentanyl was starting to wear off. He raised his head and saw that Nelder had halted and turned around to gaze at him.

"That's the whole story on this place?" Mike tilted his head toward the clinic building. The sun had risen far enough to spell out THERMALEN in upside down shadows on the ground; the last wooden E sprawled yards away. "Just some quack . . . peddling miracle cures?" The

119

banished pain was returning. It crept up his spine, already blurring his vision.

After a moment, Nelder nodded his head. "That's all there is. That's all there was—there isn't anything now."

"That's . . . too bad." He tried to smile. "Man, I could sure use one. Miracle cure, I mean. You sure . . . these magic waters don't really work?"

The caretaker wasn't in a joking mood. The black-shaded gaze regarded Mike without emotion.

"There's no way you'll ever find out, is there?" Nelder looked past him to the building. "The spring's been capped for years. For a long time—since the clinic closed down."

Nelder turned and continued walking. Mike called after him.

"Hey—"

The black gaze turned on him again, the weeds thick around Nelder's legs.

"I wanted to say thanks."

Nelder regarded him. "For what?"

Leaning his weight on the crutch, he touched the bandages around his ribs. "For fixing me up. You did a good job." He managed to bring the smile up. "That's my professional opinion."

The caretaker didn't say anything, but kept watching Mike.

He felt his strength fading. "You didn't have to do it." He could barely hear his own voice. "You could've just thrown me out on the road . . ."

Black gaze, and silence. Then: "I did it so you could leave." Nelder's voice sounded like the wind brushing the dry stalks of the weeds. "I didn't want you to die here." He started to turn away. "This isn't a good place to die."

He felt someone take his arm, holding him up. Lindy had come out of the building and now stood next to him, keeping him from falling. He watched the old man walking, mounting into the first slope of the hills, until the rocks hid him and he was gone.

Thirteen

They waited until dark, and later, to take care of business. Charlie didn't mind; he and Aitch had this cherry Mercedes, a midnight black 450 SEL, to cruise all over town in, getting something to eat and generally relaxing. He liked the smell of the leather seats, everything, a lot better than in the Detroit iron Aitch usually had him driving.

Aitch was in the rear seat with the black kid they'd picked up—black in black, it struck Charlie, still thinking about the Mercedes's polished good looks—and doing the same shit he'd done with Mike. Making people listen to that raspy old music he dug so much.

Aitch sang along with the tape. "God, that's great stuff." He brought his smiling face close to the black kid's. "Come on, you gotta admit it. Be cool and say you like it."

Up in the driver's seat, Charlie had the mirror angled so he could see what was going on. The black kid held his head high, giving Aitch a disdainful killer look from the corners of his half-lidded eyes. He looked like he had African princes in his genetics; that haughty, imperious set to his seventeen-year-old face. Even with one of those stupid high fade haircuts—Charlie didn't know whether they reminded him more of show poodles or somebody wearing a Brillo pad for a hat—the kid looked like a hard number. Or as hard as he could, given that Aitch had the snout of a Colt Diamondback shoved up into the kid's jawbone.

"Turn it up," said Aitch, without looking around. "I want our guest to get a real musical education."

Charlie turned the volume knob on the Blaupunkt up a notch. He had the fader control rolled all the way to the rear speakers, so it wouldn't be so loud around himself. He didn't see how Aitch was going to gain many converts with this whole business. Either by beating the crap out of somebody until he was just drifting in and out of consciousness, the way they had with Mike, or by putting a big old cannon alongside somebody's neck—people just weren't going to sincerely reconsider their musical tastes under those kinds of conditions.

Of course, that hadn't been the reason they'd worked over Mike, or why they were driving around with this kid. This was business. The other was just something Aitch did on the side, because he was a fun guy.

"Now just ease back and listen." Aitch rubbed the muzzle of the gun up to the point of the black kid's chin, then back to the hinge under his ear. "You don't have anything else to do right now, do you? So this is just a little free time we made in your schedule—okay? Maybe in a little while we'll talk some more."

The kid sat with his long-fingered hands carefully laid flat on top of his thighs. He had on black Nike warm-ups, with a single red stripe running down the sleeves and legs. He didn't say anything, but the cold gaze in his eyes read out that the Diamondback was the only thing standing between him and pulling the head off this crazy white motherfucker with his grating, thumping old music.

Truth to tell, he was getting pretty fuckin' tired of it

himself. Charlie wondered if Aitch would get pissed off if sometime he wore a Walkman or something on one of these little runs. Pop his own tape in, some of the stuff that Aitch sneeringly referred to as elevator music. *That's what you listen to when you go to the dentist*—Aitch stroking himself into one of his tirades. *So they can skimp on the Novocain; your head's already numb by the time they get you in the chair.* It probably wasn't a good idea. It had taken a long time just to get to this point, where Aitch wasn't always laying those lectures on him.

He checked the mirror. The kid was sitting bolt up-right—who wouldn't be, with a big nasty machine like that alongside his neck?—but Aitch had settled back in the seat, smiling with boa-constrictor contentment.

He felt the same easy looseness rolling in his gut and up and down his arms as he steered the Mercedes through the dark streets under the freeway. Before picking up the kid, they'd been out at some place farther east, drinking beer and listening to the Mayther Brothers. Them he liked—it was a kick to see some huge guy like that, doing those James Brown moves with the microphone, up on a plywood riser the size of a postage stamp. Plus they got some of those women out on the floor dancing, ones who must've been knockouts back in the sixties, in a teenybopper no-bra way, and who could still stroll their cans despite hips wider from popping a few kids. A different kick from looking up at the studio windows and watching the downtown ballet students, but still all right.

Sometimes Aitch dragged him off to see the Margo Tufo Revue, and that wasn't nearly as much fun for him. Aitch would be knocking them back and nodding his head in time to the music, lost in his own deep groove, and Charlie would be worrying. A bar audience split down the middle, half stoned rednecks and half biker dyke types, and he'd be wondering when the punch-outs started. They never did, but he got tired watching his and Aitch's back.

Tonight, right after the Maythers did "I'd Rather Go

Blind"—the slow, murderous point in their set that always made his skin tighten, like he was going to explode or something—Aitch had pushed away his empty glass and stood up, tilting his head toward the door and the cool night street outside. Time to take care of a little business.

The kid had been waiting for somebody, but not them. He'd realized he'd been set up as soon as they'd walked in the door of the Northside apartment. He was pushing himself up out of the chair, getting ready to bolt, when Aitch had flashed the Diamondback. "Let's talk," Aitch had said, smiling. "Let's go for a long drive and just . . . talk."

Up to this point, riding around in the car, the kid hadn't said anything. And Aitch hadn't talked business yet—just getting on his ass about the music thing.

"You know, it's really a shame." Aitch stroked the shaved part of the kid's skull with the gun. "It's a shame a smart kid like you doesn't appreciate this stuff. I mean, this is like your fuckin' *heritage,* man." Aitch sounded genuinely grievance-loaded. "I can't figure you guys out. You got this"—he made a little gesture with his own head, to indicate the music moaning off the speakers—"and what do you listen to? Whatever dickhead is on the radio. And that fuckin' rap music. That stuff's for assholes. Really. They make it to sell to assholes. You're not an asshole, are you?"

The kid didn't say anything. The Mercedes floated over a set of railroad tracks—there were a lot of them in this district, around the old warehouses—and the bumping joggled the gun at the side of his head. Charlie looked up at the mirror and saw that a bright sheen of sweat had broken out on the kid's brow. If he hadn't eased the Mercedes over the tracks, if he'd taken them hard, the piece could've gone off. Aitch had his finger tight on the trigger. The kid was frozen in place, except for his eyes, which leaked venom and promised to kick this white guy's ass someday.

The lecture continued. "You know, if it weren't for white people, all this stuff would've died out. Isn't that a shame? You got a couple of the old ones left, like maybe John Lee Hooker or somebody like that, but you go to one of his concerts and it's all like white college kids. And when he goes, and the rest of them all go . . . then shit, it's just going to be white folks playing and listening to this stuff. I mean, you don't give a fuck about it, do you?" Aitch poked with the gun. "Name me one. I bet you can't. Just name me one single blues man that you know about."

"Robert Cray," said the kid.

"Very *good.* I'm impressed." Aitch nodded. "You know the home boys at least, huh? Local talent. There's hope in the world. 'Course, he's gotten some radio play, but still . . ." He rubbed the gun's muzzle back and forth near the kid's ear. "I *knew* you weren't stupid. I knew you were a smart guy."

He heard the change in Aitch's voice that meant he wasn't screwing around anymore. He took a corner—they had just about gotten to the edge of the warehouse district—and worked back into it, where no one could see them. For a moment, there was a glimpse of the downtown lights shining off the river.

"Like with the artillery—am I right? I know a lot about you," said Aitch. "I know you don't ever carry a piece. Do you? That's for the foot soldiers, huh? Let *them* get busted by the cops. Smart guy like you, you want to be off the street, sitting in some nice chilled-out apartment, toting up the figures on the ol' computer—don't you?" Aitch's smile widened. "Running things. That's your style. You don't know shit about big nasty guns—like this one—except they go boom and take people's heads off. And that's smart. I got to hand it to you. Dinking around with guns when you don't have to is how you get into trouble."

The kid looked out of the corners of his eyes at Aitch. The Diamondback had traveled back under the kid's jaw.

"So how come you do stupid things? Hm?" The grievances in Aitch's voice became sharper, moved up closer to the surface. "Cutting in on somebody else's action—that was really stupid."

"Don't know what you're talking about." The black kid's jaw bumped against the gun when he spoke.

"Aw, come on." Aitch looked disgusted. "Don't pull that crap with me. You know, there's such a thing as being smart, and then there's being too smart for your own good. *Too* smart is when you think you're the only smart guy, thinking that other people don't know what's going on. That's how you got set up. The guys up above you, those L.A. heavyweights—they tell you they want a little conference, got things to discuss, business blah blah blah; go here and they'll come around and you'll have a nice little talk. Only they don't show up, it's me and my associate here that show up—are you starting to get the picture? Is it making any bells ring inside your head?"

Aitch was really sticking it to the kid. Charlie glanced up at the mirror and saw him poking the Diamondback into the kid's neck, punctuating his words.

"You know, I think I'm getting through to you." Aitch simmered down a little. "I can see the little gears going around in there. Now me and your numero unos— the guys who *really* didn't like some of your bright little ideas—we've got ourselves an arrangement. I don't step on their toes; they don't step on mine. I deal with a rather exclusive clientele. Believe it or not, everybody in the world isn't necessarily in love with that crack shit. There's a lot of people who like things . . . nice. And clean. They're not interested in some garbage a bunch of whacked-out spades are cooking up in a motel room with a blow torch and a saucepan. The people I deal with, they want pharmaceuticals. They want to see Merck, they want to see Lilly, stamped right there on the label. They want hospital action, man, sterilized, right in their own homes. And they can pay for it. I'm talking a low-volume, high-markup business. I'm not interested in price-cutting rocks down to three dollars and looking to get every welfare mother in town peddling her ass for it so I can get another gold cap put on my teeth. You understand what I'm talking about?"

The gears were turning in the kid's head, all right; Charlie could look in the mirror and see them. The kid's whole face was shiny with sweat now. Aitch's voice had gotten cold and hard and scary.

"Now my accounts—" Aitch rubbed his thumb on the curve of the Diamondback's hammer. "They don't mind being addicted—Christ, I've got some old fucks on my list who've been doing shit for half a century—and they don't even mind being a little strung out. You got enough money, you got your name on some law firm's letterhead, people tend to overlook these little things."

The tape had ended. There was just silence in the Mercedes, except for Aitch's monologue.

"These people, they sure don't want any crap that's going to *lose* them all their money, all their nice cars and corner window offices, all that good shit. They want to have their fun and *keep* everything they got, too. They want something they can maintain on. Now you take something like hospital-grade analgesics—those are class drugs. You got your synthetic opiates, take you right out. Plus you deal with me, you know it's clean, it hasn't been stepped on by every greaseball between here and Turkey. People with the money, they're willing to pay for that kind of action. And you know what else? They're loyal. They're *grateful.* So what the fuck did you think you were doing, trying to cut in on me like that? You don't even have what these people want. And trying to do it without telling the guys above you. Now *that* was stupid. What, you thought you were going to carve yourself a little empire on the side? You asshole. They handed you over to me on a stick."

The kid's silence deepened. His hands dug into the warm-ups above his knees.

127

"See? You're smart, but you don't know things." Aitch shook his head, his voice sad, even kind. "Like with the guns. I've got this piece, this revolver, upside your head, you're pissing your pants—and you know what?" He stroked the side of the kid's head with the muzzle. "The whole time, I've got the safety catch on."

The kid's eyes went wide.

"Yeah, the safety's on," said Aitch, "so I could have a little fun with you. Give you a little talk, a little warning. I'm not a hard guy." He still had the gun up to the kid's head.

Visibly, the kid melted, his shoulders slumping. A weak smile came up on his face. "Shit, man—"

"You know what else you don't know? About guns?" Aitch's voice went all quiet. "Revolvers don't have safety catches." He pulled the trigger.

"Aw, Christ." Charlie looked in the mirror and saw the mess all over the rear window and the upholstery. That fucking Aitch. "I was going to keep this car for a while."

Aitch was wiping the Diamondback's barrel off on the kid's sleeve. He looked up. "Turn the tape over, will ya?"

Fourteen

"Just relax . . ."

It was the doctor again, the one with Nelder's skull face. In his white coat and glittering spectacles. The gaunt features loomed over Mike, coming closer.

He raised his hand, shielding his eyes from the examining lamp's glare coming over the doctor's shoulder. The light put a burning halo around the doctor's skull, made his face a black mask except for the glitter of the wire frames.

The room with its glass-fronted cabinets tilted around him, the insect shape of the X-ray machine hunched in the corner.

Dreaming . . .

The doctor raised a scalpel, the same perfect instrument as before, holding it delicately with the fingers of his rubber-gloved hand. Mike shrank away from it, his spine pressing into the padding of the examining table.

"Now this won't hurt a bit . . ."

The doctor leaned down, and Mike couldn't see what he was doing. Until he straightened up and displayed the scalpel again, its point tinged red now. A red line trickled down the metal handle and touched one rubber fingertip.

"See? There's nothing to be afraid of . . ." A smile in the doctor's voice. "A simple surgical procedure . . . that's all."

That's all . . . If he closed his eyes, the words went echoing around in his head.

Dreaming . . . dreaming, that was all.

That's all . . . around and around, as he held his breath. . . . *simple surgical procedure . . .*

"See for yourself. Aren't you a doctor, too?"

He opened his eyes. His chin touched his breastbone and he saw a red line traced down his chest and stomach. Panic constricted his breath as he raised himself up on his elbows. Where the red line ended, a drop of blood welled up, then curled like a snake into his navel, into a glistening red jewel there.

The doctor's hands pressed him back down to the examining table. "There's nothing to worry about . . ."

. . . nothing to worry about . . .

He fought to raise himself, but he couldn't, even after the doctor turned away, the rubber gloves dropping the scalpel with the other instruments.

"This is how we start . . ."

The doctor laid his hands on Mike's chest, the thumbs an inch to either side of the red line. The narrow face came down closer as the doctor pushed harder, his hands spreading apart. The red line widened.

"Really very simple . . ."

He grabbed the doctor's wrist, fighting to pull himself up from the table. "No—" He heard his voice cracking, the panic bending the words. "No, you don't understand—you didn't make the incision deep enough—*it won't work—*"

"Just relax . . ."

. . . relax . . .

"No—" Tears squeezed from his eyes as he ground his teeth together.

Dreaming, he told himself again. Dreaming, that was all it was.

The flesh parted between the doctor's hands.

He looked and saw the line, a red door now, widening as the doctor gripped and pushed. The breastbone cracked, and his ribs opened like the fan of a dove's wings. The lungs lifted upward, trembling; he gasped and saw them swell in response.

"You see . . ." The doctor's hand probed inward, delicately parting a nest of yellow connective tissue. "Simple . . ."

His moan broke out of him, his spine arching, his shoulders driven back against the table.

. . . *simple* . . .

Heart welling up in its soft nest. Alive, beating faster as the adrenaline of fear seeped into the tissue.

The doctor's hand cradled it, the fingers sliding beneath. "You see?" A different adrenaline had tinged the doctor's voice. "Do you see *now?*"

"No . . ." A whimper, a child's misery. He rolled his head back, away from the sight. Squeezing his eyes shut, blocking out everything—

. . . *everything* . . .

The dream broke. His eyes opened to nothing, to blackness. He heard himself struggling for breath, his heart flapping against his breastbone, as though to escape.

His face chilled under the sweat. A ribbon of moonlight slid through the nearest window. He looked down and saw Lindy's bare arm, the skin silvered, draped across his chest. In a convulsion of disgust, he pushed her arm away. She stirred beside him but didn't wake.

He crawled away from the damp nest of blankets. Drops of sweat smeared under him, the nails of his good hand clawing at the raw planks. When he reached the door, he managed to get through, the boards scraping at his stomach. Outside, he collapsed onto his chest, breathing the cooler night air in through the dust layered on the verandah. After a few minutes, he raised his head, then dragged himself down the steps.

The track of a crippled animal showed in the dirt behind him, as though his own carcass had been pulled across the ground. His mouth filled with salt; he spat it out and saw the thick blot sinking into the gravel. The mark spread out of focus, his head growing lighter. He looked up and saw the ridge of hills, black against the night sky. The animals with the red, watching eyes ran back and forth along the crest. Then the red sparks and the stars behind them blurred and tilted.

He crawled, his hand digging into the ground to pull himself up, the stones splitting his fingertips.

Rocks spilled down an incline. Dimly, he heard them rattling down the slope, until they were swallowed by the weeds. He raised his head, the side of his face crusted with dirt and sweat. The earth fell away before him, as though the hill itself had disappeared.

He turned onto his dead arm, looking back the way he'd come. For a few seconds, his vision cleared and he saw the building in the distance below him, down at the foot of the hills. The moonlight shone through the braced letters at the building's top story. The marks of his climb lay through the broken weeds and scrabbled dirt.

He'd reached the crest of the first low ring of hills. A dry wind, which had rolled across the miles of desert, touched his face.

A small shack was centered in an open space on the other side of the hills—he could see down onto the tarpaper roof. The blue light from the moon and stars etched the details. A stone basin, like the ones in the room inside the building, sat near the shack's door. A metal pipe stuck up from the ground at one end. It had a spigot: water gushed out and splashed into that already filling the basin to its crumbling rim.

He laid his chin on the hill's crest, holding his shallow breath. There was someone down there, in the water.

The old man—Nelder. He had his back turned toward the hill. But Mike saw who it was when the figure tilted back its head and the sharp outlines of the face were touched with the moon's blue light. The old man was naked, squatting down in the water, its dark surface coming up to his ribs, the white bones of his knees sticking up. He looked more like a skeleton with a thin cloak of flesh than before. Mike could see the articulations of his spine and shoulder blades, the stringy tendons of his arms. The skin looked translucent and luminous, as if it had never been exposed to the sun, but hidden in the deep caves of the earth.

Nelder cupped his large-knuckled hands underneath the spigot, leaning his face close. The water splashed and ran down his elongated forearms, trickling from the points of his elbows. On the pale skin, the wetness looked black, glistening with an oily sheen. Light shifted in the ripples around Nelder's stomach, as though the reflection of the stars was submerged inches below the surface.

The old man leaned back from the spigot, lowering himself full-length into the water. His mouth parted, the narrow face suffused with a trancelike pleasure. As Mike watched, unseen behind the hill's crest, Nelder cupped the water in his hands, raised them and drank. The water dribbled down his chin and neck, staining the skin like ink.

The water's smell drifted to Mike. Stronger than before, sulfurous and heavy. Not with things rotting, but from life hidden and curled in upon itself.

Down below, Nelder sat up in the basin. The dark water dripped from his arms as he raised them. His hands curled into claws, the lean muscles tensed. His head tilted back in silent ecstasy.

In the darkness at the edge of the open space, the darker shapes of the animals moved, the red eyes fastened

133

upon the pale, glistening figure. One form separated from the shadows and sidled to the basin; it lapped up water from the rim. Then it raised its head, teeth bared, throat mirroring the angle of the man's a few inches away.

Mike pushed himself down from the hill's crest. Loose pebbles spilled from under him as he slid against the dirt, his one hand scrabbling for a hold to keep from rolling unchecked.

The flashlight, the one the kid had left with them, glared against the stone basins and the maze of pipes above them, casting a net of shadows into the room's damp corners. The mold patches soaked up the light, as though they were holes into the night outside.

Mike, still panting from the crawl down the hillside and then along the building's ground-floor corridor, raised himself onto the lip of one of the basins. The room's sulfur smell choked in his lungs.

Balancing his weight against the basin, he reached and tugged at the chain and padlock fastened tight around the spigot. Flakes of rust came away in his hand, but the chain stayed fast. His breath turned to sobbing as his fingers clawed at the links.

He dropped onto the floor, the paralyzed right arm caught beneath his side. The pain and dizziness washed over him.

The flashlight beam caught at something wedged in the angle of the wall and floor. He reached and closed his fingers around it, pulling it scraping across the tile toward him. He rolled onto his back, clutching a yard-long piece of rusted pipe to his chest.

A clang of metal bounced off the walls as he swung the pipe against the spigot. The impact wrenched the pipe from his hand; it skittered spinning across the floor. He crawled after it, shoving it back toward the basin.

Brownish-red flakes fell from the padlock with the next blow. He was panting with exertion, barely able to focus on the target of his swing. The next blow hit the wall beside the spigot, cracking the tile. He swung the pipe again, lurching forward to bring his weight with it.

The lock broke, dangling loose from one rusted link. He dropped the pipe and grabbed hold of the chain. He fell backward with it; after a moment's resistance, the chain rasped across the spigot handle. The metal clattered against the basin's stone side when he let go.

The handle wouldn't turn. "Come *on—*" An animal whine escaped from between his clenched teeth. "You fucking . . . motherfucker . . ." He picked up the pipe and laid another blow, the swing sending him sprawling beside the basin. The pipe hit against one spoke of the spigot handle, turning it a quarter inch. A faint noise whispered inside the metal.

Exhausted, he pulled himself back up onto the edge of the basin and grabbed the handle. He tasted blood welling from his lip as he bit down, his arm straining.

He felt the metal turning, the handle rotating another fraction of an inch. Rust scraped against rust; a fine reddish dust drifted down. Then the handle came free, turning halfway around. Frantically, he spun the handle. Nothing came from the spigot.

"Jesus . . . come on . . ." He laid the side of his face against the basin's edge. Tears pushed from under his eyelids.

The spigot rattled; the pipe leading to it shook against the wall. Then a black thread slid out, spattering against the stone beneath it.

He raised his head, hearing the wet sound. The thread doubled and blurred, then become one as he focused on it. Then a string, the pipe's rattle turning to a moan; a burst, rust flakes and hard debris exploding from the spigot— and the water gushed out, splashing into the basin.

The water coursed over his hand as he held it in the stream. It was warm, holding the earth's heat. The smell of sulfur—not nauseating now, but alive and intoxicating—built up in his head as he breathed it in, the taste of it strong on his tongue. A dark rivulet ran down his arm, transparent—he could see the paleness of his skin through it, as though it were diluted ink or a rippling grey cellophane. But where it pooled in the basin, already inches deep, the oily black turned opaque. Its surface glistened with the beam of the flashlight bouncing from the tiled ceiling.

It came faster, a frothing torrent from the spigot. The basin was already half full. As he watched, the dark water, lapping against the stone, rose toward the lip.

He lifted himself up, stomach dragging on the damp edge. He rolled shoulder first into the basin, the water surging around him. It broke over the rim and trickled down the side. Exhausted, he collapsed against the basin's sloped end. He turned his head toward his shoulder and saw the water oozing snake-like toward the drain at the center of the floor.

Eyes closed, he let his head fall back, the water touching his chin and the angle of his jaw. His mouth opened, the water seeping in at the corners of his lips. The sulfur taste pooled on his tongue, and he swallowed, feeling the warmth spread through his gullet. The water swirled around him, caressing his ribs and groin, dissolving pain. His limp arms floated upward.

For a moment, he couldn't breathe. He had slipped down far enough in the basin that the water had come to the level of his cheekbones. He coughed, sputtering, and pushed himself upright. His dead arm flopped out of the basin; the drag of the stone edge against the soft flesh of his underarm anchored him, head above the glistening surface. He relaxed again, the water flowing warm over his chest.

The back of his dead hand lay on the floor, the black snake trickling near as it ran to the drain.

His head had flopped back, eyes closed. He didn't see when the fingers of the hand outside the basin twitched, then curled slowly into a fist.

Fifteen

In the morning light, Doot worked the front wheel of the motorbike over the railroad tracks. The temperature had fallen enough during the night that wisps of steam floated off the pond at the side of the lane.

He gunned the bike toward the old clinic building. The red 'Vette was still parked out in front, like an enameled jewel set in the dirt. He didn't see any sign of that guy Mike and his girlfriend Lindy. He supposed they were still probably sacked out inside. If the guy hadn't up and croaked yet. It had been looking pretty iffy when he'd left them.

The debate about whether he should've come back out here at all was still going around in his head. It wasn't like the guy was stuck out here anymore; he had the girl and the car now. She could take care of him, whether that meant finally dragging him off to a hospital emergency room, or fetching whatever he needed while he laid up here.

Doot had spent an hour after he'd gotten up, pacing around in the kitchen of his dad's house and drinking instant coffee. Until he'd finally loaded up some stuff—a loaf of bread, a couple cans of Campbell's Soup, and another quart bottle of Pepsi—onto the bike's carrier rack.

Won't hurt, he'd figured. To check up on them. Plus there wasn't anything else to do.

The bike's engine sputtered to silence. He got off and unhooked the bungee cord from around the sack of groceries. Carrying it in the crook of one arm, he brushed past the 'Vette's tapered snout.

The dark inside the building wrapped around him as he let the boards fall back over the door. He could make out somebody sleeping, wrapped in the blankets on the floor. Blonde hair in a dust-specked ribbon of light—it was the girl Lindy. When he walked closer, he saw that she was by herself.

He set the bag down beside her and prodded her bare shoulder. "Hey."

Her eyes opened groggily, taking a few seconds to focus on him.

"Where's Mike?" Doot stood back up, looking around the lobby. "Where'd he go?"

Lindy gazed up at him in puzzlement, her hair tousled across one side of her face. Then she realized what he was talking about. She bolted upright, sweeping her hand across the rumpled blanket next to her.

"Mike?" Her voice echoed against the walls.

She scrambled to her feet, throwing the blankets aside.

"Mike, where are you?" she shouted, her voice harsh with alarm.

Both of them turned about, scanning across the empty lobby.

"I didn't see him outside."

They stood still, their breathing the only sound in the building's trapped air. Then, far away, the quick note of water dripping into water, each drop followed by silence.

Behind him, Doot heard her calling the name again, as he ran down the ground-floor corridor. Past the doors on either side, toward the burned-out section with its charred timbers crossed over daylight.

He halted, gripping the sides of the last door frame. Turning his head, he shouted back to Lindy, "Here he is."

Black, oily-looking water lapped at the bottom step. Doot splashed across the floor, the water coming up to his ankles. He reached the stone basin, water streaming in a sheet from its edge, and gripped the unconscious figure under the arms. Mike's head lolled backward.

He heard more splashing, then Lindy was beside him. The water had soaked up to the knees of her jeans. She helped him pull Mike from the basin. Mike's skin was slick, tinged with the inky water, the bandage around his ribs pink from the blood underneath. Doot had to get the man's weight onto his own shoulders before he could wrestle him out, arms flopping to either side.

A wet trail showed in the dust of the lobby floor. Doot slid Mike down onto the blankets. He stepped back, panting for breath, as Lindy knelt down, bending close over Mike.

The guy was still alive—he'd felt him breathing as he'd dragged him down the corridor—but he looked as if he'd almost drowned. Hair wet, plastered to his skull, skin streaked with the water trickling off.

"Is he going to be all right?"

"Quick." Lindy looked over her shoulder at him. "Get me something to dry him off with. Anything."

He scanned across the lobby for a second, then ran over to the nearest window and tore off the curtain hanging at its side. Dust exploded around him.

Lindy rubbed the wadded-up curtain over Mike's chest and arms. The cloth turned black, the water smearing into the dirt. Her face curdled as the sulfur smell rose up.

Doot saw Mike's arm moving, where it lay flopped on

139

the blanket. Lindy didn't notice it; she was mopping the water from Mike's face. The arm rose, bending from the elbow.

Doot opened his mouth to speak, then stopped. For a moment, he couldn't figure out what was wrong, what was different. Then he realized. *He couldn't move that arm before.* Doot watched as the fingers curled. *That was the one he couldn't move—*

Mike suddenly sat up, wrapping both arms around Lindy's waist. She gasped in surprise, a little scream cut short by Mike's pulling her tight against himself. His eyes had snapped open, a smile breaking across his face.

She pushed against his shoulders so that she could breathe. "Mike . . ." The same realization hit her. She looked down at his grasp encircling her. "Mike, your arm . . ."

Doot watched as Mike got to his feet, pulling Lindy up with him. His smile grew wider. He let go, stepping back from her. A pool of water collected around his feet as he flexed his arms. The one that had been paralyzed was still stiff, the fingers curling slower than on the other. He watched his own hands working into fists, then releasing. He held the right arm out to the side, awkwardly, like a bird's broken wing; the paralysis hadn't completely ebbed away.

He turned his head, still smiling, looking from Lindy over to Doot. Then he laughed, head thrown back, his chest straining against the bandages. The laughter bounced, echoing from the lobby's ceiling.

The guy stood outside on the building's verandah, hands on his hips, drinking in the air, looking out across the weeds and the reaches of the sun-battered landscape as though he were a king surveying his domain.

Doot slid out of the doorway and circled around behind him. He was still amazed at the change.

"How . . . how're you feeling?"

Mike glanced over his shoulder. He smiled and nodded his head. "I've never felt better." His gaze traveled back out to the mountains. "Never," he murmured, "in my whole life . . ."

This was even spookier than when the guy had looked like he was going to die. The way he was bouncing around the place, and talking and smiling with that nut gleam in his eye—Doot watched him, keeping a careful distance. One end of the bandages wrapped around his chest had come loose, dangling in a ribbon at his hip, but he didn't seem to have noticed.

The guy suddenly turned, looking straight at Doot. "You're still around, huh? How come?"

Doot shrugged. The guy's voice snapping out at him like that made him nervous. "I don't know. Just . . . curious, I guess."

"Yeah, well, tell you what." Mike tilted his head to one side. "You stick around, and I think I'll be able to find something for you to do." The smile widened. "You know . . . I think you can be real useful to me." The voice softened as he turned his gaze away. "Real useful . . ."

Mike strode across the empty lobby. He didn't see Lindy anywhere around; she was probably off somewhere, doing whatever girls did by themselves. It didn't matter. Nothing mattered except the sensation that welled up inside his chest and spread across the muscles of his arms and legs. Like blood pumping to every cell, strong and hard.

In the lobby's dim light, his foot clipped the edge of the suitcase Lindy had brought with her. Something rattled inside it. He stopped, knelt down, and threw the case's lid back.

All the good things were in there. The things that used to be so good. He ran his hand gently over the hypodermics and glass vials, the containers of orange plastic with white caps, with the brighter-colored things inside.

141

He suddenly scooped up a double handful, then laughed as he turned and threw them. The tiny objects, the small rattling things, scattered across the floor.

The water had drained away, leaving its dark, slick residue on the tiled floor. At the head of the basin, a drop formed at the spigot, then fell, wetting the stone surface beneath.

He sat on his haunches for a moment, watching as another drop oozed out. Its smooth surface was a mirror; he could see his face, distorted by the curve, eyes fastened on the dark liquid.

That drop fell, and another formed. He touched it, and the bit of water dampened his fingertip. He put it in his mouth, the sulfur taste biting sharp on his tongue.

He reached out and turned the spigot handle. Water trickled, then ran in a steady stream. A dark pool formed at the drain underneath. He gripped the basin's edge and leaned over. The water's mirror was bigger there, but rippling and surging back and forth; the reflection of his face broke into dancing fragments.

It was warm in his palms as he cupped his hands under the spigot. It trickled down his wrists to his elbows as he brought his hands up and splashed it into his face. The water ran down his neck, its tendrils slowing over his chest. He took his hands a few inches away from his face, then licked the water from them.

Doot stood out in the corridor, watching through the doorway. The guy was so into his own wavelength—some weird place in his head—that it'd been easy to creep along after him and check out what he was doing.

Which was *super* weird. This whole bit with that rotten-smelling water . . . The guy had flopped down on his knees at the side of the stone basin, like he was worshiping it or something. Looking at the little drops of water, more like drops of ink, for a long time. As though they'd hypno-

142

tized the guy. Doot had held his breath and waited to see what Mike was going to do next.

Another whole creepy bit. Drinking the water from his hands—the thought made Doot's stomach flip—and throwing his head back. Trembling, for Christ's sake, as though it were a hit too good to be believed. Scooping more and more of it from the stream coming out of the spigot, and faster, until there were rivulets running down the guy's shoulder blades.

And the creepiest thing—the guy looked *bigger*. The light wasn't too good, just what came bouncing down the corridor from the burned-out section, but Doot could have sworn it was happening. Like the guy had plugged into some sort of instant steroid action, getting pumped up, the muscles across his upper back swelling and tightening the skin. Fucking *weird.*

The guy had stopped with the drinking routine. He was still leaning over the side of the basin, head close to the stream of water. His shoulders rose and fell, gradually slowing as he caught his breath.

Doot stepped back against the corridor's wall. He didn't want Mike to catch him snooping. Especially not the way the guy was all charged up.

Mike was standing, pushing himself upright with a hand against the basin.

Time to split—Doot scooted down the corridor, toward the charred timbers at the end. He could pop out that way, where the big gaps in the walls were, and circle back around to the front of the building.

Too weird, he thought as he ducked under one blackened timber. But . . . interesting. He had to admit that much.

"Mike—maybe you should take it easy . . ."

Lindy grabbed him by the arm as he strode across the lobby. Gently—but unstoppably—he peeled her grasp from him and set her aside. Smiling as he did it. Then he was heading for the door again.

At the edge of the empty swimming pool—he'd brought the pipe length with him from the room inside the building—he planted himself in front of the valves and cocked the pipe over his shoulder like a baseball bat.

The sharp clang of metal against metal drifted, echoing into the hills. He lifted the pipe for another blow.

A half dozen more, and the broken chains looped in a tangle at the valves' base. He dropped the pipe length and took the closest wheel in both hands, his arm muscles tightening as he strained to turn it.

He heard the sudden gush of water, and smelled it. Sulfur, and the other scent, the living one, that mixed with it. He stepped to the edge of the pool and saw the dark fluid spurting from a hole a foot or so down from the last row of tile. The water fell and splashed onto the wood and trash at the bottom.

His heart grew inside him at the sight. He nodded, satisfied, then turned and gazed up at the hills.

The stick prodded at the spider. The tiny creature scuttled in a different direction, trying to avoid the sharp point thrust at it.

Nelder sat on a rock beside his shack, the stick held loosely in one hand. He poked the stick at the spider again, keeping it trapped in a small space of dust.

A shadow fell across the ground. Nelder glanced up at the figure standing a few feet away. The spider scurried around the stick, dragging a line in the dirt, and escaped into the pebbles and larger rocks.

Mike looked down at him and smiled.

A little spark of recognition, of knowing everything, passed between them. From the black lenses of Nelder's glasses to the other's narrowed gaze—a mirror set in front of another.

The old man nodded. "Now you know," he said quietly.

One corner of Mike's smile lifted. "Now I know."

The two men looked at each other, sharing the secret between them.

In the dark spaces of the earth, shaded from the sun, other eyes watched them. Sharp muzzles lifted from the cool soil of the dens and tasted the odor of sweat, and the other, drifting in the air.

Sixteen

That spooky Mike guy had gone striding up into the hills, off on Christ knew what kind of errand. Doot had peeked around the corner of the clinic building and watched him go. Something wild was going on around here—the guy sure wasn't all fucked up and half paralyzed *now*. He went up the hillside, even the steep parts, as though he were on rails.

Before that, the guy had busted off the chains around the control valves and sent the rotten-smelling inky water spilling into the swimming pool. That had been weird, too—the guy had stood there with his hands on his hips, looking all pleased with himself, like he'd discovered a gusher of oil instead of a bunch of stuff that looked like something had died in it. Doot had been able to watch the guy from his spy point at the building's front. He'd snapped his head back out of sight when Mike had turned and looked around, just in time to avoid being spotted.

He couldn't see where Mike had disappeared, way up in the hills. The water was still pouring into the swimming pool; he could hear the gurgling and splashing noises.

The pool would do, for what he wanted. He had the plastic bottle that he'd brought with him the first time. It was empty now. All he had to do was scoot out to the side of the pool, stick the bottle under the stream of water gushing from the hole, fill it up, and stick the cap on.

Doot hesitated before stepping away from the side of the building. There was no telling where Mike was right now, not the way he'd been bouncing around. And even if he were still up in the hills, he might be keeping an eye on whatever was going on down here. One way or the other, Doot didn't want the guy catching him sneaking around. He didn't trust people with glittering speed-freak eyes like that. They tended to get bent out of shape over all kinds of small shit.

He drew back from the corner of the building and sighted toward the other side. The burned-out wing: he could get back in there—and that way Mike's girlfriend wouldn't see what he was up to—and hit the little room with the spigots and basins in there. That struck him as being the safest way to go. He took a quick glance around, then headed for the blackened end of the building.

They walked higher in the hills, the dry weeds scrabbling at their legs. The sun lengthened their shadows. At the crest of the next ridge, Nelder stopped and looked back. Far below them, the clinic building looked like a doll house.

Mike stood beside him, waiting. There might be more the old man knew; he needed to hear it. To know everything.

A hot breeze kicked up around them, carrying away dust and Nelder's quiet, uninflected voice.

"You'd be smart," said the old man, "if you left now." The sunglasses gazed out over the brown landscape. "You've tasted it."

Mike laughed. "Are you kidding?" He shook his head, grinning.

Nelder glanced over at him, then looked away again. "It's not a good thing." His voice had gone softer. "I've been here a long time. I know what the water can do. It affects people . . . different ways. The weak and the strong." He fell silent for a moment. Then, in a whisper: "It wants things."

The silence spread, wrapping around the earth. Mike lifted his gaze, hearing nothing. Except his own hushed voice: "What is it?"

Nelder shook his head. "It's old. Older than men. Perhaps . . ." The black lenses turned toward Mike. "Perhaps it made men . . . made them different from what they were. In the oceans, or where the forests were always dark . . ." A slow rapture had entered the old man's voice. "Perhaps it found us there, and taught us . . ."

The spell broke, like the stem of a wineglass snapping. *This old fucker*—Mike kept his thoughts to himself. *Senile old bastard.*

"Maybe you've been out here a little too long, if you ask me."

The old man remained silent. He'd delivered his warning.

Mike rubbed the corner of his eye. "Maybe I've been out here too long. Shit, starting to see things . . ."

That brought Nelder's gaze around. "Like what?"

He shrugged. "Things . . . strange things. At night. Like I'm dreaming—but it's not dreaming. It's like they're real. Things that happened here. Like a long time ago." He looked back at Nelder, studying him. "But you were there, too. So it must've been just dreaming." He shook his head. "I don't know . . ."

"That's bad." The black glasses regarded him, two dark mirrors. "It likes you."

"What're you talking about?"

The mirrors of the black lenses held unmoving. "The water. That's what it does when it finds somebody . . . it likes. That it can do things for. That it can do things *with*.

148

Then it shows them . . . things." Nelder looked back toward the distant building. "That's what it did to me."

Mike barked a quick, scornful laugh. "Yeah, right. If you say so." *Crazy old fuck.* His own voice slowed, brooding. "All I know is there's things *I* want. And now I can get them. Those fucking punks . . ." An edge rasped below the words. "Those shits dumped me out there to die. Those sonsabitches . . ."

His face had darkened, the fury building underneath. Suddenly, he squinted and blinked, as though the bright sunlight had become too much for him. He reached up and rubbed his eyes. When he took his hand away, he stared at it.

The tips of his fingers were smeared with blood.

He rubbed his eyes again. Now he could feel it, the warm wetness leaking out like tears. The blood on his fingertips glistened red in the sun.

Nelder looked over at him, at the mask of blood streaked down from the corners of Mike's eyes and across his cheeks. Nelder's thin, weary nonsmile rose again.

"Just a little side effect." The old man tilted his head. "You're going to have to watch your temper from now on."

Mike gazed at his own hands, the smeared blood already drying. For a moment, he felt his stomach growing queasy; then it passed.

Blood was no big thing. He'd seen plenty of it.

Something moved in the hills above, a lean canine shape. The memory of the eyes glinting red in the night troubled him; he scooped up a rock and threw it.

"Get out of here, you fucker! Get out—"

Nelder reached up and restrained his arm before he could pick up another stone.

"You shouldn't do that." The old man gazed into the hills. The animal had disappeared. "They've been around here a long time, too. A *long* time. You could learn from them."

His anger, prodded by the remembrance of fear, simmered lower.

"Yeah," Mike nodded. "Okay. Watch my temper . . ."

Everything looked clear. Doot flattened himself against the corridor wall, checking it out. He couldn't see or hear anybody around, all the way down to the doors that led off to the lobby. He pushed himself away from the bricks and plaster, and slipped into the room on the other side.

The floor was still wet, with inky patches on the tiles, but most of the standing water had drained away. The room still smelled like sulfur, and worse.

He crossed over to the stone basin, the one in which they'd found Mike passed out. The spigot at the end dripped slowly, a couple of seconds between each fall and tiny splatter. He glanced over his shoulder at the door, then reached and turned the spigot's handle. It creaked through its stiffening layers of rust, then gave way. A thin stream poured out.

Catching a bit in his palm, he held it under his nose and sniffed. It smelled even more rotten up close. He rubbed his hand dry on his shirt, then picked up the plastic water bottle from where he'd set it on the floor. The water splashed inside the bottle, darkening the white plastic, as he held it under the spigot. As the bottle filled, the water gurgled, slowly changing pitch. It almost sounded like laughing.

When the water was up within an inch of the bottle's neck, he screwed the cap on and turned off the spigot. He tucked the bottle under his arm and hurried toward the steps leading up to the door.

He was strapping the bottle onto the motorbike's rack when he felt somebody behind him. He'd left his denim jacket on the seat, and now he pulled that over the bottle to hide it.

"Taking off?" It was Mike's voice.

He turned around and saw Mike come walking from the side of the building. Mike's face was damp, as well as that green hospital-type shirt he'd put on; he looked as if he'd scrubbed himself, maybe at the edge of the swimming pool, and then used the shirt to wipe off the inky water.

Doot nodded. "Yeah. I got some stuff to take care of."

"I meant what I said." Mike squinted against the sun, his eyes red-rimmed. "You do a few things for me, and I'll make it worth your while." He dug into his pocket and pulled out some money, bills folded over. "We're going to need a few things around here—food, something to drink. You know, like you've already been bringing out."

He took the money from Mike's hand. The guy hadn't had it before, he was pretty sure; it must've been some that Lindy had brought with her. He tucked it into his own pocket.

Mike peered at him. "Nobody knows I'm out here, do they? I mean, you haven't told anybody."

Doot shook his head.

"We likely to see anyone?"

Another shake. "Nobody ever comes around here."

Satisfied, Mike nodded. "Good—let's keep it that way." He turned and walked back toward the clinic building.

Doot waited until the guy had gone inside before he snugged the jacket under the bungee cord. Then he climbed on the motorbike and fired it up. The empty landscape swallowed the bike's rasp and the clattering echo from the front of the building. In a couple of seconds a dust cloud was rolling up behind as he headed down the lane to the road.

She was waiting for him. She had cleaned herself up, put on a change of clothes from the suitcase. Making herself nice for him. That was one of her major job skills.

Mike stood at the edge of the blankets, looking down at Lindy. She had also helped herself to the stash, what was left in the case. Lying on her back, one hand flopped to the side, palm upward—she was out cold. Or as close to it as didn't matter. Mouth open, breathing slow.

Her eyelids trembled but didn't open when he touched her. He pushed her top across her stomach and higher, exposing her breasts. His hand curved around one, the ball of his thumb stroking the nipple. She made a small sound as she drew her breath deeper, her back arching up from the blanket beneath her. He watched, noting her reactions with clinical detachment.

He took his hand from her breast and laid the point of his forefinger in the middle of her sternum, just underneath the rucked-up edge of her top. Then he drew a slow line down, dragging his finger between her breasts, all the way to her navel; just hard enough to leave a white trace on her skin, which slowly turned pink again.

For a few minutes longer, he sat beside her, watching. She shifted uncomfortably, as though the sharp point of his gaze had penetrated her fog.

The dreaming . . . The memory of it came back to him. Of that other woman, who had smiled and touched herself. Deeper inside. Offering herself to him, where the red flesh trembled and grew warm from the blood flowing beneath . . .

Just like being back in med school. He smiled, thinking about it. Like being in anatomy class, only instead of the cold cadaver of some street creep with a cirrhotic liver, something warm and soft, that moved and breathed. That yielded to the soft probing of the knife, welcoming it, drawing it inside her, the red moisture touching his hand . . .

He let his smile fade. Sitting back from her, he folded his arms on his knees.

Nice and easy . . . The old man's voice, whispering inside his head.

There were some other things he had to take care of first. And then he was going to think about this some more. About red, soft things that moved and breathed.

He promised himself. Resting his chin on his forearm and gazing at the sleeping woman—*real soon.* He nodded, his chin rubbing against his arm. There was a lot he was going to think about.

Seventeen

The screen door slammed behind Doot as he stepped into the house, out of the baking afternoon sun and into the relative cool. At least it was quiet in here now.

Back when Lindy had shown up and asked for him—that golden moment—he'd managed to clear off Garza and the rest of his buddies. They'd been too dazzled by the sight in the flesh of a total number like her, as though she'd stepped out of the TV screen, to have put up any argument. Not just dazzled, but even a little scared—Doot still got a kick out of that, just thinking about it. What'd they think she was going to do, eat 'em up with her little white teeth? Christ, you would've thought they'd *volunteer* for that.

Maybe it was the fear of the unknown. There were a couple of girls in the high school who tried to pull it off, but you knew that underneath the hard-edged makeup and the drop-dead expressions, they were the same ones you'd gone through grade school with, back when they'd been scheming on getting their first training bras.

There were still bits of party debris around, though.

An empty beer can clattered away when his foot hit it. He'd have to finish getting this place cleared up and aired out—it still smelled like stale cigarette smoke and spilled beer—before his dad got back. Though if his dad showed up and the place still smelled like the Lysol atom bomb had gone off, he'd know that something had gone on here. Not to mention the dead giveaway of the missing cases of beer.

Shit—he'd have to think about it later. Right now he had something else on his mind. He carried the plastic water bottle, its contents sloshing back and forth, back to his bedroom.

A big utility table, the kind with the metal legs that folded up if anybody wanted to move it, served as a desk. It practically stretched from one side of the bedroom to the other; its whole six-foot length was covered with books and magazines, paper and all the other crap he accumulated. The good stuff, like all those library discards that Anne had paid a nickel apiece for and given to him—stacks of Gabriel García Marquez, a beat-up Kafka collection—had all sunk with their own weight through the levels, leaving a bunch of *Playboys* and silly-ass comic books floating on the surface. People around here thought that if you read *The Dark Knight,* it made you an intellectual.

Doot cleared a space on the table with his elbow, shoving a whole stack of stuff onto the floor. He set the bottle down, then sat on the bed a couple of feet away, between a pillow and a mound of his dirty laundry. He cupped his chin in his hands, looking at the white plastic, tinged darker by its contents.

On the wall above the table hung a poster of a Lamborghini Countach, shot three-quarters profile on a black background. A girl wearing nothing but a pussy-binder bikini and a full-face helmet lounged against the front left fender. Anne had used a heavy yellow marking pen to draw in a speech balloon coming from the woman: "I used to have existential angst, before I found this bucket to carry my brains around in." The words were a little hard to read against the shiny black.

He leaned forward to pick up the bottle and unscrewed the cap. The sulfur stink oozed out into the room. He dipped a finger into the bottle's neck and tasted the water.

"Christ." It made him gag. He scraped his tongue against his front teeth, trying to get the taste off.

Setting the bottle back down, he looked around the bedroom. He pushed himself up from the bed and walked over to his dresser.

A ten-gallon aquarium tank sat on top. Rust specked the chrome edges; the water, murky with algae, had evaporated a couple of inches down from the top, leaving white-streaked glass above. The air pump beside the tank sputtered and wheezed, sending up a thin stream of bubbles in one corner.

Doot tapped on the glass with his fingernail. "Hey— you guys still in there?" He sprinkled in a few bits of food every morning, more out of habit than anything else, but he hadn't actually checked on the tank's inhabitants in a long time. He'd grown out of his tropical-fish phase a couple years back, when a friend had cleaned out a tank and given him a pair of cichlids, a Jack Dempsey and a grey-striped one that he hadn't known the name of. Both of which had proceeded to annihilate practically everything in the tank—those fucking cichlids were killers.

A flash of pink moved through the tank's gloom. The survivors, two gouramis, were still swimming about. With nothing else in there with them, they had grown to a good size; they looked big as the palm of a baby's hand, and the same color.

He stood looking at the fish, as a minute ticked by. Then he went off to the kitchen, and came back with a roll of paper towels.

A double layer on the tabletop; he dug out an X-Acto

knife from one of the cardboard boxes underneath and laid it down beside the plastic bottle.

"Come on, boy . . ." He splashed his hand around in the tank, cornering one of the fish. He carried the wriggling thing to the table and dropped it on the paper towels. It flopped back and forth, bending in its middle.

He picked up the knife. He took a deep breath and blew it out.

"Hate to do this to ya, fella." He shook his head, then brought the knife down, slowly and carefully. The point sank into the wet flesh, and he winced.

The sight of the fish thrashing, blood seeping into the paper towels, made him feel sick. He'd done one deep cut, a little over an inch long. The fish's innards showed through the new opening. The towels reddened, soaking up more.

He bit his lip, watching the fish's agony. None of this seemed like such a good idea now.

It finally lay still. He poked it with his finger. The fish twitched. It was alive, but just barely.

From the kitchen, he brought a clear glass mixing bowl, filled halfway with water from the tap. He set it down beside the dead fish. The plastic bottle already had its cap off; he picked it up and poured a splash into the bowl. He stopped when the water was tinged grey, as though somebody had emptied an ink pen into it. Picking the fish up by its back fin, he dropped it into the bowl. Blood from the cut seeped out and made a cloud around it as it sank.

He stepped back to watch.

The dying fish drifted in the murky water. It looked broken, hinged in the middle. The staring eyes came round toward Doot.

"Aw, fuck." He felt like an idiot. Five minutes had passed; he'd timed it by the alarm clock on top of the dresser. The time had gone by, and he'd felt sicker and sicker. The poor little bastard was probably dead by now.

Drowned, if the cut hadn't killed it; it seemed like a stupid way for a fish to go.

He felt even stupider. He sat down heavily on the side of the bed, shaking his head, disgusted with himself. He had killed an innocent gourami that hadn't wanted to do anything except paddle back and forth in a dirty ten-gallon tank for the rest of its life, *and* had proved what a jerk he was for making up and believing weird shit about that rotten water from out at the old clinic. This was turning out to be a long day. He flopped back onto the pillow, picking up an old *Watchmen* from the mess beside the bed and holding it in front of his eyes. He stared at the same page without turning it, not even trying to read the words.

Water splashed; he heard it. He lowered the comic and looked over toward the dresser. Probably left the lid off the tank, he figured. If the other gourami jumped out and expired on the floor, that'd be consistent with everything else that had happened.

The lid was on the tank. He could see the gourami swimming back and forth behind the green-mired glass.

Wait a minute. He swung his feet over and sat up on the bed, gripping the mattress with both hands. On the table, just a few feet away from him, in the bowl with the dark-tinged water . . .

The fish, the gourami he'd cut open with the X-Acto knife, barreled back and forth, its tail thrashing the water. Little dark flecks slopped over the rim.

"Sonuva*bitch.*" He stood up and looked down at the bowl in amazement. "You little sucker."

In the dark water, the fish surged back and forth, its tail whipping in powerful strokes.

The trailers looked shabby, like cheap boxcars for an abandoned railroad line. The sign out at the front of the park called them mobile homes, but there weren't any of the fancy double-wides with covered carports that better-off people had. These were *trailers.*

All of them seemed to have sagging clotheslines strung with women's underwear—old bras and strange-looking panty girdles with dead elastic. They looked strange to Doot, at least. They were a long way from what you saw in a Frederick's of Hollywood catalog.

And why did all the trailers have broken Big Wheels sitting in the too-long grass around them? He couldn't figure that one out. Didn't any of these kids ever get a *new* Big Wheel? And if it wasn't that, it was Bert and Ernie dolls, and Big Bird, that all looked as if they'd gone to war and come back with limbs shot off. Like the kids didn't play with them, but used them for target practice with their daddies' guns.

The motorbike sputtered down the trailer park's central lane. One old bat in a faded housedress and cat's-eye glasses, sitting sprawled in a lawn chair with busted webbing, glared at him as he went past.

He parked the bike at the end of the lane. From the carrier rack he unfastened a cardboard box. The water bottle was in there, sloshing around, down a couple of inches from when he'd first filled it up.

Noise poured out of the trailer's screen door. He could hear children squabbling—little kids, like five or six years old, their voices pitched so high it hurt his ears—and a TV set tuned to the soaps. He knocked on the door's thin aluminum frame, adding its clatter on top of the rest.

"Yo, Anne"—he knocked again—"you home?"

One of the kids started crying, a sobbing heat-irritated wail. A fan was droning in a window opposite, but not accomplishing much. These tin cans were like ovens, Doot knew.

"Just a minute!" The shout came from deeper inside the trailer.

He stood waiting, the box in his arms. One of the

kids, face damp with recent tears, came up to the screen and looked out at him.

Anne had to push the kid out of the way to get to the door. Her face lit up when she saw him.

"Hey, Doot—how you been?" She unlatched the door and swung it open. "Come on in."

The trailer had that smell of sour milk and a trash can tucked somewhere full of used Pampers, which Doot always associated with lots of rug rats running around. There seemed to be even more of her little brothers and sisters than the last time he'd come here; Anne's step-dad should've tied a ribbon on it a long time ago. The screen door clapped shut behind him, trapping them in the trailer's dimly lit heat.

He shrugged. "Been okay, I guess." It seemed like a long time since he'd come by to see her.

She had on her usual faded jeans and too-big T-shirt. This one said Precision Castparts on it. "Whattaya got?" She nodded toward the box.

"Got something to show you." He held the box up. "Something you'll think is, uh, interesting."

"Oh?" Anne tilted her head and raised an eyebrow. "Come on back here, then."

One of the kids was flopped stomach down on the bed in Anne's room, playing with a couple of Transformers. Anne grabbed the kid's ankles and swung him around, half off the bed.

"Come on, squirt-ee-o, beat it. Me and my buddy Doot have some stuff to talk about."

She hurried him along with a hand between his shoulder blades. Soon as the kid was out the door, she sat down beside Doot on the bed.

"Hey, it's good to see you." She gave him a punch in the arm. "I haven't seen you since graduation—I mean, if you'd been there."

Her leg was right next to his, and he felt its warmth going through the two layers of denim. He got a twitch, but nothing approaching a hard-on, nothing that he had to hide. He could if he'd wanted to—he had in the past— by thinking about different pieces of her. She had a nice pair underneath the big loose t-shirt. And the legs and the butt were all nice enough, too. She'd even been the first girl he'd ever kissed, way back in sixth grade. But that had been before he'd learned what all of his buddies had already seemed to know. That you weren't supposed to go for girls who didn't wear makeup and had their hair cropped shaggy-short instead of in one of those big stiff, tangled fluffs. And who played tympani in the school orchestra, and got B's and A's—at least when she wasn't telling the English teacher to go fuck herself for calling Emily Dickinson a man-hating spinster. Most of the high school's girls had already figured that teacher out as something of a dyke, anyway. She was always standing behind their chairs when they'd be taking a test and trying to look down their blouses. The dyke label got tossed at Anne, too—probably because of the short hair and the fact she'd waited until her sophomore year to start shaving her legs—but she hadn't given a fuck about that, either. She'd told Doot a long time ago that she was planning on blowing this whole popsicle stand.

He laid his hands on top of the cardboard box. "I didn't know if you'd be here or not. I thought maybe you'd already left."

She shook her head. "Naw, those National Merit people only gave me a partial scholarship. I gotta stay here till September, maybe get a job and save up some money."

"You still going to go premed?"

"Yeah. Going to try to, at any rate."

Doot unfolded the box's flaps. "That's why I brought this over. I figured it was something you'd think was, um, pretty wild."

She made space on her desk in the room's corner, not shoving the books and papers off but stacking them neatly on the floor. Doot started taking the things out of the box and setting them out.

Anne picked up the plastic bottle with the dark water rolling back and forth inside. She unscrewed the cap and sniffed.

"Jeez!" Her nose wrinkled in disgust. "What's this stuff?"

"Hold on. You'll see." He had brought a couple of paper towels and laid them on the desk top. From the box he took a jar filled with clear tap water. The other gourami from his aquarium swam around in the jar. He reached in—the jar's mouth was just big enough to squeeze his wrist through—and caught the fish. He laid it wriggling on the paper towels.

Anne watched him dubiously as he picked up the X-Acto knife. He'd wiped its blade clean.

"You know, Doot, I've seen dissections before." She folded her arms across her breasts. "Remember, when we were lab partners in biology class? We did the little froggie on the board?" She shrugged. "I mean, I did the little froggie. You chickened out."

He didn't answer her. Knife in hand, he bent over the fish on the desk.

A shake of her head. "It's not really, you know, ethical to go cutting up some poor animal, for no good reason—"

He brought the knife point down. "I got a good reason. Just hang on."

A moment later, he stepped back from the desk. The knife's edge was bloodied. He reached down and lifted the clear glass mixing bowl from the cardboard box.

"You'll see . . ."

The tap water splashed into the bowl. Then he poured from the plastic bottle until the water was tinged grey. He stirred it with his hand, then dropped in the gourami. It floated a couple of inches below the surface, bleeding and twitching.

Anne bent down, bringing her face close to the side of the bowl. The fish had stopped moving, drifting now in the cloud of its own blood.

"Way to go." She turned her head, looking up at Doot. "You've killed some poor goddamn guppy. Am I supposed to applaud now, or what?"

He smiled, tapping the edge of the bowl with his finger. "Hang on."

The fish looked dead now, the cut raw in its side. Anne stepped away, shaking her head. "I don't know, Doot. Maybe you've been out in the sun too long . . ."

A splash of water. Then another, as though someone had flicked the surface with a finger.

Anne looked over her shoulder, eyes widening. "What the fuck—"

They both bent down, on either side of the bowl. He saw her face bent and magnified, the amazed look even bigger.

"Sonuvabitch," said Anne. "That's *wild . . .*"

Between their faces, the fish swam back and forth in the dark-tinged water, swerving against the bowl's curved glass.

Eighteen

"It's quiet out here, you know?" Lindy laid her head against Mike's shoulder. Her last hit was fading away, leaving her in peace. "Real quiet," she murmured. "I've never been anywhere it's this quiet."

They were sitting on the steps outside the clinic, the ones leading up to the verandah. The sun had just started to lower behind the hills, pouring a pink-tinged radiance across the dry valley fields. A hawk drew a slow wheel in the distant sky.

She glanced at Mike beside her, but he didn't seem to have heard her. His face was all dark and broody.

"I always lived in the city." The chemical drift made the words come rolling out of her. "With everybody screaming at you all the time. Not like it is here."

She closed her eyes, so she could just feel him next to her and not have to see him scowling all slit-eyed at the landscape.

"I could learn to like it out here . . . It's so peaceful. You know what I mean."

Her head snapped to the side as Mike shoved her

away from himself. She opened her eyes and saw him looking with disgust at her.

"What the fuck are you talking about?" The corner of his mouth curled. "Are you kidding? This fucking place is a dump. You want to become like the assholes who live out here?" Flecks of spit showed white on his lips as he yelled at her. "Like that stupid kid that comes around? Is that what you want?" He turned away from her, shoulders hunched. "Yeah, peace and quiet—peace and quiet until your fuckin' brain turns to Jell-o."

She had shrunk back from him, from the force of his wrath. Trembling, she watched him squeeze his hands into white-knuckled fists.

Doot gave Anne the binoculars. They were a pair his dad used for spotting deer whenever he went out during hunting season. "Down there," he said, pointing.

Lying on her stomach beside him, Anne propped herself up on her elbows and scanned the territory below. She spoke as she kept the binoculars up to her eyes.

"You got it from that old place?" She peered into the rubber eyecups. "Where?"

They were keeping low in the dry grass at the top of the hill, to avoid being spotted. Doot slapped away a bug that had been itching at his chest. They'd had to wait until Anne's mother had come home from work, to take over watching all the younger kids, before they'd been able to come out here, Anne riding behind him on the motorbike.

"There's like a room, down on the ground floor. Off toward the side, over where it's all burned and shit." He nudged her shoulder. "Over there. That's where the water's piped in. And there's that swimming pool—there, behind the building. He busted the locks off and started filling that today." The dark water lapped at the pool's tiled edge; it sparkled, looking like a polished bit of coal from up here.

Anne turned her head, swinging the binoculars

around. She held their focus on the tiny figures of Mike and Lindy down below. Doot lifted his head, to see better.

The two people had been sitting on the verandah steps; now Mike was standing up. He was shouting something, but Doot couldn't make out what it was at this distance. Lindy cringed back from his anger.

Anne studied the scene. "That's the guy?"

Doot nodded. "Yeah. We gotta be careful about him. I think he's kinda . . . you know . . . dangerous."

She lowered the binoculars and looked at him. "And he told you he was a doctor?"

"Yeah. That's what he said, at least."

Anne shook her head as she raised the binoculars to her eyes again. "Sure makes you want to think twice about your career choices."

He didn't mind her keeping the binoculars. Looking down there without them, and seeing that Mike guy stomping around, and Lindy cowering away from his shouting, was giving him a funny feeling in his stomach.

"I just meant—"

Mike's anger had flared out of control. Lindy had never seen him like that before, with his face all red and throwing his hands up, the fingers curled and shaking.

"You just meant; you just meant what!" He cocked one hand back as though he were about to strike her. "A day out here in this shit pile, and you think you're fuckin' Heidi or something!"

He shoved her aside, sending her sprawling across the steps as he stormed up them and into the building. The boards over the door slapped back into place. Lindy sobbed, feeling a hot burst of tears on her face.

A moment later, he reappeared. She turned and looked up, seeing him standing above her with her little purse in his hand. He fished out her car keys, then threw the purse down, its contents scattering across the verandah.

"I got business to take care of." He strode down the steps without looking at her. "I'll see you later."

She pushed herself up on her hands, watching him go.

Doot didn't need the binoculars to see what was going on. Mike had knocked Lindy flat, and now he was roaring off in the red 'Vette. A cloud of dust rolled behind the car as it headed down the road.

Anne took the binoculars away from her eyes. "How bad did you say that guy was hurt?"

"He was *all* messed up." He didn't look at Anne, but down toward the building, where Lindy was sprawled across the steps. Probably crying, he figured.

"Yeah, well, he looked like he's feeling all right now." Anne made a scornful noise. "The sonuvabitch."

"I told you," said Doot. "I told you that's what it does."

Anne rolled over on her back, resting the binoculars on her stomach. She nodded as she looked at him.

"You know, Doot—this is crazy. I mean, some kind of magic water . . . It sounds like a tourist attraction or something."

"Hey—you *saw* it. You saw what it does."

She shrugged. "I don't know . . . a tropical fish, and this guy out here . . . it's not what you'd call great scientific evidence, is it? Maybe this guy wasn't hurt as bad as you thought he was. I mean, it's not like *you're* a doctor, or something."

He felt his face growing heated. "I've *seen* it. It's true."

A shake of her head. "Okay, maybe it's true; maybe there's some kind of miracle water bubbling out of the ground out here. You can raise the dead with it . . . I don't know." Her voice went softer and lower. "What I want to know is, what's it matter to you?"

"Huh?" The question took him aback. "What do you mean?"

167

"I mean, why's it so important for you to believe all this?"

He stared at her in amazement. "It's . . . it's important. It's like . . . a discovery . . ."

"Come on." She sat up so she could look him in the eye. "There's a whole wide world out there you haven't discovered." Her voice went low again. "When we were in school, you were the one who wanted to be a doctor."

Silent, he turned his face away.

"You wanted to be a lot of things."

He shook his head, staring at the ground in front of him. "Yeah, well . . . I can't. Okay?" He looked up at her. "I gotta help my dad with his business. There's all the paperwork to take care of while he's out on the road. And if he buys another rig . . . he's going to need another driver. There's all that stuff I gotta think about."

"That's bullshit." Anne's face clouded with anger. "The town's full of unemployed drivers—he needs one, he can hire one. And he can fill out his own forms, just like he's always done. He doesn't need you to do that. You're the one who needs the excuse, so you can hang around here forever, acting like a dumb shit in front of all those so-called friends of yours. Never getting out and going anywhere, never becoming anything. Because you're afraid to."

Doot scrambled up from the ground. He stood over her, shouting.

"I don't even know why I bothered showing you! You don't want to believe me—that's fine. You never wanted to believe me about anything, anyway!"

He strode down the hillside, dust kicking up around him.

"Shit." Anne rolled onto her back and gazed up at the cloudless sky. "You really fucked that one up." A grasshopper, the only other thing to hear her voice, rasped its hind legs, then flew off.

* * *

168

The road, the thin ribbon of the county highway, cut straight through the flat, dry landscape. He didn't have anything to do except aim the 'Vette for the horizon and push down the accelerator. The wind streaming over the insect-marked glass buffeted Mike's face.

His hands gripped the steering wheel as though trying to twist it apart. Teeth grinding down hard—*that stupid cunt, fuck her, fuck all of them*—he squinted into the sun.

A tear broke and ran down his cheek. He felt the sudden wetness and took one hand from the wheel. He dabbed at the tear.

When he looked at his hand, his fingertips were spotted with red. He rubbed his cheek, then brought his hand away.

His palm was smeared red.

The sick feeling at the pit of his stomach didn't hit him. This time, he smiled.

Her face was damp and puffy from crying. She looked up and saw the boy standing there, at the corner of the building. His jeans and shirt were coated with the hill's dust.

Lindy sat up on the verandah's top step and rubbed her face with the palm of her hand, smearing the tears dry. With a toss of her head, she shook her hair back away from her face.

Doot stayed where he was, yards away from her. "You okay?"

She nodded. "Yeah. I'm fine." She made a sound that could have been a laugh, but wasn't. "Can't you tell?"

He walked up to the bottom of the steps. "Can I get you anything?"

"No . . ." A shake of her head. Her nose had reddened; she sniffed loudly. "Just don't . . . just don't go away . . ."

He mounted the steps and sat down beside her in the striped shade of the building's overhang. There was a sweet smell that came from her. She must've put perfume on, or something like that, Doot figured. Something girls did. She had done it for that Mike guy, out here in the middle of nowhere.

Her face was still streaked from the tears, a black smudge at the corner of one eye from her makeup.

"He scares me," she said in a small voice. "He's all different now . . ."

Doot didn't know what to say. He put his hands on his knees and pressed down hard.

"I've never seen him like this before . . ."

She laid her head on his shoulder. He felt its light weight there, a pressure and the trembling as she breathed, each breath almost a sob. He put his arm around her shoulders, and suddenly her face was against his chest, her hair trailing against his chin, and she was crying. Her body shook with the force of her weeping; he wrapped his arms tighter around her to hold it in.

Then she pushed away from him, her hands flat on his chest, the straightening of her arms breaking his hold.

"I can't take this shit anymore." Her face had turned into something hard underneath the tears' wetness. She rubbed with her palm again, harder this time, pushing the skin white. "I've gotta feel better than this."

Lindy jumped to her feet. In a second, she had pulled the boards over the door aside and had slipped into the building's dark interior.

He followed her inside. Dust hung in the building's stale-smelling air. In one of the ribbons of light, he saw her kneeling down by the blankets, pawing through the suitcase. She found what she was looking for; she slapped a trio of capsules into her mouth and swallowed them dry.

She was breathing heavily as he stepped up behind her. Her head turned and she opened her eyes, looking over her shoulder at him. The caps were already having an effect on her, even before they could have dissolved into her bloodstream. Her face smoothed, became slack, as though the muscles beneath the skin had been sliced loose from the bone.

A smile, wet at one corner. "Want some?" The words came out slow.

Doot shook his head. As he watched, she sprawled back on the blanket, arms flung out.

"I know," she murmured, "what would make me feel even better . . ."

She reached up and grabbed his hand, tugging him down toward herself.

Nineteen

It was a long way home. Anne still had the binoculars that Doot had brought along; she'd looped their thin leather strap over her shoulder so that they hung at her hip as she walked. She'd have to get hold of him, get them back to him sometime soon. Or maybe just go over to his dad's house and leave them on the back door handle where he'd be sure to find them. Dusty and thirsty, she climbed the steps to the trailer's screen door. She'd decided that she'd think about it later.

The youngest of her brothers and sisters were watching something dumb on the TV, with beefy-looking guys in short-sleeved cop uniforms. She picked up the remote as she walked by them and punched up Dan Rather; they squealed in protest, and she flipped the control back over to them.

Her mom was flaked out on the daybed, still in her white nurse's assistant uniform, the clumpy air-pillow shoes kicked off. Anne eased the door of her own bedroom shut so as not to wake her.

Doot's tropical fish still swam around in the bowl on

the desk. The water had cleared a bit, but was still tinged grey. The fish, pink and shiny, stroked back and forth. When she brought her face down and looked straight at it, she thought she could see a thin white line on its side, where the cut had healed.

Maybe... She shook her head as she straightened up. She didn't know what to think about it.

Carefully, trying not to slop the water over the rim, she picked up the bowl and set it on the little table by her bed. She went back to the desk and sat down, pulling a stack of books toward her. They were all college-level texts, physiology and anatomy, with yellow USED stickers on the spine. She found her marker in the top one and spread the book open, leaning her face in her hands as she read.

She could hear the splashing of the fish in the bowl. Once, after a couple of minutes, she glanced over her shoulder and watched it swimming back and forth. Then she turned back to the textbook.

The fish swam, slicing through the tinged water. A trail of blood followed after it, like a red thread that widened, became faint, and dissolved.

The 'Vette needed gas. Mike glanced at the gauge and saw that it read nearly empty. Lindy, that stupid twat, must have come barreling out from the city without even stopping. The way she kept her head fogged up, it was a wonder that she hadn't rolled to a halt, the engine sputtering dead, somewhere along the highway.

He wouldn't have any choice: the next gas station he saw would have to be it. And it had better fucking be open—the digital clock on the dash had already gone past seven. These fucking hicks out here turned in early.

A sign showed up ahead, a square of back-lit yellow plastic against the reddening sky.

He pulled the 'Vette in by the pumps. Some off-brand

of gas, with an Indian's profile in ancient, flaking paint. The store had neon beer signs in the windows.

The screen door banged shut behind him. A teenage boy sat behind the cash register, reading a copy of *Thrasher.*

"I need a fill-up out there." Mike pointed with his thumb.

The kid nodded, not taking his eyes off the magazine.

"Like now," he snapped. "Okay?"

The kid's head jerked up. He took one open-mouthed look at Mike, then scooted out from behind the register. The magazine slid off the stool and onto the floor. Mike could hear the kid fumbling with the pump nozzle and the 'Vette's gas cap.

There was a Coke machine by the door. He fed in a couple of quarters and a can rattled down. As he took a long pull from it, he heard laughter and voices behind him. He rubbed the cold can against his face, then glanced over his shoulder.

At the far end of the store was a glass-doored cooler stacked with six-packs of beer. And a counter with red linoleum, worn through in patches to the black beneath by years of elbows rubbing on it. There were two men there now, the heels of their dusty work boots hooked in the spotted chrome rungs of the stools. They tipped sweating brown bottles up to their faces, then slammed them down and laughed at whatever the woman on the other side of the counter said. She had blond hair and black eyebrows, and a crepe paper neck. She laughed, too, her breasts shaking, the freckled skin shining with sweat.

Mike lowered the Coke from his own face, turning and looking at the two men. They didn't see him; they were having too good a time.

He'd seen them before. It took him a few seconds to remember where and when.

A voice spoke inside his head, the words wavering and fading, louder and then softer.

. . . get rid of him . . . haul him back out to where you found him . . .

Now he knew. He remembered the one face, that of the guy with the louder braying laugh; he remembered that one real well. He watched the two men knocking back their beers and horsing around with the woman.

The screen door opened and slapped shut behind him. The teenage boy stood a couple of feet away from him.

"That's, uh, fourteen-fifty . . ."

Mike kept his eye on the two men as he dug a couple of bills, a ten and a five, out of his pocket and handed them to the teenager. "Keep the change." He drained the last of the Coke, then crumpled the can in his fist and tossed it into the box at the side of the machine.

Outside, the sky's red had started to turn black. He leaned his hands against the still-warm hood of the 'Vette and gazed down the road.

Harley fumbled at his shirt pocket.

"Fuck—forgot my smokes."

He and his buddy had just-opened bottles of Bud in front of them. Harley winked at the woman on the other side of the counter and pushed his bottle toward her.

"You just keep an eye on that for me, okay? Don't let this ol' boozehound get his slobbery lips all over it." His buddy laughed around his own upraised beer. "I'll be right back."

He slid off the stool and walked, a little unsteady, toward the screen door.

The pickup truck was out back of the store. He didn't like to leave it near the road, since the license tags had expired a couple of years ago. Didn't want some cop running a check on it. His boots scuffed in the gravelly dirt as he headed for the truck.

He pulled open the driver's-side door and climbed up on the running board. Leaning across the seat, he rummaged around in the glove compartment. He knew he had at least a couple of packs in there. He'd stocked up, buying an armload of cartons, the last time they'd left the pit mine they were stripping and had gone into town.

"Hey—"

The quiet voice came from behind him. He raised his head and looked over his shoulder. Some asshole was standing there outside the truck.

"Yeah?" His voice slopped with drunken belligerence. "What the fuck do you want?"

The man had a little smile. "You recognize me?"

Harley pushed himself upright on the truck's seat, staring at the guy in puzzlement. Somewhere . . .

Then his eyes widened. "Yeah . . ." he said in amazement. "I remember you . . ."

The man's smile grew bigger and more unpleasant. "Good," he said, his voice still soft. "I was hoping you did."

He stepped closer to the truck, hand reaching up to the door.

The sound of a horn blaring came into the store. The guy working his way through the Bud had been telling the woman behind the counter about what his second wife had gotten arrested for, right off the stage of a roadhouse near Spokane; something to do with a carton of raw eggs.

"What the fuck—" He let the story hang halfway through and looked around toward the door. The horn was still wailing away outside. It sounded like the one on Harley's pickup.

He figured he'd better check it out. With a drunk's grace, he held up one finger. "I'll be right back. Don't," he said, "go away."

The horn sounded louder when he stepped outside the store. He rounded the corner and saw the pickup in the distance, the door open and somebody—Harley, he guessed—sitting behind the wheel. And closer than that, somebody walking back toward the store, as though he'd just finished having a talk with Harley out by the truck.

The guy walked right by him, not even glancing in his direction. He turned his head, watching the guy climb into the Corvette that was parked in front of the gas pumps.

He'd seen the man before, and he remembered where. When he'd seen him, the guy had been slumped in the cab of a diesel truck, looking like he'd had the shit pretty well knocked out of him. Looking like he was about ready to die in a couple of hours.

The 'Vette's engine started up, a bass rumble underneath the wail of the pickup's horn. The guy had looked okay now, except for one thing. That was one more reason why his mouth had dropped open when he'd spotted the guy's face.

A red line, still wet and glistening, ran down one cheek, as though the man had shed a single bloody tear.

The 'Vette peeled out from in front of the store, scattering gravel as it swerved onto the road. A wordless fear squeezed his heart, and he turned and ran toward the pickup.

"Hey! What the hell's going on—"

Harley was slumped over the steering wheel, his face resting right in the center of it, his hands on either side; that was what kept the horn blaring. He stopped a few feet away, staring at Harley. There was something wrong— Harley's face was too far down, as though somehow he'd managed to shove the steering wheel's hub into his mouth. And the back of his head—the hair was all dark and shiny wet, and something poked through it. Something—he saw it now—something that was red and pulpy and soft, studded with hard, jagged-edged pieces, curved like a broken bowl.

As he looked at Harley, a last pulse of blood surged, and the bits that had been inside the skull fell away, sliding in wet red tracks down the side of the face and neck. A rough triangle of bone, with hair on one surface, rattled onto the truck's running board.

Where the back of Harley's head had been, the steering wheel's hub poked through, the chrome and plastic emblem at the center mired in a sticky web.

"Fuck!" The sight, on top of all the beer, knocked his legs out from under him. He sat down hard on the dirt, looking at what was left of Harley and hearing—a million miles in the distance—the horn still singing away.

The wind chilled the wetness on his cheek, and Mike rubbed it with one hand. Red was smeared across his fingertips when he looked at them.

That made him smile, as he tightened his grip on the 'Vette's wheel and aimed it down the road. The anger that had welled up in him, when he'd seen the asshole and had remembered who he was, had ebbed back down into its nest around his heart. But the thrill, the memory of the strength that had come bursting into his arms—that remained.

It'd been easy—like spiking a melon on a fence post. He hadn't even had to think about it, just do it. The fucker, the stupid sonuvabitch, had had time for just one gargling cry before his nose and mouth had been caved in.

That was the way to deal with stupid motherfuckers like that. Mike straightened his arms, working the muscles in his shoulders. That was the way he was going to deal with *all* the stupid motherfuckers.

He pressed the accelerator down flat, and the 'Vette leapt forward, eating up the highway to the city.

It had gotten dark enough outside that she'd had to turn on the lamp over her desk. Anne leaned her chin on one hand, the knuckle of her little finger at the corner of her mouth. She'd managed to plow through twenty pages of the anatomy text; if she kept pushing, she might make it to the neurology section by midnight.

She could hear her mother rounding up the little kids, trying to get them all to the dinette table in the trailer's kitchen.

"Annie"—her mother knocked on the bedroom door—"you want some supper?"

"No," she shouted, not taking her eyes off the textbook. "Not right now." There was an apple and a carton of yogurt on the corner of the desk. That, plus a couple forays to go make some instant coffee, would get her through.

Quiet again, or as quiet as it ever got inside the trailer—the floor shook sometimes, when all the kids were running around. She heard the splash of water behind her.

She looked over her shoulder. The circle from the desk lamp didn't reach all the way over to the bed table. All she could see was the small, dark shape of Doot's tropical fish, swimming back and forth in the bowl. In the unlit corner of the room, the water was nearly as dark.

Maybe it was hungry. She wondered what to do about that. Maybe in a little while, she could go out to the kitchen and scrounge up some bread crumbs, drop them into the bowl. Or were tropical fish supposed to eat dead flies, and stuff like that?

She folded her arms on the desk, leaning over the anatomy text. It was Doot's stupid fish, after all; if it missed a meal before she could give it back to him, it wasn't her fault. She didn't even hear the next quick splash of water from the corner of the room.

In the dark bowl, the fish moved back and forth, its mouth brushing against the glass, then its tail as it flicked itself around.

The water turned darker as blood streamed from the fish's gills, making ribbons that turned to black, dissolving lace behind it.

Twenty

The freeway's river of lights cut through the darkness. It was well past midnight by the time Mike reached the city's outskirts. He had had to slow the 'Vette down once he'd gotten onto the Interstate to keep from picking up a speed cop on his tail. Right now, he didn't feel like hassling with police; he had too much to take care of. It had taken a real effort of will, though, to keep from punching the 'Vette up to its limit.

He started switching lanes, moving over to the right. The freeway had curved into the city proper. He pulled the 'Vette out of gear and let it coast down the off-ramp, easing it to a halt at the stoplight at the bottom.

When the light changed, he drove one-handed, using the fingers of the other to comb his hair back down. He flexed the hand into a fist, then released it, feeling the muscles up into his arm, all working perfectly now. He smiled, squeezing the fist tighter.

Some people were going to be surprised to see him. The thought lifted one corner of his smile. *Really* surprised—he couldn't wait to see the look on their faces.

* * *

The knock on the apartment door woke him out of a drowsing slumber. Charlie raised his head, blinking. The TV in front of him showed Humphrey Bogart, colorized to look like either a fairy or a mortician's makeup demonstration, blowing cigarette smoke with Lauren Bacall. The two of them weren't anywhere near a door, so the sound hadn't come from there. It must've been here in the real world.

He turned his wrist, checking his watch. It wasn't even one A.M. So it couldn't be Aitch. He'd gone off to the White Eagle to catch the Paul DeLay Band, which usually meant he wouldn't be back until sunup. He had a thing going with one of the barmaids there. They'd go back to her place, since Aitch didn't believe in bringing people—women, especially—where they might see something they didn't need to know. You never knew who might also be dating a cop on the side.

Besides, Aitch would've used his own key to let himself in. So this was somebody unexpected—which was never good news. Charlie was all the way awake, with an adrenaline trickle raising the hair on his arms, when whoever it was knocked again.

He pushed himself up off the couch and went to the door. Looking through the peephole, he saw a face smiling back at him. He almost shit when he saw who it was.

"Hey, come on." The voice came muffled through the door. "I know somebody's home."

He opened the door a few inches, leaving the chain on.

"Hello, Charlie." Mike looked at him through the narrow gap. "Mind if I come in?"

Jesus fucking Christ. He couldn't believe it. The guy was just standing there, big as life. And smiling.

"Look." Mike spread his hands wide. "I'm clean." He patted the sides of his jeans. "I'm not carrying anything. Come on," he coaxed. "Just let me in and we'll talk a bit, okay? You know—I've come a long way just to say hello." The smile widened.

As though moving in a dream, Charlie unlatched the chain and swung the door open. He stepped back, keeping a careful distance as Mike came inside.

Mike shut the door behind himself. "How you been, Charlie?"

He shrugged. His thoughts were still bouncing off the walls of his skull, just seeing Mike standing there. And looking all pulled together, *healthy* even, instead of busted up and bleeding. It was like it'd been some other Mike that they'd dumped off in the boonies. The only sign that it hadn't been, that it had really been this one, was the green short-sleeved shirt, the collarless kind that doctors wear in hospitals. It was what Mike had been wearing, with his name tag stitched over the breast pocket, when they'd taken him out for the drive. The shirt looked fucked up, at any rate: the green cloth was ripped in a couple of places and stained with something that could have been old dried blood. The bottom of one jeans leg flopped loose, showing the dirty yellow of a healing bruise beneath.

Mike gazed around the apartment. "Is Aitch around? I was hoping to see both you guys."

Charlie stood behind him, feeling sweat growing cold on his own neck. "Uh—he's out."

"Yeah?" Mike looked over his shoulder at him. "Taking care of some business, huh?"

He shook his head. "No . . . just out. That's all."

Mike nodded. Smiling to himself, he prowled around the apartment. He picked up the remote for the TV; he flicked through the channels—a Bob Newhart rerun, Preparation H, a car ad shot with shiny dark menace—then flicked it off. The picture snapped to dead grey. Mike flopped down in one of the chairs at the side of the sofa.

"Hey. Take it easy, for Christ's sake." The smile tilted up at Charlie. "What are you so worked up about? Huh? We're all friends here, aren't we?"

Charlie didn't say anything. He was wondering what the hell he'd been thinking of—if anything—when he'd let the guy in. There was a gun in the back bedroom—Aitch's nasty Diamondback—but that was a long way out of reach. Something about the way Mike was looking at him made him nervous about trying to go get the gun.

Mike was still being cool and smooth, his elbows draped over the arms of the chair. "There's beer in the fridge, isn't there? There usually is. Why don't you go get us a couple of beers? Then maybe you'll relax."

He turned and went to the kitchen—anything to get away from that smile—then came back with two chilled bottles, already opened. He handed one down to Mike.

Head tilted back, Mike drank, his throat working. He lowered the bottle, fist wrapped around the sweating label. "You still look nervous," he said. "I would've thought you'd be glad to see me. Old friends, and all that. Business colleagues." The smile turned sly. "Maybe . . . maybe you're just a little surprised."

Charlie sat down in the corner of the sofa farthest away. "Well—we worked you over pretty good." This was weird, sitting around and talking about it. He took a sip of his beer. "Least, I thought we did."

Mike shrugged. "Hey. Why don't we let bygones be bygones? I can understand why you guys were a little upset with me." He leaned forward, his thumb rubbing the neck of the bottle. "That's just the way it is in business some-times. These little things happen, that's all. No reason we still can't be friends, is there? Maybe even do a little more business—hm?"

Weirder still. "Yeah, sure . . ."

" 'Yeah, sure.' " Mike's voice twisted sour. The smile showed the teeth at one corner of his mouth. "Because—after all—I know I can trust you guys. Can't I? If a little problem comes up, we can work it out. No sweat." The knuckles around the bottle had turned white. His face set harder, teeth grinding together. "You'd give a friend a chance to explain—wouldn't you? Instead of just fucking him over and dumping him off somewhere to die. You and Aitch wouldn't do something like that, would you?" His voice peaked to a knife edge. "I mean, you wouldn't do it *now—*"

The bottle in Mike's hand exploded, the brown glass crushed into the center of his fist. Foam streaked with red rolled down his wrist.

Charlie felt his spine burrowing into the sofa, his legs pushing him away from the other seated across from him. He stared as Mike, head down, his shoulders hunched, threw the bits of glass and the sopping, torn label onto the carpet. Red dripped off the ends of his fingers.

"Jesus Christ—" The words caught in his throat.

Mike had raised his head. He wasn't smiling now. His eyes were red, and wet.

The red brimmed over and ran down his cheek, a tear a razor would draw.

A spark jumped the gap in Charlie's spine, which the sight of Mike's bleeding eyes had torn, and he scrambled up from the sofa. The bottle he'd held struck the floor and spun across it, spewing out beer.

He managed to get around the side of the sofa and start for the apartment's front door, his hands already straining for the knob—

Mike's arm, the red hand at the end of it, circled his neck. The impact of Mike's spring from the chair, an animal's uncoiling leap, brought them both down. The floor knocked the breath from Charlie's lungs.

All he wanted to do was get away from the face that was like a clawed mask now, the blood tracks over the cheeks and mingling at the throat. He twisted onto his shoulder, Mike's arm dragging across his neck. He got his hands up, pushing against the red face.

The other's rage swelled, his lips drawing back from his teeth. The blood wasn't just tearing from Mike's eye but seeping from his pores; Charlie felt it blossoming underneath his own straining hands.

Mike's hand, a bit of glass still glittering in the wounded palm, reached up and clawed into Charlie's face. The thumb pressed in toward his teeth, the web between the first two fingers tight against his nostrils. He fought for breath, feeling the glass shard cutting his bottom lip.

The hand tightened, fingertips curling in. He had both of his own on Mike's wrist, but he couldn't bend it away.

His jaw snapped, the hinge breaking free under the digging point of Mike's thumb. A shaft of pain shot up through the center of his head, battering against the top of his skull.

The blind face was above him, the red welling from the eyes and dangling like a wet string across his own. A hissing noise came from between Mike's rigidly clamped teeth.

His cheek tore, the skin ripping under the point of the other's thumb. He felt a molar break, blood pulsing from the socket as the thumb lodged against the roof of his mouth.

The pain sang and burned. He couldn't see the other's face now; it was gone behind the red that washed through his own eyes.

Another breaking noise, bone snapping. He couldn't breathe. The red burst, the agony becoming a black thing that swallowed him.

The last thing—beyond pain, beyond the red that flooded his brain—the last thing he felt was the other's hand, the tips of the fingers coming together, the fist clutching the shards of bone and trembling pulp.

As though it had been an egg, crushed in his hand. Mike staggered backward a step, catching his balance. His own head had still been swimming, his pulse pounding and roaring, when he'd stood up.

He twisted his shoulder and wiped one eye clear. His lashes were sticky with blood, but he could see. He looked at his hand, the one that had grabbed hold of Charlie's face, and saw the looped clotting mire, flecked with bone. The wet stuff smeared across the front of his shirt as he wiped it off his hand.

He pulled the shirt off over his head, and used it to mop his face. The raw smell of sweat and blood caught in his breath. The shirt was soaked red in a few seconds. Looking down, he saw Charlie's corpse at his feet.

The arms were outflung, palms upward, the fingers curling. Those hands were streaked with red as well, from fighting and pushing against Mike's face.

Face—Charlie didn't have one now. The biggest piece left was a splinter of the jawbone, sticking up from the ruin. From the brow line to a flap of skin hanging over the jagged opening of the windpipe, the red bubbled, spreading and sinking into the carpet.

Mike closed his eyes, swaying where he stood, feeling the adrenaline drain from his arms—and the other, stronger currents that had surged inside him. The anger ebbed away, but the memory remained.

He smiled, letting his breath slow, his heart gathering its strength back into himself.

He dropped the shirt—a sodden rag now—on Charlie's stomach. He could wash off the rest of the blood in the bathroom. And take a shirt from the closet in the bedroom. He turned away from the thing on the floor and walked toward the rear of the apartment, leaving red footprints that grew lighter with each step.

Twenty-
ONE

He had thought—somehow—that she would look different. Doot rested on his side, his face propped up on his hand, looking at her. Or maybe he hadn't thought about it at all; it had just happened. The moonlight tracing in through the window slits turned her skin all silver. She breathed slowly, eyes closed.

Maybe he'd expected, if he had thought about it at all, that her breasts would be bigger. The way she dressed, anyone would have thought so. But they were like a child's; he could cover one with his hand, the soft lower curve resting against the side of his thumb. He reached out and pulled the edge of the blanket over them. The night air had turned cold.

She opened her eyes when he brushed a strand of her hair away from her brow. She smiled drowsily and snuggled closer to him.

"When I first saw you . . ." He didn't know if she

heard him. She looked as if she had drifted back asleep, one of her hands pressed against his bare chest. "When you came to the house," he whispered, "and you asked for me—I'd never seen anything like you. Not for real. You were like . . . like something out of a Z Z Top video."

He said it as a joke, even though it was true. He'd guessed she was awake, because her smile had started to show again.

She looked up at him. "That's sweet." She lifted her head and kissed him. "You're nice, too."

They lay together, the night sifting past them. He awoke—he didn't know if he'd fallen asleep for more than a minute—and saw that the line of moonlight had changed its angle. Now it fell a few inches away from him and the sleeping woman and on the open suitcase. The bright things inside, the hypodermics and vials, the plastic cylinders half full of capsules, shone with a dull radiance.

He eased his arm from under Lindy's weight, reached out and brought the case's lid down, softly, without making a sound. Then he pushed it away, into the dark where it couldn't be seen.

The old man walked in the hills, slow and surefooted in the night spaces. Other things walked about as well, beyond the reach of his hand, or down into the black ravines. Their red gaze seemed like the sparks of a dying fire, drifting parallel near the ground.

Nelder climbed to the top of the ridge and looked down. The building was tinged blue under the moon and stars. He could feel the living things inside it, eased into sleep or murmuring dreams. The ones who slept, who had been left there . . . they didn't know.

The other, the one of blood and darkness . . . Nelder lifted his face, breathing in the thin air. He could tell, taste, that the other one was gone.

But he'd return.

The silent animals crept down the hillside. Nelder watched them as they moved from one shadow to the next.

His clothes all smelled like cigarette smoke now, and that pissed Aitch off. That was the one thing that annoyed him about going out to hear music—you go out, you come back smelling like an ashtray. And if some place set aside a couple of tables as a no-smoking area—as if that did much good, with the air inside turned blue and hanging down from the ceiling in cumulus reefs—and some little asshole lit up right at your elbow, and you asked him— nicely, trying to be cool about it—to put it out, the little shit would goggle at you and act as if you'd just asked him to saw his whole fucking head off and hand it to you on a plate.

A couple of times he'd taken some little dickbreath outside to discuss the matter, but the bartenders had finally asked him to ease up; the ABC could yank the liquor license for running a rowdy establishment, plus it didn't look good for business to have blue ambulance lights flashing outside while the paramedics scraped somebody up from the parking lot asphalt. So nowadays he just endured, and tried to sit close to an open door, where some fresh air might straggle in.

The sun was coming up, washing across his back, as Aitch got his key out and unlocked the apartment's front door. He stepped inside and pushed the door shut behind him. When he hit the light switch and looked down and saw what was spread out on the carpet, his head snapped back.

"Shit." He scanned across the apartment, listening. Nothing.

In silence, he cautiously stepped around the yard-wide pool of blood and the thing with the ruined face at the center. He picked up the wrought-iron poker from the side of the fireplace and used it to push open the door of the bedroom.

No one. The whole apartment felt empty, empty even of that poor bastard Charlie now. But he still hauled the Diamondback out of the dresser drawer, and kept it raised as he checked out the closets and the bathroom.

In the living room, he switched on the stereo, loaded a tape into the cassette deck. Howlin' Wolf's raspy, moaning voice filled the space, a heavy human presence crawling up the walls. Aitch stood in the center of the carpet, listening. He couldn't recognize the track; the words somehow didn't make any sense, as if they weren't even in English anymore, but just keening and shouting, an animal's angry grief.

His own anger broke. He slammed the deck's eject button with the butt of his hand and grabbed the cassette inside. Something caught on an edge of machinery; a shiny brown streamer of tape fell as he threw the cassette across the room. Silence pressed against his ears.

He flopped down on the sofa, his arm with the gun dangling over the side. The flash of rage had already started to cool. He could just see the legs of Charlie's corpse from this angle. That wasn't so bad.

After a couple of minutes, he got up again and went over to look at it. The first sight, the shock of it, had made his stomach flip. Standing at the edge of the blood-soaked section of carpet, he craned his neck to see better.

It looked as if somebody had taken a hammer and chisel and had excavated the whole front of the sonuvabitch's skull. Broken pieces of bone stuck up from the red mess.

Something—it looked like a rag—had been draped over Charlie's stomach. Aitch leaned over and used the Diamondback's barrel to pick up the cloth.

A shirt, the fabric torn; there was just enough left unstained to see that it had been green. He dangled it in front of himself, studying it. Collarless, short-sleeved; a hospital scrub shirt. And with a name tag sewn over the breast pocket. Whoever had fucked Charlie up might as well have signed his work with a spray can.

He didn't even need to read the name on the tag. He dropped the shirt and went back to the bedroom. From the same drawer where he kept the Diamondback, he took out an envelope of Polaroid snapshots. Underneath the top one, which showed a black kid, punctured head lolling back against a car seat, he found the one he was looking for.

It showed dry, brown dirt and a tangle of yellow weeds in the corner. Right at the center was Mike's face, bruised and battered. The snap had been taken just far enough back to get the upper third of the scrub shirt in; the name tag showed, and the rips in the green cloth.

Aitch nodded to himself, standing by the open drawer and looking at the Polaroid. He didn't know how the fucker had done it—how he was still alive—but he had to hand it to him. He admired shit like that.

He glanced over his shoulder, through the bedroom doorway. One of Charlie's outstretched arms was visible. Aitch flipped the Polaroid back and forth across the fingers of his other hand.

He shook his head. Mike shouldn't have done that, though. There just wasn't any call for that.

It was morning, the first edge of it coming over the hills, by the time he got back to the old clinic. From the road, Mike spotted Doot's motorbike sitting out in front of the building. He switched off the 'Vette's engine as soon as he'd made the turn and let the car's silent momentum roll it on down the lane.

They didn't hear him. They were both still asleep, wrapped up in the blankets and each other's arms. He stood in the doorway, watching them. Then he stepped back and eased the boards into place without making a sound.

He was smiling as he stepped carefully down from the verandah.

It was nice to be right about things. To have known just what was going to happen. To be right about *her*—she didn't have any brains above her navel. And the kid . . . *Stupid little shit.* It was all he could do to keep from laughing as he walked along the front of the building, toward the burned-out wing.

Inside again, as he knelt by the stone basin, he turned his head and listened. Lindy and the kid were still lost in sleep—he knew it. He could tell, his hearing sharpened to every faint stirring in the air.

They didn't know. They had each other now. That was good enough . . . for them.

He turned the spigot handle and a thread of the black water trickled out. Then more, splashing on the stone beneath. He cupped his palms under the flow. In the tiled room's sparse light, the water glinted and danced over his wrists.

It slid down his throat, a living thing without form, as he tilted his head back and drank from his hands.

He closed his eyes, and rocked back and forth on his knees. A small crooning sound came from his trembling lips.

This was communion. This was love now.

Twenty-
TWO

He held her hands so she wouldn't pull away from him.

"Come on," said Doot. They knelt, facing each other, on the rumpled blankets. "We can just split. We don't have to hang around here." He brought his face down, trying to see into her eyes. "You don't have to stay—with *him.*"

With a toss of her head, Lindy shook the hair from her eyes. She glared at him, a sullen anger welling up inside her.

"Oh, yeah? It's that easy, huh?" She gave a quick, scornful laugh. "I suppose you're going to take care of me. You're going to get me the things I need—"

She jerked her hands out of his grasp. She lunged to one side, then straightened up again, dragging the suitcase across the floor. The lid flipped back, and she held up a double handful of the orange plastic containers and the small glass vials.

"You're going to get me this? Huh?" She held them up to Doot's face. "The way Mike can—"

He slapped the bright things out of her hands, and they scattered across the floor. One vial broke against the wall, oozing a wet stain into the corner.

"You don't need that shit."

Lindy regarded him in silence. Her face looked old now, the skin dulled and drawn closer to the bone beneath. "What do you know," she said finally. "What the fuck do you know about it? You're just some stupid kid. You don't know what it's like."

She turned away from him. She pawed through the blankets and found her purse, dug out some money and shoved it into his hand.

"Here. Go get some food and shit. Something to drink . . ." She sank back down on the blankets, laying her head on her arm.

He looked at her for a moment, then crumpled the money into his fist. He got to his feet and stomped away, feeling his own face taut with anger.

Outside the building, the anger fell away, replaced by surprise. Doot hadn't expected to see the 'Vette sitting out there. The car was empty; he touched its hood and found it cold. It had been parked there for a while.

So Mike must be around someplace. The skin along Doot's arms tightened as he stepped around the front of the 'Vette and into the open. *Maybe he saw us* . . . Doot turned slowly on his heel, scanning in all directions. The morning sun dazzled in his eyes. The weed-choked fields and the hills were bare of any sign of the other's presence.

Maybe Mike had gone bouncing off, with his big speed-freak grin, up into the hills to talk with the old caretaker Nelder. Or—Doot tilted his head, listening for any sound—maybe he was out back of the building, taking an early morning swim and doing double gainers into the debris-clogged pool he'd filled up with the inky water.

He heard nothing. Still gazing around, he climbed onto the bike and kicked its engine to life. He headed down the lane toward the road.

She lifted her face from the spread-open book. Blinking, swallowing a sour taste in her mouth, Anne looked around her bedroom. The morning light slanted in through the curtains. She rubbed her eyes with both hands, then reached up and switched off the desk lamp.

The fog of sleep was still heavy inside her brain. She shook her head, drawing in a deep breath. Stretching her arms above her head, she felt her spine slowly unkink. Falling asleep like that, crashed out on the desk—it wasn't the first time she'd done it—always left her stiff. Maybe a long hot shower—if the bathroom wasn't clogged with the littler kids or her mother getting ready for work—with her back curled against the spray as hard as she could get it; that might work.

Something was wrong. She turned her head, slowly, a cold finger touching her heart. Thinking about the shower, and the bathroom . . . she had listened to hear, through the trailer's thin walls, if somebody was in there already. The sound of running water, of splashing. But there wasn't any—only silence.

She looked over toward the bed and the table beside it. There was enough daylight in the room now for her to see the glass bowl sitting there. The dark-colored water was perfectly still. Nothing moved inside it.

She walked over to the bowl and bent down to peer into it. The water had become murkier, tinged with red. The oval shape of the fish hung suspended in it, drifting slowly.

The water clung to her fingers as she reached in and took the fish out. It lay on her palm, not moving. The shiny pink had turned ashen; a thick black substance oozed from underneath its gills.

With her free hand, she switched the desk lamp on again, and held the fish underneath to see it better. Her throat clenched, gagging; the sulfur smell rose from the creature, the odor worse now, as if mixed with something rotten. The dark water, mixed with red, trickled down her arm to her elbow.

The fish moved, suddenly jerking and bending double in her palm. Fright pulled her muscles back, and the fish dropped upon the desk, landing on her yellow notepad.

Blood, thinned by the water, seeped out in a widening circle on the paper.

It trembled. Anne reached down with her forefinger and touched the fish.

The grey skin swelled upward, like a balloon expanding. It split and broke open, the red stuff inside pulsing up, a blister bursting under pressure.

She snatched her finger back, a spot of red wet upon the tip. She couldn't breathe, the smell filling her mouth and throat, as she watched the creature break apart. The tiny mouth split open to vomit up more red things. The skin disintegrated, the tiny organs inside pulsing, the spine curling in a final spasm.

When it stopped moving, there was nothing but a red, uneven stain on the desk, flecked with a few bright scales. A thread of blood ran to the edge and trickled down the side.

There was some old guy out in front of the apartments, watering the lawns. Aitch figured it was the building manager. The old guy watched him as he walked past and knocked on Lindy's door.

No answer. He knocked again, louder.

"She ain't there."

Aitch turned, looking around at the old man. "You know where she went?"

The manager shrugged, watching the stream from the hose nozzle splash against the sidewalk. "Beats me," he

196

said. He didn't seem too happy about it. "I came out the other day, found her door wide open, everything inside a mess. Ain't seen her car around here, either."

"Okay." He nodded, digging out his car keys. "Thanks." He'd expected as much. Somehow Mike had gotten hold of her. She was probably out there with him right now.

The manager called after him as he walked away. "If you find her, tell her she ain't getting her damn cleaning deposit back."

Aitch smiled to himself. He figured that'd be the least of her worries.

He spent nearly the whole day lying on his bed, staring up at the ceiling. The money Lindy had shoved in his hand was crumpled up on top of his dresser.

The phone rang, a couple of different times, and somebody had knocked on the door, but Doot hadn't answered. Whoever it was could go fuck themselves. Right now, his gut felt hollowed out. It just went on feeling that way.

Only when the light coming through the bedroom had started to dim had he swung his legs over the side and sat up. He looked at the money, the wadded bills. He supposed he should just go ahead and buy some stuff with it, and take it on out to them. Let *them* sort out their own fucking personal difficulties.

You got laid out of it—so what's your problem, dweeb? He should just be grateful for that much, he figured. Instead of getting all bent out of shape because she hadn't gone running off with him into the sunset. What'd he think they were going to do, head down to Reno and get married, or some shit like that? He shook his head as he stood up. What a jerk. He stuffed the money into his jeans and headed for the door.

Ten minutes later, he went down the aisle of the Seven-Eleven, loading things up in his arms. Cans of soup and more chili, plastic bottles of mineral water—Doot couldn't think of what else to get. Maybe some more Pepsi. He headed to the cooler at the back of the store and picked up a couple of bottles, carrying them under his arm.

"Hey, Doot." Garza and a couple others from the stoner crowd, the same ones who'd been left lounging around after the party, had come in and were hanging around the magazine rack, cruising for tit shots. Garza's big sloppy smile spread across his face. "How's your girl-friend?"

Doot stopped at the head of the aisle and looked at him. "What're you talking about?"

All three of the teenagers were grinning now. "You know," said Garza, lowering the copy of Penthouse in his hands. "That wild piece of ass you got hidden away. I bet she gives head like a Hoover—"

The other two snorted laughter. The notion of somebody like Doot getting it on with a waxed-and-pol-ished number like the one that had shown up at the door and asked for him had finally struck them as hilar-ious. It hadn't really happened—at least not the asking for him part. They must've been really fucked up to have imagined it.

"Hey . . ."

Garza smirked at him. "What?"

"Hold on a second," said Doot. "I'll be right back."

He walked over to the cash register and laid the cans and plastic bottles down on the counter. The guy behind the counter was picking his teeth with a fingernail. He didn't care what went on; it wasn't his store.

Doot stopped alongside the magazine rack. "Hey, Stevie."

The other's smile faded. Something, the look in Doot's eye, made him take a step backward. But not before Doot could grab him by the back of the neck.

"I got something for you." Doot planted his other fist in Garza's stomach. Garza doubled over, right into the arc of the fist coming up into his chin. He fell backwards, arms flailing spastically; his hand caught and dragged a row of magazines off the rack.

"Fuh-*uck.*" Goggle-eyed, Garza's buddies stared at him laid out on the linoleum floor, a split-beaver centerfold of the Pet of the Month fluttering open on his chest. They looked up at Doot, then backed away toward the door. They finally broke and scrambled outside, running across the asphalt parking lot.

The cash register guy had already rung everything up and bagged it. Doot walked back over to the counter, pulling the money from his jeans pocket.

He was strapping the bag onto the motorbike's carrier rack when he heard more running steps, coming toward him this time. He looked up and saw Anne, breathless, coming to a stop.

"Doot—where have you been?" She grabbed his arm. She panted for a couple of seconds, pushing her hair away from her brow with her other hand. "I've been looking all over for you! I've got to talk to you—"

He finished tightening the bungee cord over the top of the bag, snapping the hooks together. "I don't have time to talk." He pulled his arm out of her grasp.

She grabbed him again, both arms, tugging him around to face her.

"It's that stuff, that water you showed me." Her face was still red, from running to find him. She looked straight into his eyes. "There's something wrong . . . it does something . . ."

He shoved her away, hard enough to stagger her back a couple of steps. "I thought you were the one who didn't believe in all that." He climbed onto the bike and started the engine.

"Doot—wait . . ."

She ran after him, but he was already beyond her reach. She stood watching as the bike scattered gravel, crossing the dirt strip onto the road.

Twenty-
THREE

He lifted his head from his dark sleep and dreaming. Sitting on the floor of the tiled room; the smell, the taste of the water heavy in his throat and lungs; arms wrapped around his knees, sheltering the steady hammer of his pulse.

The girl again—he'd seen her, the laughing mouth red and wet as blood. The skin of her bare throat and breasts a perfect transparent ivory that yielded to his touch but moved with no breath beneath. And it had been night in the dreaming, great rolling fields of it outside the examining room windows, the mountains shapes that ate the stars. The animals of the red eyes had paced and watched, their gaze lifted intently to the building they circled around.

Here, she'd said, pulling back from him, teasing. She'd slid away from the examining table and his embrace. The smell of his own fevered sweat had choked him as he'd watched her pull something—not one of the blue glass bottles, or a chrome sharp-edged tool—from one of the cabinets on the wall. A book, with lined pages and flowing script in black India ink. *See?* She'd held the book low against her breasts, the small bleeding wounds of her nipples just above the paper white as her flesh. He raised himself up on one elbow. *Look*—her smile had shown the points of her teeth. *See for yourself.*

Dreaming. He had woken, with her smile and the book still there inside his head. But not the words written in it. That was the secret.

Mike touched his chest with the flat of his hand. The shirt, the one he'd taken from Aitch's closet, was still wet from when he'd drunk and spilled the water from his palms. A white shirt, the front discolored with a dark, smeared blossom.

Kneeling, he rubbed his hand across the bottom of the stone basin, then licked the moistness from his fingers. The taste uncoiled on his tongue, then slid down his throat.

He turned his head, looking up at the ceiling. And through it, to the floor above. He could already see it, waiting for him there. He stood up, wiping his hands against his hips.

She'd heard the crashing sounds from upstairs. They'd pulled Lindy from sleep, a chemical haze jerked away from her by a sudden rush of fright. Her eyes opened wide as she lay on her back, hearing something else smash into the floor above.

"Mike—what is it—"

At a flying run, she'd taken the stairs, the sounds growing louder with each step. Now she stood in the doorway of the old clinic's examining room, watching Mike rip through everything there.

He didn't turn to look at her. He toppled the examining table onto its side and ran his hands over the rust-specked chrome beneath. With a manic fury, he crossed to one of the wall cabinets and swept the glass bottles off the shelves. They exploded on the floor, the shards grinding beneath his feet.

"It's here . . ." His voice came through his clenched teeth. "I know it is . . ."

"Mike—"

He shot her a look of seething anger. With one step, he was across the room; he slapped her hard enough to knock her back against the doorframe. She felt herself sliding down it, hands clutching the wall behind. In the thin curved mirror of one of the examining table's legs, she saw her face with the red imprint of his hand.

Mike had already returned to his search. The antique X-ray machine tilted, then crashed to the floor as he shoved it aside. It was followed by one of the pharmaceutical cabinets, wrenched free from the wall and thrown behind him.

He stopped for a moment, panting for breath. Dizzied from the blow of his hand, Lindy watched him, her back against the bottom of the door.

A niche was sunk into the wall, in the center of the space where the cabinet had been mounted. Edges of rough plaster were framed on either side by the building's timbers. Mike stepped closer to the hole, his stomach pressing against the countertop beneath. He reached into it and pulled something out that he held with both hands as he looked down at it.

He was smiling when his gaze came up and fastened on Lindy's face, as if seeing her there for the first time. Sweat plastered his hair to his forehead and neck.

"Look." He squatted down in front of her, holding out the thing he'd found. His voice trembled with excitement.

She tasted salt in her mouth and knew it was blood. Her tongue had cut against her teeth when he slapped her. She looked down and saw that it was a book he held.

The leather cover was cracked and fire-scorched, with the single word Registry in faded gilt lettering.

Mike opened the book, leafing through the pages, stiff and yellowed with age, the edges blackened by ash. She could see, upside-down, the old-style handwriting, full of swooping flourishes. People's names, then other words, and dates—the years were all in the 1890's.

His finger traced one of the lines. "You see," he murmured, voice softened by his fascination. "They'd put down what they came here for." He touched another word. "Their ailments. What they were hoping to be cured of. Vapors and fits . . ." He looked up with his smile. "Female troubles . . ."

She kept still, trying not even to breathe, as he paged further through the book. Her face still ached, but the dizziness had ebbed away.

A piece of paper that had been creased and stuck in the registry—he took it out and unfolded it, the browned surfaces rustling in his hands.

He nodded, eyes closed in satisfaction. "This is it. She told me . . ."

Lindy didn't know what he was talking about. The way he was acting . . . She wondered if she could slide out of his reach, without his seeing her, and out into the hallway and away from him. Her hand reached to the side of the doorway, pulling her a couple of inches closer to it.

Mike's eyes opened. He held the unfolded piece of paper out to her. "See for yourself."

The paper looked like some kind of poster, an advertisement. For the clinic—the word THERMALENE, in big ornate lettering, filled the top space. Underneath were gray-toned, old prints, framed in ovals like the pictures she remembered seeing in her grandmother's photo albums. A big one of the clinic building itself and smaller ones of the room with the stone basins and the lobby, with potted palms stationed by deep sofas and armchairs.

"There." Mike's finger touched the paper. "See it?"

At the bottom, another oval, with a man's face. Wearing a doctor's white coat—the shoulders of it were just visible. The man had dark hair, parted in the middle, so he looked younger; but he looked just like the old man who was the caretaker here. The same skull face, the flesh tight against the bone. And without the dark glasses, small gold rims instead—the ancient portrait gazed out directly at her.

Mike's finger traced the words underneath the man's face. " 'Doctor Wilhelm Nelder,' " he read aloud. " 'Founder and chief physician.' "

She didn't understand. All she knew was that a wild, frightening joy had bloomed inside Mike.

He took back the paper, folding it and putting it in his shirt pocket. He nodded, lost in thought, as though she no longer existed for him. "Now," he murmured. "Now I know . . ."

He stood up and left the examining room, leaving her crouched upon the floor.

The old man was sitting on the rock outside his shack—where Mike had seen him before, when he'd gone up into the hills.

Nelder looked up at the sound of pebbles and dust shifting down the slope. Sun glinted off the dark lenses over his eyes. He made no move as the visitor made his way down to him.

He looked up at Mike, standing before him. And the piece of paper, browned with age, that Mike held out. Nelder glanced at the paper, but didn't touch it.

"There's more than what you told me." Mike tossed the paper onto the ground. "About the water. A lot more."

Nelder shrugged, his gaunt face expressionless. "There's more to a lot of things."

Mike prodded the paper with his foot. The oval-framed picture, of a young, thin-faced man, gazed up.

205

"You've lived an awful long time . . . *Doctor* Nelder. When you add it all up—what does it come to? A couple hundred years? Something like that. That's a long time. A long time to keep yourself alive. And a long time to be sitting on something like this. Keeping it to yourself."

The old man stood up and faced Mike.

"You'll have to leave now." A fine tremor, the skin growing even paler, touched the skeletal face. "Immediately. The water . . ." Nelder's voice trembled and broke. "It heals, but then it changes. I know; I have been here a long time. I know what it wants." Fervor pitched the words higher. "It wants bad things, dark things like itself. It made me do terrible . . . things . . ."

Mike gazed at the old man, a smile of contempt turning on his own face.

Nelder looked away from him. The years weighed upon his shoulders, bowing his spine.

"But it made me want to know things, the things *it* knows . . ." A whisper now. "There was blood all over, and they looked at me, and they would scream . . . The water kept them alive, but they kept on screaming and screaming . . . I had to stop. I had to stop everything."

Nelder turned and grabbed Mike's arm, the long, large-knuckled fingers squeezing into the flesh. "That's why I set fire to the clinic. To end it; to end everything. And then when it was over, when everything was gone . . . the bad things, the screaming . . . I had to stay. To guard it. To keep anyone from finding it again." The voice screeched up into Mike's face. "I had to stay, and go on drinking it, and bathing in it, letting it inside me, letting it go on living and wanting . . ."

Mike could see his own sneering face reflected in the dark glasses.

"Bullshit." The stupid old fuck; the stupid *scared* old fuck—Mike felt disgust growing in his gut. "You're afraid. It's kept you alive, but you got old, and now you're afraid." He shook his head. "But I'm not."

He tried to pull away from Nelder's grasp, but the old man's hands clung even tighter to his arm.

"No—you have to leave! Immediately!"

The anger surged up inside him, and he struck the old man across the face, backhanded. Nelder hung on to him, the bony hands clenching stronger than he could have imagined. His vision reddened, as he felt the blood come weeping from his eyes, a red sweat seeping from the pores of his face. With the anger came his own strength, the muscles swelling under his dampening skin. Another blow sent Nelder's dark glasses flying onto the ground. The lenses crackled as they broke against the rocks.

He could barely see through the red haze, but it was enough. Nelder had no eyes; where they should have been, nothing but two deep sockets, red darkening to black, going back into his skull. Something wet moved at the base of the two holes, with a gaze that burned into Mike's head, to that same thing at the center of his brain.

His teeth clamped together as he struggled to peel Nelder's hands from him. Suddenly, the old man's strength ebbed; he seemed to crumple and shrink as Mike gripped the hard knobs of his shoulders.

Then the old man came apart in his hands.

Nelder's shirt split, exposing the white, ridged chest. The drum-tight skin tore open, peeling away from the bones and tendons beneath. The ribs cracked, spilling out the lungs and heart, soft trembling masses suspended in yellow sinew.

Skin hung in tattered strips from Nelder's bowels, the looped intestines dangling lower.

Mike felt his fingers sink into the thin layers of skin. The weeping flesh fell away from him, the tapered masses of the arm muscles pulling away from the shoulder and elbow joints. The knife edge of Nelder's skull broke through the face, drawing out the taut, striated ribbons around the mouth and eye sockets.

He let go of the thing, casting it away from him. For

a few seconds, it writhed upon the ground, more red segments detaching from the carcass. The legs snapped at the hips and knees, the tattered ankles lengthening from the blood-soaked trousers. Then it lay still, the blind red face pressed into the dust.

He stood above it, gazing down and drawing one deep breath after another, the anger retreating once more to his spine. With the arm of his shirt, he wiped the blood from his face.

There was water in the stone basin by the shack's door. He knelt down and splashed it up with his hands, opening his mouth to let the sulfur taste run down his throat. He scooped up more with his cupped palms and drank it, tilting his head back, the sun full in his eyes. Inside him, beneath his heart, the water spread, filtering into his arms and legs, restoring him.

He went back to Nelder's corpse and regarded it for a moment. Then he reached down and grabbed its wrists, where the bones and tendons lay exposed. The arms stretched as he dragged the corpse over the ground, but they didn't tear loose; the connective tissue tightened, a web across the collarbone and upper ribs.

Carefully—he didn't want to lose any part of it—he dragged the red, bedraggled thing up into the path through the hills, the way he had come.

The dark water was hidden by the layer of charred timbers and other rubble floating on its surface. Mike squatted down by the swimming pool's edge. He reached down and cleared an open space, pushing the debris away from the tiled side.

He eased Nelder's corpse into the water, the skull with its blind eyesockets going under first, then the torso with its dangling viscera. The limbs, torn and elongated by the rocks of the hills, drifted for a moment, then sank into the blackness and disappeared.

Mike stood up, watching the rubble cover the water's

surface again. A trail of blood led to the edge; that was the only sign of what he'd just done.

It had made sense; he didn't even have to think about it. He knew it was what the water wanted. The old man had belonged to it for so long—he should return to it.

He smiled. He was happy . . . when *it* was happy.

He looked over his shoulder. At the clinic building. There were more things in there. Promised to him: things to find out, to know. That no one else knew.

Bending down, he scooped up a handful of the water from the pool's edge and drank it. Then he walked toward the building.

In the dark, the soft, torn thing drifted. The water filled its mouth and crept into its lungs. It lost buoyancy, and fell, its arms wavering above its head like strands of seaweed. Its blood mingled with the water, a cloud seeping from around its heart. The eyeless skull turned upward, toward the thin, diminished rays of sunlight that penetrated the surface.

That was the other world up there, where things—things such as it had been—moved around, their blood neatly bound into themselves.

This was its world now.

It drifted, the water caressing its groin and spine. Easeful peace. It drifted, and waited.

She was on her hands and knees, scrabbling across the lobby floor. Looking for the stuff that had been thrown across the space, and shoving the vials and orange plastic containers into the suitcase when she found them.

That was stupid of her—Mike stood with his arms folded across his chest, watching her. She should've just split, if that was what she wanted to do. Now it was too late.

Lindy suddenly looked up and saw him standing in

the doorway. Her mouth fell open, eyes widening with fear.

He sauntered toward her. "Going somewhere?"

Still kneeling on the floor, she scooted back away from him.

Mike bent down and picked something up from the floor, something she'd missed. He raised it up to show her.

"You know"—the point of the hypodermic glittered in one of the room's shafts of light—"I think you've gotten a little overexcited . . ."

Lindy scrambled to her feet. She turned to run away, but he was right on her. He grabbed her by one arm, jerking her around to face him.

"Mike . . ." She struggled, trying to pull her wrist out of his grasp. "Don't . . ."

He threw her down to the floor. She sprawled there, facedown, while he stepped over to the suitcase. He quickly pawed through it and found what he was looking for. He turned back toward Lindy as he plunged the needle through the seal on one of the glass vials.

"I think maybe you need a little something to calm you down."

She cowered away from him as he approached with the hypodermic.

"Hey . . ." He smiled as he grabbed her arm and pulled him up toward her. "You can trust me. I'm a doctor."

He sank the point into the vein at the crook of her elbow.

Twenty-FOUR

He found the spot easily enough. He recognized the outcroppings of rock several yards back from the road.

Aitch pulled the big Caddy over to the side, the tires crunching over gravel. He left the tape deck and the air-conditioning on as he got out of the car. The late afternoon heat squatted down on him, the highway's vanishing point shimmering beneath a silver mirage.

Sunglasses dangling in his hand, he looked around the area. Just as bleak as when he'd come out before, with Charlie. This time, he was the only human presence.

He kicked the dust at the roadside. A set of tire tracks, only partially sifted in, and another, wider set of marks, probably from some kind of truck. Part of the ground was discolored, stiffened into a thin crust. That was Mike's blood, he figured, from when they'd dumped him off.

That was the only sign left of him. No picked bones

inside rags, no pieces of skin dried to leather. Aitch put his sunglasses back on and headed for the car.

In the cooled space, with the tape's volume turned up, he reached over and opened the glove compartment. The Diamondback lay on its side there, all chambers loaded. Just the sight of it satisfied him, for now.

He snapped the compartment's lid closed and straightened back up behind the wheel. Dropping the transmission into gear, he pulled back onto the road.

A bunch of teenagers hanging around a hamburger stand—the place hadn't switched on its neon yet, though the evening was already swallowing up the last of the daylight. The bluish light from the fluorescents inside spilled through the windows across the kids' faces.

They all looked over at Aitch as he pulled up and got out of the Caddy. A few of them, with carefully bored expressions, sat on the fenders of their cars and pickup trucks.

He stopped in front of them. "I'm looking for a young lady," he announced.

A couple of the teenagers snickered.

He didn't give a shit. "Drives a red Corvette. Maybe you've seen it around."

One of the kids, his jaw darkened with a spreading bruise, nodded. "Yeah, we've seen her."

"Know where she is now?"

The kid looked sullen and didn't reply.

He took his wallet from his hip pocket. "It's worth something to me."

The kid glanced around at his friends, then back to him. "There's an old place. Out that way." He pointed down one of the roads branching off.

"What kind of place?"

A shrug. "Just . . . a big old place. Like it was a hospital or something. It's all boarded up." The kid thought some more. "There's a sign up on top of it."

Aitch dug out a fiver and handed it to the kid. "There you go." He knew they were all staring at him as he walked back to the car.

When he first spotted it, he switched off the Caddy's headlights. The moon had risen high enough to keep the strip of road visible.

A building with a sign on top of it; cut-out letters, at an angle that he couldn't read them. And dark, just a black shape against the hills.

The moon glistened off a pond, lying to the side of a lane that turned from the road. A heavy, sour-egg odor hung in the night air. Aitch killed the engine. For a moment longer, he sat with the window rolled down, listening. Then he took the Diamondback out of the glove compartment and slipped it into his jacket pocket.

He crouched down by the stone basins. He had stripped to his jeans, his feet bare—it felt better that way. In the thin light that penetrated from the burned walls outside the room's door, his damp skin glowed as though polished with oil. His hair was plastered close to his skull, dark tendrils trailing on his neck.

Mike lifted his head, the water trickling from the corners of his mouth. He listened, slowly turning his ear toward the faint noise he'd perceived. There was something out there, moving around. Not the animals of the sharp-pointed jaws and red eyes that were always out there, watching and sliding through the stony hills; something else. Or somebody—he could smell the trace of human sweat, different from his or Lindy's. A visitor.

The thought made him smile. He had a good idea who it was. He'd left his calling card, the mark of what he'd done, as an invitation. There was no way Aitch would be able to resist coming out here.

Fine. He ran his tongue over his lips, tasting the dark water beaded there. He'd been waiting for this.

* * *

He should've brought a flashlight. Aitch stood just inside the building's front door—he'd found the boards already pried loose—and let his eyes adjust to the dark. The Diamondback's weight filled his hand.

Streaks of moonlight slanted in through the covered windows. He heard the slow, shallow breathing at the same moment that he saw the figure lying on the floor. Blond hair spilled across a rumpled blanket.

He knew she was fucked up even before he prodded her with his foot. Lindy moaned, a low sound like a creature dying in the tides of a chemical ocean. The hypodermic lay next to the outflung arm, the same red on its point—it looked black in the room's partial spectrum—as was dotted in the curve of her arm.

Aitch took the Diamondback out and extended it down toward her forehead. He could already see the results, the blood splattered across the walls the same as Charlie's had been.

"Mike . . ." Her lips barely moved as she murmured the name.

Aitch raised the gun and stepped back from her. There would be plenty of time to take care of her later. Right now, he didn't want that sonuvabitch to be warned that he was here. He gazed around the dark lobby until he spotted the dim light spilling down the stairs from above.

On the landing halfway up the curving sweep of stairs, he looked out the window at the moon-glazed hills. He drew back, lifting the gun, when he saw something outside, looking back at him. Red eyes, glinting like tiny mirrors—he saw the black, doglike silhouettes moving over the stones and let the muscles of his shoulders and arms ease.

He reached the head of the stairs and gazed down a corridor of numbered doors. The moonlight spilled through a window at the end of the hallway.

One of the doors stood open a few inches. Aitch

stepped toward it, his back sliding against the wall, the gun raised in expectation.

The door didn't have a number like the others, but a clouded glass window instead, with a few gold-leaf letters still visible on it. He used his free hand to push the door all the way into the room behind it.

Some kind of medical office—it looked as if a fight had taken place there. Broken glass glittered on the floor, and an examining table had been knocked over on its side. Aitch stood inside the doorway, looking around the room, the gun's snout following the track of his gaze.

"Aitch . . ."

The whisper came from behind him. He whirled about, hand tightening on the Diamondback's grip. He saw nothing—the voice had been so soft that he could have imagined it. A step took him back to the door, where he looked out to the corridor.

Something hit him, a blow to the shoulder and chest, so fast that he didn't see it coming. He landed sprawling on his arm, skidding a few feet down the hallway. Rolling onto his back, he saw Mike hurtling toward him, the blue light from the window glistening on the bare torso.

Mike grabbed the front of Aitch's jacket and lifted him to his feet. The face a couple of inches from his was contorted with a grin that drew the cords tight in Mike's neck. He slammed Aitch against the wall, then again, the ancient plaster cracking behind his head and spine. The gun flew from his hand as his arms flung outward. Dazed, he heard it clatter into the darkness farther down the hallway.

"Good to see you, Aitch . . ." Mike held him up, whispering in his ear. "You weren't home when I came by." One of Mike's hands let go of his shoulder, balled into a fist, and punched hard into his gut. "Glad you got my message."

The other hand pinning him to the wall let go, and he slumped down, gasping for breath. Mike grabbed his hair, lifting his head to catch the crack of a knee across his jaw.

Aitch sprawled across the floor. A corner of his bloodied mouth slid over wet stone. He could barely see, at the limit of the world tilting above him, Mike's face, eyes alight with triumph.

The fucker wasn't dead; he knew that. Mike could hear Aitch's ragged breathing, see the flutter of his eyelids, the whites rolled up beneath.

He'd dragged the sonuvabitch down the stairs, Aitch's head bouncing against each step. And outside, to the edge of the swimming pool behind the building. Now he picked Aitch up under the arms, holding him close to his own face.

A line of blood trickled from the corner of Aitch's mouth. His eyes slowly wobbled into focus.

Mike held him erect with one hand. With the other, he tenderly stroked Aitch's face.

"Aitch . . ." He kept his voice soft. "I don't forget my friends."

He straightened his arm, his hand letting go. Aitch lifted backward, then hit the layer of rubble on the water's surface. The back of his head struck one of the charred timbers. Aitch moaned and rolled to his side; the debris parted under his weight, and he slid partway into the darkness. The water swelled upward, a small wave surging against the tiles at the side. Aitch's hand, the last part of him visible, dragged across the wood, then disappeared.

Mike turned away from the pool. Then he heard something behind him. He looked over his shoulder.

With a splash, Aitch breached the water's surface, his head tilted back, mouth open to gasp for air. His arms flailed as he struggled for the edge of the pool. Just as he reached it, two red arms, things of skinned muscle and tendons, emerged and wrapped themselves around his neck. They tightened their grip, pulling Aitch back, the tips of his fingers smearing against the tiles.

216

His struggle lifted his chest out of the water, his hands straining against the shifting rubble. The thing fastened onto him rose as well, the dark liquid mingling with blood streaming from its empty eyesockets. Aitch saw it then, the blind face pressed close to his, as though the lipless mouth were moving against his for a kiss.

Nelder's skull, the tattered remnants of flesh dangling from it, grinned as it dragged Aitch back under the water.

Mike watched, his own breath stopped with fascination. He stood at the edge of the pool, watching the struggle sink out of view.

He knelt down, staring into the small opening that had been created. Below, the elongated shadow of the Nelder-thing tore at Aitch's throat; red bubbles frothed at the water's surface. The hands of bone ripped the soft flesh open, and Aitch's arms slowly floated wide, the hands uncurling.

The water calmed as the red stain spread, until it was still again.

Enthralled, Mike squatted back on his heels. With one hand, he reached out and brushed away some more of the obscuring debris. Aitch's pallid corpse rotated as it floated lower, the cloud of blood blossoming from its throat. The pool's other occupant moved away.

The Nelder-thing's head rose a few inches above the water's surface. The eye sockets turned toward Mike. He knew it could see him somehow. It knew he was there.

"You're alive," whispered Mike. Wonder, and a fierce joy, burst in his heart. "You're still alive."

He scooped up some of the water and watched it trickling down his wrist.

"It's keeping you alive . . ."

He reached farther out and trailed his fingers through the water mingled with Aitch's blood. The Nelder-thing hissed and drew back from Mike's hand.

The water dripped from the point of his elbow. He

cupped his palm to his mouth. The water's sweet taste was mixed with salt.

He stood up from the pool's edge. The Nelder-thing drifted, the water lapping at the rim of its eyesockets. The skull face turned, following his movements.

"Well, well, Doctor Nelder . . ." He smiled at the thing. "This is an . . . *interesting* medical development. Interesting . . ." He nodded, the thoughts moving at an irrevocable pace inside his own head. "What's needed now is—"

He turned, looking at the clinic building's dark shape.

"Yes . . ." He rolled the thick residue of the water and blood on his tongue. "Some further experiments—that's what." He gave a final glance at the pool and the things in it, then walked away.

Twenty-
FIVE

He picked her up in his arms. The shot had started to wear off. Lindy roused from her stupor, eyes fluttering open. Mike's face came into focus, and she gave a small cry, pushing weakly against his bare chest with her fists.

"There, there . . ." He made his voice go soft and soothing. "Don't worry." He kissed her on the cheek. "I'll make it all better."

The way he talked and looked at her frightened her even more. She struggled futilely in his grasp as he carried her out of the lobby and down the stone steps.

"Here we go." The white-tiled room, with its encrustations of mold black in the partial moonlight, tilted about her. He suddenly let go of her, and she fell, gasping in surprise.

Water splashed around her. Her elbow struck the rim of the basin, sending a sharp electric jolt up her arm. The dark water surged against the sides, then slapped back into her face, choking her with its sulfur odor. The shock of the sudden dunking brought her fully conscious; she struggled even more frantically, hands scrabbling at the stone. Mike's hand at her breastbone pushed her back down into the water.

Her hair floated about her face as her breath bubbled out of her mouth. The water invaded her nose and throat, dizzying her with its fumes.

Mike dragged her up from the basin, his hands digging into her arms. She gulped in the room's close, humid air, the water sluicing down her face.

"You're a very lucky young lady!" Mike's eyes gleamed as he shouted at her. "You don't know how lucky!" He shook her like a wet rag doll, her head flopping back and forth.

His voice increased in fervor. "This is your golden opportunity—you're going to get the full treatment!" His face trembled and swam in her blurred vision. "You want medicine? I'll give you medicine! Something better than all the pills and shit in the world! Something that'll cure you for good, you stupid little cunt!"

She dangled limply in his grasp. "Mike . . . please . . ."

With a sneer, he flung her down into the basin, then reached down again and raised her to a sitting position. He cupped the dark water in one hand and brought it to her mouth. Lindy choked and gagged as he tilted her head back and forced her to drink.

He let her collapse over the basin's side, the water dribbling from the sides of her mouth. It moved, like something uncoiling, deep in the base of her stomach. He'd gone on, over and over, bringing his hand to her face, each time pouring another palmful down her throat. She tried to vomit, but nothing came up.

"Come on." Mike's voice, above her, sounded pitying now. "This is where you get to make your big contribution to medical science."

He grasped her under the arms and lifted her from the basin. Her legs dragged over the stone rim.

The light was better up in the examining room, the moon sliding in through the window. He could see what he was doing. Mike laid her limp form down on the floor, then uprighted the examining table. He bent down and picked Lindy up, placing her on the padded surface.

From the table's underside dangled the original restraining straps, the leather cracked but still serviceable. He pulled the rusted buckles tight around her wrists and ankles, spreading her legs apart.

Her clothes were sodden, darkened with the water. With a pair of bandage scissors he found on the counter, he cut them loose along her ribs and hips, then pulled the wet rags out from beneath her.

Groggily, her eyes opened, gaze scanning across the room's ceiling. He turned his back to her and searched through the rattling instruments in the chrome tray.

Her eyes widened and she screamed when he stepped close to her with the rust-specked scalpel raised in his hand.

He leaned over her. "Now, now . . . just relax." The smile and the soothing voice again. "This won't hurt. At least not for long."

The scream dwindled to sobbing and whimpering as he brought the edge of the scalpel down to the bare soft flesh of her abdomen.

"I just need to know . . . everything." He drew a red line across her stomach. "All about how it works . . . what it does. All the little changes . . ."

Fascinated, he watched the line of red widen, a jewel-like drop trickling down to the damp triangle of hair between her legs. He had never seen anything so beautiful; he had never seen *her* so beautiful before.

He could fall in love all over again. With her, with the way she'd be when he was done. Why was she afraid?

Her skin glowed, luminous. He raised his head: the room around him had brightened, the lamp over the table radiating a fierce brilliance. It dazzled him for a moment; he lifted his hand to shield his eyes.

He saw them then, in the room with him. A white-coated figure, a gaunt, skull-like face watching him. Nelder—but with watery blue eyes behind gold-rimmed spectacles, and black hair slicked down and parted in the middle. The way he'd looked in the old oval-framed picture.

Beside Nelder stood the nurse, the young one, in the old-fashioned uniform, the white winged hat on her head. She smiled at him, her eyes half shaded, demure and mysterious. He felt his groin clench as he looked at her.

Around them, the examining room was new again, the battering of time erased. The walls burned with the flood of light.

The young nurse held out a tray of gleaming chrome. Nelder nodded his head toward it.

"Go on . . ." His whisper cut through the room's perfect silence. "You're the doctor . . ."

Mike closed his eyes, the moment expanding inside him, unlocking his heart.

The time grew larger, a world with himself at the center. He heard the sounds of running outside the room, across the lobby floor and up the stairs, and in the hallway. But not human; instead, the quick, almost silent surge of the animals, their red gaze and their fur darkened to black by the water. Leaping against the walls, copulating in their glory, the male biting the female's neck until the blood flowed across his teeth.

The world became small again, became just this room. He looked at the shining tools on the tray, their delicate edges. He didn't need any of them. He turned back toward the subject on the table, raising the red-tipped scalpel.

* * *

The building's night shadow fell across him as he pulled the motorbike up in front. When Doot switched off the racketing engine, the hills' silence flowed back together, complete and unbroken again.

On the bike's carrier rack, the stuff he'd bought at the store was still strapped down with the bungee cord. He left it there as he walked—cautiously—around the front of the 'Vette and up the verandah stairs.

He pushed the boards over the door aside, not knowing what to expect inside.

"Lindy?" He looked around the empty space. The blankets and the open suitcase were still there. But no one answered him.

He walked farther into the dimly lit space, hands spread wide, gaze flicking nervously from one corner to the next. His foot touched the edge of the blankets; he poked them with the toe of his shoe and something rolled out from them, clattering on the floor.

Bending down, he picked the object up. A syringe, the plunger pressed all the way inside. He looked around the room, his heart speeding.

He heard something, a faint noise coming from beyond the lobby's ceiling. His gaze went up to the carved beams. A rustling sound, but wet at the same time. He dropped the syringe and ran toward the grand staircase.

The noise came from down the hallway. Doot stopped at the head of the stairs, gulping to catch his breath. In the moonlight coming in through the window, he saw the door of the examining room standing open.

He pushed open the door and stood back to look inside. He saw no one, but the sound was louder. Something breathing—he took a step into the room.

Behind him, a slurred voice spoke, the word barely understandable. His name—

"Doot . . ."

He whirled about and saw it lying on the examining

table. His hands scrabbled at the door as he backed away, his stomach crawling upward into his throat.

The red thing on the table still had the shape of a human being, legs spread apart, arms lifted beside its head. Leather straps, slick with blood, held the wrists and ankles in place. The skin had been stripped away, hanging in neat-edged flaps down the table's side. The long bunches of muscle lay exposed, laced in their nets of tendons. At the thing's center, its viscera nested in an intricate coil; the veined fist of the heart pulsed behind the spider cage of the ribs.

Lidless eyes, the pain and shock visible in them, stared from the wet ruins of the face. The mouth worked against red-smeared teeth, trying to say his name again.

A scream froze in his throat when he saw the fall of golden hair, streaked now with blood, cascading off the head of the examining table.

One of her hands tugged against its leather strap, reaching for him. Bits of flayed tissue dangled from between the fingers.

He felt his own head exploding, as though the room and the red thing inside it had swollen his skull to the bursting point. Dizzy, a taste of vomit in his mouth, he fumbled at the door behind him. He managed to scrape his spine along its edge and then stumble backwards into the hallway.

What had been Lindy made a soft, mewing cry. The sound followed him as he collapsed to the floor. He crawled blindly toward the stairs.

The reactions of the thing in the pool were well worth studying. Mike crouched there, his hands full of red, soft objects. Their fluids oozed slowly down his wrists. He dangled a spongey kidney section over the open space in the water. Beneath the surface, empty eye sockets followed the motion. He dropped the dissected fragment; as soon as it hit, the Nelder-thing drew it under, paddling a few feet away with its bone hands, so it could worry the piece undisturbed.

It didn't seem to eat the bits he dropped in. The Nelder-thing's digestive parts were largely nonfunctional now; its stomach floated like a balloon outside of the abdominal cavity, the intestines trailing behind like party streamers. But—Mike observed this carefully, bending close to the water to see—it still apparently had some capacity to *savor*. The skull's exposed teeth didn't tear apart the scraps, but sank into them, as though it could draw out some ineffable substance, sweeter than blood.

Interesting—he supposed a paper could be written on the subject and submitted to one of the medical journals. He didn't suppose he'd ever do that, though. That saddened him a little. But these things were secrets; the water had promised him, and then shown him, and that should be enough.

He dropped into the water the last of the pieces he'd extracted from the other thing, the one upstairs in the building. A memory troubled him, of the thing's face before he had started. It had kept crying out his name, but he didn't know why. Another mystery. The Nelder-thing scooped the pieces under, then retreated beneath the layer of debris.

Other things were watching him, the wolf shapes pacing in the hills. He could feel the pressure of their red-eyed gaze upon his back. That made him smile. Now he knew the same things they did.

He lifted his head. A faint, distant sound had touched his hearing. He turned, looking toward the building behind him. Something was moving around in there. Silently, he rose from the pool's edge and padded across the dirt and rocks, along the building's side.

The motorbike—he spotted it parked out front. The kid had come back.

Mike nodded to himself, his smile stretching back the

225

corners of his mouth. That was okay. The kid could be *interesting* as well.

He reached to the back pocket of his jeans and pulled out the crusted scalpel. With unhurried ease, he loped up the verandah steps.

The panic had caught him, tearing away all control. Doot had fallen down the stairs, catching hold of the banister rail before he hit the landing halfway down. He pulled himself up with it and crouched, listening.

"Doot . . ." Another voice called his name. Mike's voice. "Hey, Doot—where are you, Doot?"

He shrank back into the shadow beneath the landing's window. He saw Mike, the skin of his chest wet and shining, step into the center of the lobby. Something that shone even brighter, beneath dark mottling, dangled in Mike's hand.

"Come on, Doot—" Mike's gaze swept across the space. "Let's *talk.*"

He froze against the wall. If he tried to dart back up the stairs, Mike would hear him. And come after him, cornering him in the room with Lindy's eviscerated form.

Mike turned away from the staircase, prowling toward the other side of the lobby. Doot pushed himself upright, then smashed his forearm against the landing window. Glass exploded into the darkness. He scrambled out over the jagged points of the sill. The shards cut at his fingers as he hung alongside the building. He let go, and dropped. The impact with the ground jarred his legs and spine; he rolled onto his side, his face scuffing into the dirt. Staggering, he got to his feet.

The darkness hid him. He glanced over his shoulder as he ran, and saw Mike's silhouette already in the window. Mike swung his legs over the sill, then pushed himself away from the frame.

He heard the heavy thud of Mike landing on the ground beneath the window. Now he couldn't see him. His heart pounding in his throat, Doot scanned the open space around him for a way to escape.

He'd managed to run a dozen, maybe twenty yards away from the building. He could go on running, into the hills. But their flanks were washed bare by the moonlight—Mike would spot him easily there and come bounding after, Mike's quick strides outmatching his exhausted flight. All he had to do was trip over a rock, and the scalpel blade would be right at his throat.

A place to hide—and quickly. One second had already been sliced away; he couldn't lose any more.

The swimming pool—he spotted it off to the side of the building. He ran toward it.

For a moment, he looked down at the dark, trash-covered surface. Then, with a final glance back over his shoulder, he stooped down and lowered himself into the water, holding onto the pool's raised edge. The warm, sulfurous fumes lay heavy against his mouth and nose. With the water up to his chin, he could just look over the tiled rim.

Mike was out there, slowly prowling across the clinic grounds. The blue light sparkled along the edge of the scalpel.

"Okay, Doot." Mike halted and looked around. "You're really pissing me off now."

He lowered his head. He could just see Mike's grip squeezing the scalpel's handle, knuckles whitening.

"Doot . . . you don't want to make me mad." The blade jutted from the clenched fist. Mike's jaw-heavy face pushed forward, his shoulders hunching against his shirt's taut fabric. "I'm telling you . . ."

Doot shrank back from the edge of the pool, the water coming up over his mouth.

The water stirred. He felt, and heard, the shifting in the overlapping layer of burned timbers and the other debris.

He jerked his head around, with the sudden realization that something was in the pool with him. A skull wearing a mask of tattered flesh sprang up from the surface. Hands like hooks carved from bone grabbed onto his neck, dragging him away from the the pool's side.

An arm of dangling wet things circled his throat, cutting off his shout as it pulled him beneath the water. His own hands clutched at the arm, and he felt his fingers sink through the strings of flesh.

His breath burst from his lungs. The dark water flooded into his mouth.

He heard the scream, cut off in the first second, and the sound of the struggle coming from the water. The splashing noise sounded faint in the distance; he had walked nearly to the edge of the hills, searching for the kid. Mike turned his head, listening; his smile broke into a laugh.

The scalpel dangled loosely in his hand as he walked back toward the pool. Everything was interesting now.

Twenty-SIX

She had kept running, even after a stitch in her side, like the sudden thrust of a knife, had nearly bent her double. In the dark, with only the moonlight revealing the long straight road, Anne spotted the black shape of the old clinic building against the hills. Gasping for breath, she stopped for a moment, leaning over with her hands against her knees. Then she straightened up and sprinted for the head of the dirt lane.

The sounds of water splashing and a scream cut off short hit her when she was only a couple of yards away from the front of the building. It came from somewhere behind, the cry echoing from the barren hillside. She ran toward it.

The pool's surface churned to a black froth, the timbers and junk heaving against the sides. Something was in there, thrashing underneath. She saw Doot's face break into the air, his mouth open, eyes wild; something that looked like ropes knotted over bone had wrapped around his throat. His hands tore frantically at the choking hold.

"Doot—over here!" Anne knelt at the side of the pool, stretching her hand out. He saw her and let go of the raw thing at his neck. His hands grabbed hold of hers and clutched desperately; she had to brace herself and pull back to keep from being dragged in.

The thing didn't release its grasp on Doot. As he came closer to the pool's edge, the other drew up with him, its skull and chest rising up from the water. The sight of it struck her gut and brain, dizzying and nauseating her. A flayed carcass that was still alive somehow, the water pouring from the empty eye sockets and across its lipless mouth.

And it saw her. Something red at the bottom of the sockets trained upon her face, with an avid hunger that made her cringe. The instinct to let go of Doot's hands clinging to hers and just curl into a ball, hiding her eyes from seeing it, swept across her.

The grip on Doot's neck loosened for a second; he took one hand from hers, and tore the arm of dangling flesh away. The thing hissed in fury, its claws scrabbling at him. Doot drew his legs up and kicked out at the thing, landing one blow in the center of its chest, his foot sinking into the squirming heart. The thing splashed backwards, disjointed arms flailing.

Doot heaved himself over the edge of the pool. Anne grabbed him by the elbows and pulled him the rest of the way. He collapsed onto his side, gagging and spewing up the water that he'd swallowed. A dark puddle, laced with the strings of his spit, spread underneath his face.

The thing in the pool had retreated, the water lapping at the bottom edge of the eye sockets. Its blind gaze held on the human figures now beyond its reach.

There wasn't time to find out what the thing was, or what had happened here. That could all wait until later.

Doot was on his hands and knees now, the dark water dripping from his face.

"Come on." She grabbed his arm and tried to pull him to his feet. "We've got to get out of here—"

"No."

For a second, she thought that Doot had spoken. But it wasn't his voice—the word came out cold and hard. Then she jerked around and saw the man standing behind her.

She had seen him before, through the binoculars. He was bare-chested now, his skin glistening wet, stained as though with dark oil. The man smiled at her, his lips drawing back from the points of his teeth.

"You're not going anywhere." The man spoke quietly, his gaze penetrating into hers.

Doot raised his head, feebly bringing a hand up to fend the man off as he stepped forward. The man brushed him aside and grabbed hold of Anne, his hands pinning her arms close to her body. He picked her up—easily, as though she weighed no more than a cat.

For a moment, she gazed down at the hair plastered tight to the man's skull, then she felt herself flying in air as he threw her.

She hit the water backwards, one of her hands striking a piece of wood. The water surged away from her, then came together over her face. In its blackness, she clawed desperately upward, her face finally breaking the surface.

At the side of the pool, the man was lifting Doot upright, drawing him gently by his forearms. "Come on," said the man. "We're going to have a little talk . . ."

That was all she saw of them. She had a split-second's perception of something gliding through the water toward her, the push of the water against her ribs. Then it lunged; the ropy arms clasped around her breasts and pulled her under the surface. The water with its sulfur stink washed over her face. She dug her fingers into the arms and felt the soft flesh part beneath. But the thing's arms held tight, squeezing the breath from her, as its weight swarmed over her, bearing her down into the pool's depths.

"Doot . . ." A hand stroked his face. "I wasn't going to hurt you." A soothing voice, somewhere at the edge of his consciousness. "I need you, Doot."

He managed to open his eyes. The walls of the examining room slowly worked into focus. He felt the ridge of the doorsill against his spine, his hands flopped loose against the floor. A puddle of the dark water spread around him.

Mike's soft voice went on; he was kneeling right beside him, running a gentle hand across his brow.

"I need your help, Doot. I can't do it all by myself. I need somebody's help." Mike lowered his head, to gaze straight into Doot's eyes. "Somebody who knows, who understands. You understand now, don't you?"

Mike rose to his feet and stepped back. Doot looked down at himself in growing wonder. He spread his arms wide, his damp palms upturned.

He had never felt like this before.

She'd managed to twist about in its grasp, shoving her hands against the exposed breastbone. A push, and her head broke the water's surface; she gulped air into her burning lungs.

The skull's mouth opened wide as the thing forced its arms tighter around her arched spine. Her hand slipped from the chest and caught against the curve of its jaw; a layer of skin tore like sodden paper under her palm.

With a brittle noise, the jaw's hinge broke loose, the bottom row of teeth slewing to one side. A tendon stretched, then snapped, and the U-shaped bone came away in her hand, shreds of flesh drifting between her fingers in the water.

The open hole into the thing's throat bubbled, gargling a muted cry of pain. Its arms spasmed, releasing her;

232

her shoulders fell back onto the layer of floating debris. The jawbone splashed into the water, bobbing up like a sea creature with dangling tendrils.

Anne clawed past the tangled rubble, her hand finally striking the tiled rim of the pool. She clambered onto her elbows, the rim digging into the stomach. Before she could kick her legs to thrust herself the rest of the way, she felt the thing's hands clamp onto her shins. Her breasts dragged across the pool's edge as the skeletal thing pulled her back into the water. Her fingers dug in but found no hold.

A spoked circle of metal, a foot away—she grabbed for it, her fingers hooking around the bottom curve. She tightened her grip, squeezing the iron into her fist. With a kick against the thing behind her, she got her other hand onto the wheel.

The thing didn't let go. She looked over her shoulder and saw the skull's face, the bottom half torn away, straining toward her. Panting in fear and exhaustion, she held the wheel with one hand, grabbing a spoke with the other, pulling herself another inch out of the water.

The wheel creaked, metal moving through rust. Her weight, and the strength of the thing holding onto her, turned the wheel a few degrees; the spoke slanted downward now. She gasped, feeling it slide through her fingers, the corrosion flaking away in her grip. Her waist slipped back over the pool's rim. She grabbed for the next spoke, getting both hands onto it, edges of pitted metal biting her palms.

With a higher-pitched scraping noise, the wheel spun free, rotating a quarter turn. Anne caught herself on the bottom, pulling herself far enough that she could hook her arm through, pressing her face against the wheel's hub. Her legs were still caught in the water. A surge of fear and revulsion shook her, and a burst of tears flooded the dark water away from her eyes.

The thing in the pool drew itself up her legs, the bone

233

points of its fingers clawing across the small of her back.

Somewhere—she could hear it but didn't know what it meant—there was the sound of water gushing, a surge splashing onto dry ground and rocks. She clung to the iron wheel, the last of her strength ebbing.

Mike's smile floated closer to him.

"You've tasted it now—haven't you, Doot?" The gaze fastened onto his, as Mike stepped closer. "There, in the pool. You've drunk it. You know what I'm talking about. You can feel it."

He did feel it. Now he knew—he closed his eyes, leaning the back of his head against the wall. The muscles of his arms and chest burned, the heat intoxicating him. The taste in his mouth was of something alive, sweet and empowering.

His hands curled into fists. He looked at them, as if he'd never seen them before. Not like this—the intricate net of veins spread through the flesh, the cords tightening. The stain of the dark water twined into the crooks of his elbows.

Mike leaned over him, savoring the glow seeping from his skin.

"It's good, isn't it, Doot?"

He clenched his jaw, a shiver spreading up from his groin into the muscles of his neck.

"Yeah . . ." His whisper slid from between his teeth.

Mike's smile widened, as he watched the transformation.

"We can do it . . . anything we want . . ." The voice curled around his ear, sliding into his brain. "Just the two of us, Doot . . . the two of us . . . and the water . . ."

He drew back, pointing to something a few feet away in the room.

"Things like that . . ." Mike's finger trembled. "They don't mean anything to us now. They're nothing . . . They don't matter, Doot . . . we do."

Doot pushed himself up from the floor. He stepped toward the examining table.

There was something beautiful on it.

A thing of blood, and tissue that wept blood. The concealing skin had been peeled away—the thing lay on it as if it were a red sheet that draped toward the floor—and the soft, joyful intricacies had been exposed. The great muscles of the thighs, the nest of coiled intestines, the fist of the heart, clenching and releasing . . .

The face, its real face, the red secret known at last . . .

Golden hair, streaked and stiffened with blood, tumbled from the top edge of the table.

Doot gazed at it, his head filling with delight and a leaping certainty, then beyond, as though the limits of his skull were no more, a new world turning in his grasp.

One of its wet hands strained against the leather strap, reaching for him. It grasped hold of his forearm, the red fingers tightening.

He looked down at the hand, the world shrinking to it and nothing else. Somewhere beyond, the flayed lips moved.

It said his name.

The world exploded, his gut heaving in a sudden contraction of nausea and anger. He jerked his arm away from its grasp.

"No!"

The arm continued in a slashing backhand arc, the blow landing across Mike's chest and sending him sprawling backwards.

Twenty-SEVEN

It let go of her. Anne felt the sudden release of her legs and heard the splash as the thing flailed backwards in the water.

She clung to the iron wheel and looked behind her at the pool. The water's level had gone down nearly a foot from the tiled rim; the layer of burned timbers and other debris shifted, scraping against the sides.

The thing of bone and torn flesh had paddled back, into the center of the pool's open space. Its jawless skull turned from side to side, the empty sockets staring at what was happening. A hissing noise came from the open hole of its throat, and the skeletal hands struck the black surface in fury.

Now she could pull herself all the way out of the pool. She scrambled upright, using the wheel and the metal housing behind it to steady herself. Her shirt clung to her, the night air chilling her skin. The water dripped from her clothes, spreading in a puddle around her feet.

The sound of gurgling and splashing came louder to her. *The drain*—she turned and ran her hands over the curve of the iron wheel. She grabbed it, pushing against the spokes until it had gone all the way around and come to a solid stop. The noise of water gushing onto the ground, somewhere nearby, grew to a torrent. In the pool, the debris took a sudden lurch downward. The thing's hiss rose to a shrill wail.

Mike fell back against the examining room counter. His arm swept across the ancient surgical instruments, sending them clattering to the floor. He caught himself against the counter's edge with both hands. His face contorted with rage when he raised his head and looked at Doot.

He reached down to the floor and came up with a rust-bladed scalpel in his grip. The point of it came straight at Doot's throat as Mike lunged across the room.

Doot caught Mike's arm in both his hands. For a moment, they were locked against each other, Mike's face straining close to his. Mike's eyes turned wet and red, then tears of blood trickled from the corners.

They fell against the examining table, toppling it over. The thing strapped to it screamed in pain, fingers clawing toward her own ravaged flesh.

The scalpel flew out of Mike's grip, skittering across the floor. He forced both hands around Doot's neck, bearing him down.

Doot fought for breath, pushing up against Mike's chest. Suddenly, the face above him, teeth clamped together in its frenzy, blurred with red. He felt his own tears, thick and warm, coursing over his cheeks. He blinked, clearing his sight for a second, and saw in the dark mirrors at the centers of Mike's eyes his own face, the eyes leaking blood.

A wave of anger swept out from his heart, and his arms straightened, tossing Mike back, breaking the hold on his throat. His hands caught on Mike's face, thumbs pressing against the ridges of the cheekbones.

The skin tore.

He felt his hands slide into wet, trembling flesh, as Mike's skin peeled back from his mouth and red eyes, wadding into folds at his ears. Mike tilted his head back, the raw face pulling the tendons of the neck through their splitting cover.

Doot grabbed the other's arms and pushed. Mike's shoulders arched backward, breaking open his chest. The wet skin tore down the center, the muscles beneath breaking to reveal the ribs, the lungs and heart at the core.

Mike screamed, fury mixed with agony.

The flesh of the arms parted in Doot's grip, skin shredding into tatters over the muscle and sinew.

Mike curled into a ball, red hands clutching at his own flesh, as though trying to hold it in, to stop the process of disintegration.

Doot wiped his face with his arm as he staggered to his feet. He looked down at the thing writhing in front of him.

It couldn't stand; the ragged split that had burst open its chest now ran all the way down its abdomen, spilling out the loops of intestine. Inside the blood-soaked jeans, the pelvic bones cracked, jerking the legs apart, a puppet with cut strings. Blood trickled across the ankles as it scrabbled at the floor.

The exposed lungs labored, as the hands pushed the chest, organs sagging against the ribs, up from the puddle beneath it. The red eyes, insane in their wounded mask, fastened their gaze on Doot. The raw facial muscles constricted as it reached a hand toward him. An obscene mewling came from the red mouth, the sound mixing with the pain-filled whimpering of the thing strapped to the overturned examining table.

Doot backed toward the door. His hands found it, and he turned and staggered into the hallway. Mike, the thing his torn flesh had become, crawled after him, the protruding bones of one hand scraping across Doot's leg.

He kicked the groping fingers away and ran for the stairs.

On the landing, stopping to catch his breath—he heard the howling then, another animal sound mingling with the ones coming from above. Through the broken-out window, he saw the red, watching eyes, like points of fire. The dark wolf shapes ran at the crest of the hills, or stood still and raised their throats to the night sky, the wild notes of their voices overlapping into one cry of exultation.

He stumbled from the last step of the grand staircase, into the lobby. He looked up at the carved beams of the ceiling. He could hear, from above, Lindy's whimpering, the sound leaking out of her like the blood oozing from her flesh. And closer, the mewling—hate and desire beyond words—of the other thing, crawling toward the head of the stairs.

Doot stepped back, hands outstretched, the sounds of pain and madness swirling about him. He turned and ran toward the door.

The motorbike—it stood only a few yards away from the verandah steps. He picked the small machine up in his arms and staggered back with it toward the building.

Inside, he screwed open the gas cap and tossed it away. He tilted the bike upside down, holding it by the wheels to keep it in position. The gasoline gurgled, pouring out of the tank; it spread in a widening pool around his feet.

The last drops spilled out, the fumes rising to his nostrils. He let the bike drop onto its side.

"Doot . . ."

A voice, no longer human, screamed his name. He looked up and saw Mike, the thing of tattered flesh and red bone, at the staircase landing. The wet, red eyes glimmered with an avid frenzy. It flopped its broken-jointed hips over the next steps down, pushing itself forward with its crippled legs. A hand lifted, straining toward Doot, the skin of the palm dangling in shreds. It held something, a piece of bright metal. The scalpel.

There were matches in the brown paper sack, ones he'd brought with all the other stuff. Doot ripped the sack open and found the box, spilling half of them on the floor as he tore off the wrapper.

He backed away to the door, leaving a trail of gasoline footprints. With his spine against the boards, he lit one match and held it to the book until the others had burst into flame. He tossed it to the wet slick shining in the sliver of moonlight from the windows.

A wave of heat brushed across his face as the gasoline turned to flame. At the sides of the lobby, the dry rotten curtains caught, the fire leaping through them up to the ceiling. The splintered panels between the beams smoldered for only a second before bursting alight.

Doot raised his hand against the heat, fiercer now. A curtain of flame and black, roiling smoke filled the space. He fumbled behind himself, squeezing past the boards over the door. The cool night air rushed over him as he staggered out onto the verandah.

He fell to his knees in the dirt beyond the steps. He managed to crawl a few more yards, his shadow lengthening in the growing orange light, a flickering radiance from the burning building. Then he collapsed onto his shoulder in the dust.

Rolling onto his back, Doot pushed himself up onto his elbows. The entire front of the building was engulfed in flames. The windows of the second story cracked from the heat, raining down brilliant shards of glass.

He got to his feet, the fire shoving him back. With a roar, the boards over the entrance fell away, a gout of flame rolling out. The heat hit his face and chest, blinding him.

When he opened his eyes, shielding them with his upraised arm, he saw the thing crawling through the center of the fire. Still alive, but now a mass of charred flesh wrapped in flames and smoke. In the burning doorway, it raised its blackened face. The raw sockets where the eyes had been could still see somehow; its empty gaze fastened onto Doot. The mewling sound, of hunger and rage, seeped through the cracked fragments of teeth.

It raised its hand, now only a stump of bone, two fingers and a fused thumb gripping the scalpel. The mewling shrieked up in pitch, to a cry of animal hate, as the thing crawled across the verandah's smoldering planks.

Then it died.

It curled into an eviscerated husk, pitching forward onto the steps. The legs curled up into the chest, the bones of the knees cracking through the ribs, breaking the shriveled lungs apart. The heart, a black fist, clenched a final time, then dangled loose in its web of connective tissue.

The blind face gaped up at the flames towering above. The hand's stump flopped against the bottom step, the scalpel falling into the dust.

He found her by the edge of the swimming pool. The burning building lit the grounds and the hillside with a fierce, shifting orange radiance.

Doot lifted Anne up, her limp arms trailing across the iron wheel of the pool's valve controls. Exhausted and soaked through, she clung to him, the dark water puddling at her feet.

Running toward her, he had heard the sound of the water running from the pool's drain into the stone-lined culvert. Already the gushing noise had dwindled to a slow trickling.

He heard another sound, as he wrapped his arms around Anne. A hissing, broken by something almost like

241

sobbing—the last noises of a dying creature. It came from inside the pool.

Doot looked over the tiled rim, holding Anne away from the sight. The pool was almost drained of the dark water now. The Nelder-thing lay at the bottom, its elongated carcass caught in the wet, charred timbers and debris. The arms of bone and raw stringy muscle moved, the clawlike hands flopping back and forth. It lifted its skull head, the gaunt jawless face gaping open, the throat dark and empty as the eye sockets.

He pulled her away from the pool, onto the dirt.

The flames' orange light danced across the dark puddle from which they'd stepped.

His gaze fastened onto the shimmering wetness. Anne pushed herself back from his chest, her eyes searching his face.

"Doot!" Alarm grew in her voice. "Doot, what is it?"

He let go of her and knelt by the pool, drawing his hand through the thin layer of water. He stood up, holding his wet palm close to his face. The sulfur smell rose into his nostrils.

The world turned silent. Beyond the roar of the fire leaping into the sky—another silence, that of things watching, and waiting.

The creatures in the hills—they had ceased their howling. But they were still there. He felt the pressure of their expectant gaze, intent upon his every movement.

He licked the water from his palm. Its sweetness burst inside his head. His blood sang, a shrill high note, as it surged into the muscles of his arms and chest.

Anne grabbed his shoulders, bringing her face close to his. "Doot, are you okay?"

He closed his eyes, then opened them; his tongue drew across the moisture on his lips. He looked past her, to the darkness in the hills.

He nodded, slowly. "I've never . . . felt better . . ."

Pushing her aside, he strode toward the culvert, and

the pool's drain pipe. He knelt down, cupping his hands under the trickling flow. He gazed down at the dark water filling his palms, the thin rivulets running down his wrists. Then he raised it toward his mouth, to drink.

Something hit his hands, dashing the water out onto the dirt.

His head jerked around, the muscles of his shoulders and arms bunching. Teeth clenched, he gazed up in fury at Anne.

She grabbed hold of his wrists, bending over him. "Doot . . ." She looked into his eyes, pleading with him. "Don't . . ." Her grip tightened, straining against the swelling muscle of his arm drawing back to strike her. "Do you want to end up like them?"

His arm froze in place, the clenched fist raised above her head.

The water trickled from between his fingers, running to his elbow. He looked away from her, to the black, shining thread, radiant in the burning light.

Then he cried out, head tilted back, throwing his hand out in front of him. The black drops scattered onto the dust.

After

Thin smoke drifted in the early morning light. He brought the Peterbilt to a halt, then pushed open the cab door. At the head of the lane, he stood looking at the smoldering ruins.

Then the trucker spotted the figures lying on the ground in front of what had been the old clinic building. He ran toward them, already knowing that one of them was his son.

"Jesus fucking Christ!"

It looked even worse when he got up close. There was a Corvette parked near the burned building, the red paint of its fender and hood blistered from the heat. And in the charred rubble sprawled a blackened corpse, barely recognizable as having been human, the stumps of its hands clawing out from the ashes.

The trucker knelt down and lifted Doot's head. His son's eyes dragged open; they pulled a glimmer of recognition into focus, then started to fade away again. The trucker stood, bringing Doot up with him. Doot hung, limp from exhaustion, against his father.

He brushed his hand against Doot's brow. "What the hell happened out here?"

Doot opened his mouth, as though about to speak, then shook his head. It would have to wait.

The other figure, a girl he recognized now from Doot's high school, had stirred, raising her face from the ground. Her clothes were sodden and stained dark. The trucker left his son wobbling for a moment, and helped the girl to her feet.

"You all right?" He bent down to look in her eyes.

A nod. "I'm . . ." She drew a deep breath. "We're okay."

He walked them toward the truck, one on either side, their arms thrown over his shoulders.

Doot stopped halfway up the lane. He turned his head, looking back at the remains of the building. This close to him, the trucker studied his son's face. He hadn't ever seen him like this. No longer a gangly kid, but—different. Older, and harder, as though the fire had melted something out of him.

"What is it, son?" He tried to see into Doot's eyes. "What's wrong?"

Doot's gaze went out to the empty hills. He shook his head, slowly.

"Nothing." His voice quiet. "I just want to get out of here."

Then he turned back toward his father and the girl, and smiled—his real smile—and walked with them toward the truck.

The hawk circled in the radiant sky. The scent of fire and smoke had drawn it; sometimes, when the endless sweeps of dry grass burned, the flames drove the small, tender creatures out into the open. Or when the fire was gone, leaving nothing but the blackened valley fields, the dead things brought out others to feed on the scorched carcasses. Then the hawk could wheel about, and dive, and eat his fill.

But not this time. There were dead things in the ashes—one burned, a thing of ash itself; the other still wet and red, soft hanging meat on the arms clawing up from the bottom of the empty pool. The pieces of another lay mired in the thick, shallow water. But nothing would approach these things to pick apart the bones and find the bits that could be eaten. The dead things smelled of death, and worse; their decay seeped into the earth and poisoned it.

The hawk's wings stroked the air, lifting it above the dry hills. Its razor eye saw a shack below, in a small open space. And a stone basin, filled near to its edge with dark, oily-looking water. The water shimmered with circular ripples from the slow dripping of the spigot at the basin's head.

The hawk spiraled upward. But it could still see. Everything—that was its nature. It saw a lean wolf shape come out of the shaded recesses of the hills. The animal put its paws on the basin's edge and leaned its sharp-pointed muzzle over. It drank, tongue lapping up the water.

Sitting back on its haunches, the wolf shape watched the distant hawk, the red eyes following the slow curve inscribed against the sky. Then it eased away, back to join the others, out of the mounting heat.

The hawk drifted away, scanning the ground for the small life that fed its own. It rose in the sky, the level earth falling away, the empty space held in the hawk's bright, unblinking vision.

Slow hours passed, or didn't pass; nothing saw or marked them.

The dark water reached the rim of the basin, trembled, then with the next drop that fell, spilled over the side, a thin line running down the stone.

It didn't seep into the ground. A twisting, snakelike shape formed, a black thing without eyes. For a moment it was still.

Then it moved, inching across the dry earth.